## SCALES OF JUSTICE

NUNSPARDON MANOR—elegant home of the Lacklanders who wish to hide what old Sir Harold had written in his memoirs...

UPLANDS—a decaying manse where a retired commander nurses his brandy, and his deeply wounded pride...

JACOB'S COTTAGE—where old Octavius Danberry-Phinn surrounds himself with his cats and his bitterness...

HAMMER FARM—the showcase where Col. Cartarette exhibits his second wife, a social-climbing young beauty with a history all her own...

Old houses, all with old secrets—which would have remained buried, if *murder* had not suddenly occurred in the valley...

"A handsome bit of craftsmanship—a classical detective story, with lots of suspects."
—The London *Times*

# SCALES OF JUSTICE
## NGAIO
## MARSH

A JOVE BOOK

Back-cover photograph by Mannering and Associates Ltd.

First Jove edition published March 1980

10  9  8  7  6  5  4  3  2  1

Printed in the United States of America

Jove books are published by Jove Publications, Inc.,
200 Madison Avenue, New York, NY 10016

*For Stella*

# CHAPTER 1

## Swevenings

Nurse Kettle pushed her bicycle to the top of Watt's Hill
and there paused. Sweating lightly, she looked down on the
village of Swevenings. Smoke rose in cosy plumes from one or
two chimneys; roofs cuddled into surrounding greenery. The
Chyne, a trout stream, meandered through meadow and
coppice and slid blamelessly under two bridges. It was a
circumspect landscape. Not a faux-pas, architectural or
horticultural, marred the seemliness of the prospect.

"Really," Nurse Kettle thought with satisfaction, "it is as
pretty as a picture," and she remembered all the pretty
pictures Lady Lacklander had made in irresolute water-
colour, some from this very spot. She was reminded, too, of
those illustrated maps that one finds in the Underground with
houses, trees and occupational figures amusingly dotted
about them. Seen from above like this, Swevenings resembled

such a map. Nurse Kettle looked down at the orderly pattern of field, hedge, stream and land, and fancifully imposed upon it the curling labels and carefully naive figures that are proper to picture-maps.

From Watt's Hill, Watt's Lane ran steeply and obliquely into the valley. Between the lane and the Chyne was contained a hillside divided into three stripes, each garnished with trees, gardens and a house of considerable age. These properties belonged to three of the principal householders of Swevenings: Mr. Danberry-Phinn, Commander Syce and Colonel Cartarette.

Nurse Kettle's map, she reflected, would have a little picture of Mr. Danberry-Phinn at Jacob's Cottage surrounded by his cats, and one of Commander Syce at Uplands, shooting off his bow and arrow. Next door at Hammer Farm (only it wasn't a farm now but had been much converted) it would show Mrs. Cartarette in a garden chair with a cocktail-shaker, and Rose Cartarette, her stepdaughter, gracefully weeding. Her attention sharpened. There, in point of fact, deep down in the actual landscape, *was* Colonel Cartarette himself, a Lilliputian figure, moving along his rented stretch of the Chyne, east of Bottom Bridge, and followed at a respectful distance by his spaniel Skip. His creel was slung over his shoulder and his rod was in his hand.

"The evening rise," Nurse Kettle reflected; "he's after the Old 'Un," and she added to her imaginary map the picture of an enormous trout near Bottom Bridge with a curly label above it bearing a legend: "The Old 'Un."

On the far side of the valley on the private golf course at Nunspardon Manor there would be Mr. George Lacklander, doing a solitary round with a glance (thought the gossip-loving Nurse Kettle) across the valley at Mrs. Cartarette. Lacklander's son, Dr. Mark, would be shown with his black bag in his hand and a stork, perhaps, quaintly flying overhead. And to complete, as it were, the gentry, there would be old Lady Lacklander, bog-bottomed on a sketching stool, and her husband, Sir Harold, on a bed of sickness, alas, in his great room, the roof of which, after the manner of pictorial maps, had been removed to display him.

In the map it would be demonstrated how Watt's Lane, wandering to the right and bending back again, neatly divided the gentry from what Nurse Kettle called the "ordinary folk." To the west lay the Danbery-Phinn, the Syce, the Cartarette and above all the Lacklander demesnes. Neatly disposed along the east margin of Watt's Lane were five conscientiously preserved thatched cottages, the village shop and across Monk's Bridge, the church and rectory and the Boy and Donkey.

And that was all. No Pulls-In for Carmen, no Olde Bunne Shoppes (which Nurse Kettle had learned to despise), no spurious half-timbering marred the perfection of Swevenings. Nurse Kettle, bringing her panting friends up to the top of Watt's Hill, would point with her little finger at the valley and observe triumphantly, "'Where every prospect pleases,'" without completing the quotation, because in Swevenings not even Man was Vile.

With a look of pleasure on her shining and kindly face she mounted her bicycle and began to coast down Watt's Lane. Hedges and trees flew by. The road surface improved and on her left appeared the quickset hedge of Jacob's Cottage. From the far side came the voice of Mr. Octavius Danberry-Phinn.

"Adorable!" Mr. Danberry-Phinn was saying. "Queen of Delight! Fish!" He was answered by the trill of feline voices.

Nurse Kettle turned to the footpath, dexterously backpeddalled, wobbled uncouthly and brought herself to anchor at Mr. Danberry-Phinn's gate.

"Good evening," she said, clinging to the gate and retaining her seat. She looked through the entrance cut in the deep hedge. There was Mr. Danberry-Phinn in his Elizabethan garden giving supper to his cats. In Swevenings, Mr. Phinn (he allowed his nearer acquaintances to neglect the hyphen) was generally considered to be more than a little eccentric, but Nurse Kettle was used to him and didn't find him at all disconcerting. He wore a smoking cap, tasselled, embroidered with beads and falling to pieces. On top of this was

3

perched a pair of ready-made reading glasses, which he now removed and gaily waved at her.

"You appear," he said, "like some exotic deity mounted on an engine quaintly devised by Inigo Jones. Good evening to you, Nurse Kettle. Pray, what has become of your automobile?"

"She's having a spot of beauty treatment and a minor op'." Mr. Phinn flinched at this relentless breeziness, but Nurse Kettle, unaware of his reaction, carried heartily on, "And how's the world treating you? Feeding your kitties, I see."

"The Persons of the House," Mr. Phinn acquiesced, "now, as you observe, sup. Fatima." he cried, squatting on his plump haunches, "*Femme fatale*. Miss Paddy-Paws! A morsel more of haddock? Eat up, my heavenly felines." Eight cats of varying kinds responded but slightly to these overtures, being occupied with eight dishes of haddock. The ninth, a mother cat, had completed her meal and was at her toilet. She blinked once at Mr. Phinn and with a tender and gentle expression stretched herself out for the accommodation of her three fat kittens.

"The celestial milk-bar is now open," Mr. Phinn pointed out with a wave of his hand.

Nurse Kettle chuckled obligingly. "No nonsense about *her,* at least," she said. "Pity some human mums I could name haven't got the same idea," she added with an air of professional candour. "Clever pussy!"

"The name," Mr. Phinn corrected tartly, "is Thomasina Twitchett, Thomasina modulating from Thomas and arising out of the usual mistake and Twitchett..." He bared his crazy-looking head. "*Hommage a la Divine Potter*. The boy-children are Ptolemy Alexis. The girl-child who suffers from a marked mother-fixation is Edie."

"Edie?" Nurse Kettle repeated doubtfully.

"Edie Puss, of course," Mr. Phinn rejoined and looked fixedly at her.

Nurse Kettle, who knew that one must cry out against puns, ejaculated, "How you *dare! Honestly!*"

Mr. Phinn gave a short cackle of laughter and changed the subject.

"What errand of therapeutic mercy," he asked, "has set you darkling in the saddle? What pain and anguish wring which brow?"

"Well, I've one or two calls," said Nurse Kettle, "but the long and the short of me is that I'm on my way to spend the night at the big house. Relieving with the old gentleman, you know."

She looked across the valley to Nunspardon Manor.

"Ah, yes," said Mr. Phinn softly. "Dear me! May one enquire...? Is Sir Harold...?"

"He's seventy-five," said Nurse Kettle briskly, "and he's very tired. Still, you never know with cardiacs. He may perk up again."

"Indeed?"

"Oh, yes. We've got a day-nurse for him but there's no night-nurse to be had anywhere so I'm stop-gapping. To help Dr. Mark out, really."

"Dr. Mark Lacklander is attending his grandfather?"

"Yes. He has a second opinion but more for his own satisfaction than anything else. But there! Talking out of school! I'm ashamed of you, Kettle."

"I'm very discreet," said Mr. Phinn.

"So'm I, really. Well, I suppose I had better go on me way rejoicing."

Nurse Kettle did a tentative back-pedal and started to wriggle her foot out of the interstices in Mr. Phinn's garden gate. He disengaged a sated kitten from its mother and rubbed it against his ill-shaven cheek.

"Is he conscious?" he asked.

"Off and on. Bit confused. There now! Gossiping again! Talking of gossip," said Nurse Kettle with a twinkle, "I see the Colonel's out for the evening rise."

An extraordinary change at once took place in Mr. Phinn. His face became suffused with purple, his eyes glittered and he bared his teeth in a canine grin.

"A hideous curse upon his sport," he said. "Where is he?"

"Just below the bridge."

"Let him venture a handspan above it and I'll report him to the authorities. What fly has he mounted? Has he caught anything?"

"I couldn't see," said Nurse Kettle, already regretting her part in the conversation, "from the top of Watt's Hill."

Mr. Phinn replaced the kitten.

"It is a dreadful thing to say about a fellow-creature," he said, "a shocking thing. But I do say advisedly and deliberately that I suspect Colonel Cartarette of having recourse to improper practices."

It was Nurse Kettle's turn to blush.

"I am sure I don't know to what you refer," she said.

"Bread! Worms!" said Mr. Phinn, spreading his arms. "Anything! Tickling, even! I'd put it as low as that."

"I'm sure you're mistaken."

"It is not my habit, Miss Kettle, to mistake the wanton extravagances of infatuated humankind. Look, if you will, at Cartarette's associates. Look, if your stomach is strong enough to sustain the experience, at Commander Syce."

"Good gracious me, what has the poor Commander done!"

"That man," Mr. Phinn said, turning pale and pointing with one hand to the mother-cat and with the other in the direction of the valley, "that intemperate filibuster, who divides his leisure between alcohol and the idiotic pursuit of archery, that wardroom cupid, my God, murdered the mother of Thomasina Twitchett."

"Not deliberately, I'm sure."

"How can you be sure?"

Mr. Phinn leant over his garden gate and grasped the handlebars of Nurse Kettle's bicycle. The tassel of his smoking cap fell over his face and he blew it impatiently aside. His voice began to trace the pattern of a much-repeated, highly relished narrative.

"In the cool of the evening Madame Thoms, for such was her name, was wont to promenade in the bottom meadow. Being great with kit, she presented a considerable target.

Syce, flushed no doubt with wine, and flattering himself he cut the devil of a figure, is to be pictured upon his archery lawn. The instrument of destruction, a bow with the drawing-power, I am told of sixty pounds, in in his grip and the lust of blood in his heart. He shot an arrow in the air," Mr. Phinn concluded, "and if you tell me that it fell to earth he knew not where, I shall flatly refuse to believe you. His target, his deliberate mark, I am persuaded, was my exquisite cat. Thomasina, my fur of furs, I am speaking of your mama."

The mother-cat blinked at Mr. Phinn and so did Nurse Kettle.

"I must *say*," she thought, "he really *is* a little off," and since she had a kind heart, she was filled with a vague pity for him.

"Living alone," she thought, "with only those cats. It's not to be wondered at, really."

She gave him her brightest professional smile and one of her standard valedictions.

"Ah, well," said Nurse Kettle, letting go her anchorage on the gate, "be good, and if you can't be good, be careful."

"Care," Mr. Danberry-Phinn countered with a look of real intemperance in his eye, "killed the cat. I am not likely to forget it. Good evening to you, Nurse Kettle."

*ii*

Mr. Phinn was a widower, but Commander Syce was a bachelor. He lived next to Mr. Phinn in a Georgian house called Uplands, small and yet too big for Commander Syce, who had inherited it from an uncle. He was looked after by an ex-naval rating and his wife. The greater part of the grounds had been allowed to run to seed, but the kitchen-garden was kept up by the married couple and the archery lawn by Commander Syce himself. It overlooked the valley of the Chyne and was, apparently, his only interest. At one end in fine weather, stood a target on an easel, and at the other on summer evenings, from as far away as Nunspardon,

Commander Syce could be observed, in the classic pose, shooting a round from his sixty-pound bow. He was reputed to be a fine marksman, and it was noticed that however much his gait might waver, his stance, once he had opened his chest and stretched his bow, was that of a rock. He lived a solitary and aimless life. People would have inclined to be sorry for him if he had made any sign that he would welcome their sympathy. He did not do so and indeed at the smallest attempt at friendliness would sheer off, go about and make away as fast as possible. Although never seen in the bar, Commander Syce was a heroic supporter of the pub. Indeed, as Nurse Kettle pedalled up his overgrown drive, she encountered the lad from the Boy and Donkey pedalling down it with his bottle-carrier empty before him.

"There's the Boy," thought Nurse Kettle, rather pleased with herself for putting it that way, "and I'm very much afraid he's just paid a visit to the Donkey."

She, herself, had a bottle for Commander Syce, but it came from the chemist at Chyning. As she approached the house, she heard the sound of steps on the gravel and saw him limping away round the far end, his bow in his hand and his quiver girt about his waist. Nurse Kettle pedalled after him.

"Hi!" she called out brightly. "Good evening, Commander!"

Her bicycle wobbled and she dismounted.

Syce turned, hesitated for a moment and then came towards her.

He was a fairish, sunburned man who had run to seed. He still reeked of the navy and, as Nurse Kettle noticed when he drew nearer, of whisky. His eyes, blue and bewildered, stared into hers.

"Sorry," he said rapidly. "Good evening. I beg your pardon."

"Dr. Mark," she said, "asked me to drop in while I was passing and leave your prescription for you. There we are. The mixture as before."

He took it from her with a darting movement of his hand. "Most awfully kind," he said. "Frightfully sorry. Nothing urgent."

"No bother at all," Nurse Kettle rejoined, noticing the tremor of his hand. "I see you're going to have a shoot."

"Oh, yes. Yes," he said loudly, and backed away from her. "Well thank you, thank you, thank you."

"I'm calling in at Hammer. Perhaps you won't mind my trespassing. There's a footpath down to the right-of-way, isn't there?"

"Of course. Please do. Allow me."

He thrust his medicine into a pocket of his coat, took hold of her bicycle and laid his bow along the saddle and handlebars.

"Now *I'm* being the nuisance," said Nurse Kettle cheerfully. "Shall I carry your bow?"

He shied away from her and began to wheel the bicycle round the end of the house. She followed him, carrying the bow and talking in the comfortable voice she used for nervous patients. They came out on the archery lawn and upon a surprising and lovely view over the little valley of the Chyne. The trout stream shone like pewter in the evening light, meadows lay as rich as velvet on either side, the trees looked like pin-cushions, and a sort of heraldic glow turned the whole landscape into the semblance of an illuminated illustration to some forgotten romance. There was Major Cartarette winding in his line below Bottom Bridge and there up the hill on the Nunspardon golf course were old Lady Lacklander and her elderly son George, taking a postprandial stroll.

"*What* a clear evening," Nurse Kettle exclaimed with pleasure. "And *how* close everything looks. Do tell me, Commander," she went on, noticing that he seemed to flinch at this form of address, "with this bow of yours could you shoot an arrow into Lady Lacklander?"

Syce darted a look at the almost square figure across the little valley. He muttered something about a clout at two hundred and forty yards and limped on. Nurse Kettle, chagrined by his manner, thought, "What you need, my dear, is a bit of gingering up."

He pushed her bicycle down an untidy path through an overgrown shrubbery and she stumped after him.

"I have been told," she said, "that once upon a time you hit

**9**

a mark you didn't bargain for, down there."

Syce stopped dead. She saw that beads of sweat had formed on the back of his neck. "Alcoholic," she thought. "Flabby. Shame. He must have been a fine man when he looked after himself!"

"Great grief!" Syce cried out, thumping his fist on the seat of her bicycle. "You mean the bloody cat!"

"Well!"

"Great grief, it was an accident. I've told the old perisher! An accident! I *like* cats."

He swung round and faced her. His eyes were misted and his lips trembled. "I *like* cats," he repeated.

"We all make mistakes," said Nurse Kettle, comfortably.

He held his hand out for the bow and pointed to a little gate at the end of the path.

"There's the gate into Hammer," he said, and added with exquisite awkwardness, "I beg your pardon; I'm very poor company as you see. Thank you for bringing the stuff. Thank you, thank you."

She gave him the bow and took charge of her bicycle. "Dr. Mark Lacklander may be very young," she said bluffly, "but he's as capable a G.P. as I've come across in thirty years' nursing. If I were you, Commander, I'd have a good down-to-earth chinwag with him. Much obliged for the assistance. Good evening to you."

She pushed her bicycle through the gate into the well-tended coppice belonging to Hammer Farm and along a path that ran between herbaceous borders. As she made her way towards the house, she heard behind her at Uplands the twang of a bowstring and the "tock" of an arrow in a target.

"Poor chap," Nurse Kettle muttered, partly in a huff and partly compassionate. "Poor chap! Nothing to keep him out of mischief," and with a sense of vague uneasiness she wheeled her bicycle in the direction of the Cartarettes' rose garden, where she could hear the snip of garden secateurs and a woman's voice quietly singing.

"That'll be either *Mrs*.," thought Nurse Kettle, "or the stepdaughter. Pretty tune."

A man's voice joined in, making a second part.

# SCALES OF JUSTICE

*Come away, come away, death,*
*And in sad cypress let me be laid.*

The words, thought Nurse Kettle, were a trifle morbid, but the general effect was nice. The rose garden was enclosed behind quickset hedges and hidden from her, but the path she had taken led into it, and she must continue if she was to reach the house. Her rubber-shod feet made little sound on the flagstones, and the bicycle discreetly clicked along beside her. She had an odd feeling that she was about to break in on a scene of exquisite intimacy. She approached a green archway, and as she did so, the woman's voice broke off from its song and said, "that's my favourite of all."

"Strange," said a man's voice that fetched Nurse Kettle up with a jolt, "strange, isn't it, in a comedy, to make the love song so sad! Don't you think so, Rose? Rose...Darling..."

Nurse Kettle tinkled her bicycle bell, passed through the green archway and looked to her right. She discovered Miss Rose Cartarette and Dr. Mark Lacklander gazing into each other's eyes with unmistakable significance.

### iii

Miss Cartarette had been cutting roses and laying them in the basket held by Dr. Lacklander. Dr. Lacklander blushed to the roots of his hair and said, "Good God! Good heavens! Good evening," and Miss Cartarette said, "Oh, hullo, Nurse. Good evening." She, too, blushed, but more delicately than Dr. Lacklander.

Nurse Kettle said, "Good evening, Miss Rose. Good evening, Doctor. Hope it's all right my taking the short cut." She glanced with decorum at Dr. Lacklander. "The child with the abscess," she said, in explanation of her own appearance.

"Ah, yes," Dr. Lacklander said. "I've had a look at her. It's your gardener's little girl, Rose."

They both began to talk to Nurse Kettle, who listened with an expression of good humour. She was a romantic woman and took pleasure in the look of excitement on Dr. Lacklander's face and of shyness on Rose's.

"Nurse Kettle," Dr. Lacklander said rapidly, "like a perfect angel, is going to look after my grandfather tonight. I don't know what we should have done without her."

"*And* by that same token," Nurse Kettle added, "I'd better go on me way rejoicing or I shall be late on duty."

They smiled and nodded at her. She squared her shoulders, glanced in a jocular manner at her bicycle and stumped off with it through the rose garden.

"Well," she thought, "if that's not a case, I've never seen young love before. Blow me down flat, but I never guessed! Fancy!"

As much refreshed by this incident as she would have been by a good strong cup of tea, she made her way to the gardener's cottage, her last port of call before going up to Nunspardon.

When her figure, stoutly clad in her District Nurse's uniform, had bobbed its way out of the enclosed garden, Rose Cartarette and Mark Lacklander looked at each other and laughed nervously.

Lacklander said, "She's a fantastically good sort, old Kettle, but at that particular moment I could have done without her. I mustn't stay, I suppose."

"Don't you want to see papa?"

"Yes. But I shouldn't wait. Not that one can do anything much for the grandparent, but they like me to be there."

"I'll tell Daddy as soon as he comes in. He'll go up at once, of course."

"We'd be very grateful. Grandfather sets great store by his coming."

Mark Lacklander looked at Rose over the basket he carried and said unsteadily, "Darling."

"Don't," she said. "Honestly; don't."

"No? Are you warning me off, Rose? Is it all a dead loss?"

She made a small ineloquent gesture, tried to speak and said nothing.

"Well," Lacklander said, "I may as well tell you that I was

**12**

going to ask if you'd marry me. I love you dearly, and I thought we seemed to sort of suit. Was I wrong about that?"

"No," Rose said.

"Well, I know I wasn't. Obviously, we suit. So for pity's sake what's up? Don't tell me you love me like a brother, because I can't believe it."

"You needn't try to."

"Well, then?"

"I can't think of getting engaged, much less married."

"Ah!" Lacklander ejaculated. "Now, we're coming to it! This is going to be what I suspected. O, for God's sake let me get rid of this bloody basket! Here. Come over to the bench. I'm not going till I've cleared this up."

She followed him and they sat down together on a garden seat with the basket of roses at their feet. He took her by the wrist and stripped the heavy glove off her hand. "Now, tell me," he demanded, "do you love me?"

"You needn't bellow it at me like that. Yes, I do."

"Rose, darling! I was so panicked you'd say you didn't."

"Please listen, Mark. You're not going to agree with a syllable of this, but please listen."

"All right, I know what it's going to be but . . . all right."

"You can see what it's like here. I mean the domestic set-up. You must have seen for yourself how much difference it makes to Daddy my being on tap."

"You are so funny when you use colloquialisms . . . a little girl shutting her eyes and firing off a pop-gun. All right; your father likes to have you about. So he well might and so he still would if we married. We'd probably live half our time at Nunspardon."

"It's much more than that." Rose hesitated. She had drawn away from him and sat with her hands pressed together between her knees. She wore a long housedress. Her hair was drawn back into a knot at the base of her neck, but a single fine strand had escaped and shone on her forehead. She used very little make-up and could afford this economy for she was a beautiful girl.

She said, "It's simply that his second marriage hasn't been a success. If I left him now he'd really and truly have nothing to live for. Really."

"Nonsense," Mark said uneasily.

"He's never been able to do without me. Even when I was little. Nanny and I and my governess all following the drum. So many countries and journeys. And then after the war when he was given all those special jobs—Vienna and Rome and Paris. I never went to school, because he hated the idea of separation."

"All wrong, of course. Only half a life."

"No, no, no, that's not true, honestly. It was a wonderfully rich life. I saw and heard and learnt all sorts of splendid things other girls miss."

"All the same..."

"No, honestly, it was grand."

"You shouldn't have been allowed to get under your own steam."

"It wasn't a case of being allowed! I was allowed almost anything I wanted. And when I did get under my own steam just see what happened! He was sent with that mission to Singapore and I stayed in Grenoble and took a course at the university. He was delayed and delayed...and I found out afterwards that he was wretchedly at a loose end. And then...it was while he was there...he met Kitty."

Lacklander closed his well-kept doctor's hand over the lower half of his face and behind it made an indeterminate sound.

"Well," Rose said, "it turned out as badly as it possibly could, and it goes on getting worse, and if I'd been there I don't think it would have happened."

"Why not? He'd have been just as likely to meet her. And even if he hadn't, my heavenly and darling Rose, you cannot be allowed to think of yourself as a twister of the tail of fate."

"If I'd been there..."

"Now *look* here!" said Lacklander. "Look at it like this. If you removed yourself to Nunspardon as my wife, he and your stepmother might get together in a quick come-back."

"O, no," Rose said. "No, Mark. There's not a chance of that."

"How do you know? Listen. We're in love. I love you so desperately much it's almost more than I can endure. I know I shall never meet anybody else who could make me so happy and, incredible though it may seem, I don't believe you will either. I won't be put off, Rose. You shall marry me and if your father's life here is too unsatisfactory, well, we'll find some way of improving it. Perhaps if they part company he could come to us."

"Never! Don't you see! He couldn't bear it. He'd feel sort of extraneous."

"I'm going to talk to him. I shall tell him I want to marry you."

"No, Mark, darling! No ... please ..."

His hand closed momentarily over hers. Then he was on his feet and had taken up the basket of roses. "Good evening, Mrs. Cartarette," he said. "We're robbing your garden for my grandmother. You're very much ahead of us at Hammer with your roses."

Kitty Cartarette had turned in by the green archway and was looking thoughtfully at them.

*iv*

The second Mrs. Cartarette did not match her Edwardian name. She did not look like a Kitty. She was so fair that without her make-up she would have seemed bleached. Her figure was well disciplined and her face had been skillfully drawn up into a beautifully cared-for mask. Her greatest asset was her acquired inscrutability. This, of itself, made a *femme fatale* of Kitty Cartarette. She had, as it were, been manipulated into a menace. She was dressed with some elaboration and, presumably because she was in the garden, she wore gloves.

"How nice to see you, Mark," she said. "I thought I heard your voices. Is this a professional call?"

Mark said, "Partly so at least. I ran down with a message for

Colonel Cartarette, and I had a look at your gardener's small girl."

"How too kind," she said, glancing from Mark to her stepdaughter. She moved up to him and with her gloved hand took a dark rose from the basket and held it against her mouth.

"What a smell!" she said. "Almost improper, it's so strong. Maurice is not in, he won't be long. Shall we go up?"

She led the way to the house. Exotic wafts of something that was not roses drifted in her wake. She kept her torso rigid as she walked and slightly swayed her hips. "Very expensive," Mark Lacklander thought, "but not entirely exclusive. Why on earth did he marry her?"

Mrs. Cartarette's pin heels tapped along the flagstone path to a group of garden furniture heaped with cushions. A tray with a decanter and brandy glasses was set out on a white iron table. She let herself down on a swinging seat, put up her feet, and arranged herself for Mark to look at.

"Poorest Rose," she said, glancing at her stepdaughter, "you're wearing such suitable gloves. Do cope with your scratchy namesakes for Mark. A box perhaps."

"Please don't bother," Mark said. "I'll take them as they are."

"We can't allow that," Mrs. Cartarette murmured. "You doctors mustn't scratch your lovely hands, you know."

Rose took the basket from him. He watched her go into the house and turned abruptly at the sound of Mrs. Cartarette's voice.

"Let's have a little drink, shall we?" she said. "That's Maurice's pet brandy and meant to be too wonderful. Give me an infinitesimal drop and yourself a nice big one. I really prefer *creme de menthe*, but Maurice and Rose think it a common taste, so I have to restrain my carnal appetite."

Mark gave her the brandy. "I won't, if you don't mind," he said. "I'm by way of being on duty."

"Really? Who are you going to hover over, apart from the gardener's child?"

"My grandfather," Mark said.

"How awful of me not to realize," she rejoined with the

utmost composure. "How is Sir Harold?"

"Not so well this evening, I'm afraid. In fact I must get back. If I go by the river path, perhaps I'll meet the Colonel."

"Almost sure to I should think," she agreed indifferently, "unless he's poaching for that fable fish on Mr. Phinn's preserves, which, of course, he's much too county to think of doing, whatever the old boy may say to the contrary."

Mark said formally, "I'll go that way, then, and hope to see him."

She waved her rose at him in dismissal and held out her left hand in a gesture that he found distressingly second-rate. He took it with his own left and shook it crisply.

"Will you give your father a message for me?" she said. "I know how worried he must be about your grandfather. Do tell him I wish so much one could help."

The hand inside the glove gave his a sharp little squeeze and was withdrawn. "Don't forget," she said.

Rose came back with the flowers in a box. Mark thought, "I can't leave her like this, half-way through a proposal, damn it." He said coolly, "Come and meet your father. You don't take enough exercise."

"I live in a state of almost perpetual motion," she rejoined, "and I'm not suitably shod or dressed for the river path."

Mrs. Cartarette gave a little laugh. "Poor Mark!" she murmured. "But in any case, Rose, here *comes* your father."

Colonel Cartarette had emerged from a spinney half-way down the hill and was climbing up through the rough grass below the lawn. He was followed by his spaniel Skip, an old, obedient dog. The evening light had faded to a bleached greyness. Stivered grass, trees, lawns, flowers and the mildly curving thread of the shadowed trout stream joined in an announcement of oncoming night. Through this setting Colonel Cartarette moved as if he were an expression both of its substance and its spirit. It was as if from the remote past, through a quiet progression of dusks, his figure had come up from the valley of the Chyne.

When he saw the group by the lawn he lifted his hand in greeting. Mark went down to meet him. Rose, aware of her stepmother's heightened curiosity, watched him with profound misgiving.

Colonel Cartarette was a native of Swevenings. His instincts were those of a countryman and he had never quite lost his air of belonging to the soil. His tastes, however, were for the arts and his talents for the conduct of government services in foreign places. This odd assortment of elements had set no particular mark upon their host. It was not until he spoke that something of his personality appeared.

"Good evening, Mark," he called as soon as they were within comfortable earshot of each other. "My dear chap, what do you think! I've damned near bagged the Old 'Un."

"No!" Mark shouted with appropriate enthusiasm.

"I assure you! The Old 'Un! below the bridge in his usual lurk, you know. I could see him . . ."

And as he panted up the hill, the Colonel completed his classic tale of a management strike, a Homeric struggle and a broken cast. Mark, in spite of his own preoccupations, listened with interest. The Old 'Un was famous in Swevenings: a trout of magnitude and cunning, the despair and desire of every rod in the district.

". . . so I lost him," the Colonel ended, opening his eyes very wide and at the same time grinning for sympathy at Mark. "What a thing! By Jove, if I'd got him I really believe old Phinn would have murdered me."

"Are you still at war, sir?"

"Afraid so. The chap's impossible, you know. Good God, he's accused me in so many words of poaching. Mad! How's your grandfather?"

Mark said, "He's failing pretty rapidly, I'm afraid. There's nothing we can do. It's on his account I'm here, sir." And he delivered his message.

"I'll come at once," the Colonel said. "Better drive round. Just give me a minute or two to clean up. Come round with me, won't you?"

But Mark felt suddenly that he could not face another encounter with Rose and said he would go home at once by the river path and would prepare his grandfather for the Colonel's arrival.

He stood for a moment looking back through the dusk towards the house. He saw Rose gather up the full skirt of her house-coat and run across the lawn, and he saw her father set down his creel and rod, take off his hat and wait for her, his bald head gleaming. She joined her hands behind his neck and kissed him. They went on towards the house arm-in-arm. Mrs. Cartarette's hammock had begun to swing to and fro.

Mark turned away and walked quickly down into the valley and across Bottom Bridge.

The Old 'Un, with Colonel Cartarette's cast in his jaw, lurked tranquilly under the bridge.

CHAPTER **II**

Nunspardon

Sir Harold Lacklander watched Nurse Kettle as she moved about his room. Mark had given him something that had reduced his nightmare of discomfort and for the moment he seemed to enjoy the tragic self-importance that is the prerogative of the very ill. He preferred Nurse Kettle to the day-nurse. She was, after all, a native of the neighbouring village of Chyning, and this gave him the same satisfaction as the knowledge that the flowers on his table came out of the Nunspardon conservatories.

He knew now that he was dying. His grandson had not told him in so many words, but he had read the fact of death in the boy's face and in the behaviour of his own wife and son. Seven years ago he had been furious when Mark wished to become a doctor: a Lacklander and the only grandson. He had made it as difficult as he could for Mark. But he was glad now to have the Lacklander nose bending over him and the Lacklander hands doing the things doctors seemed to think necessary. He would have taken a sort of pleasure in the eminence to which approaching death had raised him if he had not been tormented by the most grievous of all ills. He had a sense of guilt upon him.

"Long time," he said. He used as few words as possible because with every one he uttered it was as if he squandered a measure of his dwindling capital. Nurse Kettle placed herself where he could see and hear her easily and said, "Doctor Mark says the Colonel will be here quite soon. He's been fishing."

"Luck?"

"I don't know. He'll tell you."

"Old 'Un."

"Ah," said Nurse Kettle comfortably, "they won't catch him in a hurry."

The wraith of a chuckle drifted up from the bed and was followed by an anxious sigh. She looked closely at the face that seemed during that day to have receded from its own bones.

"All right?" she asked.

The lacklustre eyes searched hers. "Papers?" the voice asked.

"I found them just where you said. They're on the table over there."

"Here."

"If it makes you feel more comfortable." She moved into the shadows at the far end of the great room and returned carrying a package, tied and sealed, which she put on his bedside table.

"Memoirs," he whispered.

"Fancy," said Nurse Kettle. "There must be a deal of work in them. I think it's lovely to be an author. And now I'm going to leave you to have a little rest."

She bent down and looked at him. He stared back anxiously. She nodded and smiled and then moved away and took up an illustrated paper. For a time there were no sounds in the great bedroom but the breathing of the patient and the rustle of a turned page.

The door opened. Nurse Kettle stood up and put her hands behind her back as Mark Lacklander came into the room. He was followed by Colonel Cartarette.

"All right, Nurse?" Mark asked quietly.

"Pretty much," she murmured. "Fretting. He'll be glad to see the Colonel."

"I'll just have a word with him first."

He walked down the room to the enormous bed. His grandfather stared anxiously up at him and Mark, taking the restless old hand in his, said at once, "Here's the Colonel, Grandfather. You're quite ready for him, aren't you?"

"Yes. Now."

"Right." Mark kept his fingers on his grandfather's wrist. Colonel Cartarette straightened his shoulders and joined him.

"Hullo, Cartarette," said Sir Harold so loudly and clearly that Nurse Kettle made a little exclamation. "Nice of you to come."

"Hullo, sir," said the Colonel, who was by twenty-five years the younger. "Sorry you're feeling so cheap. Mark says you want to see me."

"Yes." The eyes turned towards the bedside table. "Those things," he said. "Take them, will you? Now."

"They're memoirs," Mark said.

"Do you want me to read them?" Cartarette asked, stooping over the bed.

"If you will." There was a pause. Mark put the package into Colonel Cartarette's hands. The old man's eyes watched in what seemed to be an agony of interest.

"I think," Mark said, "that Grandfather hopes you will edit the memoirs, sir."

"I'll ... Of course," the Colonel said after an infinitesimal pause. "I'll be delighted; if you think you can trust me."

"Trust you. Implicitly. Implicitly. One other thing. Do you mind, Mark?"

"Of course not, Grandfather. Nurse, shall we have a word?"

Nurse Kettle followed Mark out of the room. They stood together on a dark landing at the head of a wide stairway.

"I don't think," Mark said, "that it will be much longer."

"Wonderful, though, how he's perked up for the Colonel."

"He'd set his will on it. I think," Mark said, "that he will now relinquish his life."

Nurse Kettle agreed. "Funny how they can hang on and funny how they will give up."

In the hall below a door opened and light flooded up the stairs. Mark looked over the banister and saw the enormously broad figure of his grandmother. Her hand flashed as it closed on the stair rail. She began heavily to ascend. He could hear her labored breathing.

"Steady does it, Gar," he said.

Lady Lacklander paused and looked up. "Ha!" she said. "It's the doctor, is it?" Mark grinned at the sardonic overtone.

She arrived on the landing. The train of her old velvet dinner dress followed her, and the diamonds which every evening she absent-mindedly stuck about her enormous bosom burned and winked as it rose and fell.

"Good evening, Miss Kettle," she panted. "Good of you to come and help my poor old boy. How is he, Mark? Has Maurice Cartarette arrived? Why are you both closeted together out here?"

"The Colonel's here, Gar. Grandfather wanted to have a word privately with him, so Nurse and I left them together."

"Something about those damned memoirs," said Lady Lacklander vexedly. "I suppose, in that case, I'd better not go in."

"I don't think they'll be long."

There was a large Jacobean chair on the landing. He pulled it forward. She let herself down into it, shuffled her astonishingly small feet out of a pair of old slippers and looked critically at them.

"Your father," she said, "has gone to sleep in the drawing-room muttering that he would like to see Maurice." She shifted her great bulk towards Nurse Kettle. "Now, before you settle to your watch, you kind soul," she said, "you won't mind saving my mammoth legs a journey. Jog down to the drawing-room, rouse my lethargic son, tell him the

Colonel's here and make him give you a drink and a sandwich. Um?"

"Yes, of course, Lady Lacklander," said Nurse Kettle and descended briskly. "Wanted to get rid of me," she thought, "but it was tactfully done."

"Nice woman, Kettle," Lady Lacklander grunted. "She knows I wanted to be rid of her. Mark, what is it that's making your grandfather unhappy?"

"Is he unhappy, Gar?"

"Don't hedge. He's worried to death...." She stopped short. Her jewelled hands twitched in her lap. "He's troubled in his mind," she said, "and for the second occasion in our married life I'm at a loss to know why. Is it something to do with Maurice and the memoirs?"

"Apparently. He wants the Colonel to edit them."

"The first occasion," Lady Lacklander muttered, "was twenty years ago and it made me perfectly miserable. And now, when the time has come for us to part company ... and it has come, child, hasn't it?"

"Yes, darling, I think so. He's very tired."

"I know. And I'm not. I'm seventy-five and grotesquely fat, but I have a zest for life. There are still," Lady Lacklander said with a change in her rather wheezy voice, "there are still things to be tidied up. George, for example."

"What's my poor papa doing that needs a tidying hand?" Mark asked gently.

"Your poor papa," she said, "is fifty and a widower and a Lacklander. Three ominous circumstances."

"Which can't be altered, even by you."

"They can, however, be ... Maurice! What is it?"

Colonel Cartarette had opened the door and stood on the threshold with the packages still under his arm.

"Can you come, Mark? Quickly."

Mark went past him into the bedroom. Lady Lacklander had risen and followed with more celerity than he would have thought possible. Colonel Cartarette stopped her in the doorway.

"My dear," he said, "wait a moment."

"Not a second," she said strongly. "Let me in, Maurice."

A bell rang persistently in the hall below. Nurse Kettle, followed by a tall man in evening clothes, came hurrying up the stairs.

Colonel Cartarette stood on the landing and watched them go in.

Lady Lacklander was already at her husband's bedside. Mark supported him with his right arm and with his left hand kept his thumb on a bell-push that lay on the bed. Sir Harold's mouth was open and he was fetching his breath in a series of half-yawns. There was a movement under the bedclothes that seemed to be made by a continuous flexion and extension of his leg. Lady Lacklander stood massively beside him and took both his hands between hers.

"I'm here, Hal," she said.

Nurse Kettle had appeared with a glass in her hand.

"Brandy," she said. "Old-fashioned but good."

Mark held it to his grandfather's open mouth. "Try," he said. "It'll help. Try."

The mouth closed over the rim.

"He's got a little," Mark said. "I'll give an injection."

Nurse Kettle took his place. Mark turned away and found himself face-to-face with his father.

"Can I do anything?" George Lacklander asked.

"Only wait here, if you will, Father."

"Here's George, Hal," Lady Lacklander said. "We're all here with you, my dear."

From behind the mask against Nurse Kettle's shoulder came a stutter, "Vic—Vic . . . Vic," as if the pulse that was soon to run down had become semi-articulate like a clock. They looked at each other in dismay.

"What is it?" Lady Lacklander asked. "What is it, Hal?"

"Somebody called Vic?" Nurse Kettle suggested brightly.

"There is nobody called Vic," said George Lacklander and sounded impatient. "For God's sake, Mark, can't you help him?"

"In a moment," Mark said from the far end of the room. "Vic . . ."

"The vicar?" Lady Lacklander asked, pressing his hand and bending over him. "Do you want the vicar to come, Hal?"

His eyes stared up into hers. Something like a smile twitched at the corners of the gaping mouth. The head moved slightly.

Mark came back with the syringe and gave the injection. After a moment Nurse Kettle moved away. There was something in her manner that gave definition to the scene. Lady Lacklander and her son and grandson drew closer to the bed. She had taken her husband's hands again.

"What is it, Hal? What is it, my dearest?" she asked. "Is it the vicar?"

With a distinctness that astonished them he whispered, "After all, you never know," and with his gaze still fixed on his wife he then died.

*ii*

On the late afternoon three days after his father's funeral, Sir George Lacklander sat in the study at Nunspardon going through the contents of the files and the desk. He was a handsome man with a look of conventional distinction. He had been dark but was now grizzled in the most becoming way possible with grey wings at his temples and a plume above his forehead. Inevitably, his mouth was firm and the nose above it appropriately hooked. He was, in short, rather like an illustration of an English gentleman in an American magazine. He had arrived at the dangerous age for such men, being now fifty years old and remarkably vigorous.

Sir Harold had left everything in apple-pie order, and his son anticipated little trouble. As he turned over the pages of his father's diaries, it occurred to him that as a family they richly deserved their too-much-publicized nicknames of "Lucky Lacklanders." How lucky, for instance, that the eighth baronet, an immensely wealthy man, had developed a passion for precious stones and invested in them to such an extent that they constituted a vast realizable fortune in themselves. How lucky that their famous racing stables were so phenomenally successful. How uniquely and fantastically lucky they had been in that no fewer than three times in the past century a Lacklander had won the most famous of all sweepstakes. It was true, of course, that he himself might be said to have had a piece of ill-fortune when his wife had died in giving birth to Mark, but as he remembered her, and he had to confess he no longer remembered her at all distinctly, she had been a disappointingly dull woman. Nothing like...But here he checked himself smartly and swept up his moustache with his thumb and forefinger. He was disconcerted when at this precise moment the butler came in to say that Colonel Cartarette had called and would like to see him. In a vague way the visit suggested a judgment. He took up a firm position on the hearthrug.

"Hullo, Maurice," he said when the Colonel came in. "Glad to see you." He looked self-consciously into the Colonel's face and with a changed voice said, "Anything wrong?"

"Well, yes," the Colonel said. "A hell of a lot actually. I'm sorry to bother you, George, so soon after your trouble and all that, but the truth is I'm so damned worried that I feel I've got to share my responsibility with you."

"Me!" Sir George ejaculated, apparently with relief and a kind of astonishment. The Colonel took two envelopes from his pocket and laid them on the desk. Sir George saw that they were addressed in his father's writing.

"Read the letter first," the Colonel said, indicating the smaller of the two envelopes. George gave him a wondering look. He screwed in his eyeglass, drew a single sheet of paper from the envelope, and began to read. As he did so, his mouth fell gently open and his expression grew increasingly blank. Once he looked up at the troubled Colonel as if to ask a question but seemed to change his mind and fell again to reading.

At last the paper dropped from his fingers and his monocle from his eye to his waistcoat.

"I don't," he said, "understand a word of it."

"You will," the Colonel said, "when you have looked at this." He drew a thin sheaf of manuscript out of the larger envelope and placed it before George Lacklander. "It will take you ten minutes to read. If you don't mind, I'll wait."

"My dear fellow! Do sit down. What am I thinking of. A cigar! A drink."

"No thank you, George. I'll smoke a cigarette. No, don't move. I've got one."

George gave him a wondering look, replaced his eyeglass and began to read again. As he did so, his face went through as many changes of expression as those depicted in strip-advertisements. He was a rubicund man, but the fresh colour drained out of his face. His mouth lost its firmness and his eyes their assurance. When he raised a sheet of manuscript, it quivered in his grasp.

Once, before he had read to the end, he did speak. "But it's not true," he said. "We've always known what happened. It was well known." He touched his lips with his fingers and read on to the end. When the last page had fallen on the others, Colonel Cartarette gathered them up and put them into their envelope.

"I'm damned sorry, George," he said. "God knows I didn't want to land you with all this."

"I can't see, now, why you've done it. Why bring it to me? Why do anything but throw it at the back of the fire?"

Cartarette said sombrely, "I see you haven't listened to me. I told you. I've thought it over very carefully. He's left the decision with me and I've decided I must publish . . ." he held up the long envelope . . . "this. I must, George. Any other course would be impossible."

"But have you thought what it will do to us? Have you thought? It . . . it's *un*thinkable. You're an old friend, Maurice. My father trusted you with this business because he thought of you as a friend. In a way," George added, struggling with an idea that was a little too big for him, "in a way he's bequeathed you our destiny."

"A most unwelcome legacy if it were so, but of course it's not. You're putting it altogether too high. I know, believe me,

George, I know, how painful and distressing this will be to you all, but I think the public will take a more charitable view than you might suppose."

"And since when," George demanded with a greater command of rhetoric than might have been expected of him, "since when have the Lacklanders stood cap-in-hand, waiting upon the charity of the public?"

Colonel Cartarette's response to this was a helpless gesture. "I'm terribly sorry," he said, "but I'm afraid that that sentiment has the advantage of sounding well and meaning nothing."

"Don't be so bloody supercilious."

"All right, George, all right."

"The more I think of this the worse it gets. Look here, Maurice, if for no other reason, in common decency..."

"I've tried to take common decency as my criterion."

"It'll kill my mother."

"It will distress her very deeply, I know. I've thought of her, too."

"And Mark? Ruin! A young man! My son! Starting his career."

"There was another young man, an only son, who was starting on his career."

"He's dead!" George cried out. "He can't suffer. He's dead."

"And *his* name? And *his* father?"

"I can't chop logic with you. I'm a simple sort of bloke with, I daresay, very unfashionable standards. I believe in the loyalty of friends and in the old families sticking together."

"At whatever the cost to other friends and other old families? Come off it, George," said the Colonel.

The colour flooded back into George's face until it was empurpled. He said in an unrecognizable voice, "Give me my father's manuscript. Give me that envelope. I demand it."

"I can't, old boy. Good God, do you suppose that if I could chuck it away or burn it with anything like a clear conscience I wouldn't do it? I tell you I hate this job."

He returned the envelope to the breast pocket of his coat.

"You're free, of course," he said, "to talk this over with Lady Lacklander and Mark. Your father made no reservations about that. By the way, I've brought a copy of his letter in case you decide to tell them about it. Here it is." The Colonel produced a third envelope, laid it on the desk and moved towards the door. "And George," he said, "I beg you to believe I am sorry. I'm deeply sorry. If I could see any other way, I'd thankfully take it. What?"

George Lacklander had made an inarticulate noise. He now pointed a heavy finger at the Colonel.

"After this," he said, "I needn't tell you that any question of an understanding between your girl and my boy is at an end."

The Colonel was so quiet for so long that both men became aware of the ticking of the clock on the chimney breast.

"I didn't know," he said at last, "that there was any question of an understanding. I think you must be mistaken."

"I assure you that I am not. However, we needn't discuss it. Mark . . . and Rose, I am sure . . . will both see that it is quite out of the question. No doubt you are as ready to ruin her chances as you are to destroy our happiness." For a moment he watched the Colonel's blank face. "She's head over heels in love with him," he added; "you can take my word for it."

"If Mark has told you this . . ."

"Who says Mark told me? . . . I . . . I . . ."

The full, rather florid voice faltered and petered out. "Indeed," the Colonel said. "Then may I ask where you got your information?"

They stared at each other and, curiously, the look of startled conjecture which had appeared on George Lacklander's face was reflected on the Colonel's. "It couldn't matter less, in any case," the Colonel said. "Your informant, I am sure, is entirely mistaken. There's no point in my staying. Goodbye."

He went out. George, transfixed, saw him walk past the window. A sort of panic came over him. He dragged the telephone across his desk and with an unsteady hand dialled Colonel Cartarette's number. A woman's voice answered.

"Kitty!" he said. "Kitty, is that you?"

*iii*

Colonel Cartarette went home by the right-of-way known as the River Path. It ran through Nunspardon from the top end of Watt's Lane skirting the Lacklander's private golf course. It wound down to Bottom Bridge and up the opposite side to the Cartarette's spinney. From thence it crossed the lower portion of Commander Syce's and Mr. Phinn's demesnes and rejoined Watt's Lane just below the crest of Watt's Hill.

The Colonel was feeling miserable. He was weighed down by his responsibliity and upset by his falling out with George Lacklander, who, pompous old ass though the Colonel thought him, was a lifetime friend. Worst of all, he was wretchedly disturbed by the suggestion that Rose had fallen in love with Mark and by the inference, which he couldn't help drawing, that George Lacklander had collected this information from the Colonel's wife.

As he walked down the hillside, he looked across the little valley into the gardens of Jacob's Cottage, Uplands and Hammer Farm. There was Mr. Phinn dodging about with a cat on his shoulder: "like a blasted old warlock," thought the Colonel, who had fallen out with Mr. Phinn over the trout stream, and there was poor Syce blazing away with his bow and arrow at his padded target. And there, at Hammer, was Kitty. With a characteristic movement of her hips she had emerged from the house in skintight velvet trousers and a flame-coloured top. Her long cigarette-holder was in her hand. She seemed to look across the valley at Nunspardon. The Colonel felt a sickening jolt under his diaphragm. "How I could!" he thought (though subconsciously). "How I could!" Rose was at her evening employment cutting off the deadheads in the garden. He sighed and looked up to the crest of the hill, and there plodding homewards, pushing her bicycle up Watt's Lane, her uniform and hat appearing in gaps and vanishing behind hedges, was Nurse Kettle. "In

Swevenings," thought the Colonel, "she crops up like a recurring decimal."

He came to the foot of the hill and to the Bottom Bridge. The bridge divided his fishing from Mr. Danberry-Phinn's: he had the lower reaches and Mr. Phinn the upper. It was about the waters exactly under Bottom Bridge that they had fallen out. The Colonel crossed from Mr. Phinn's side to his own, folded his arms on the stone parapet and gazed into the sliding green world beneath. At first he stared absently, but after a moment his attention sharpened. In the left bank of the Chyne near a broken-down boatshed where an old punt was moored, there was a hole. In its depths eddied and lurked a shadow among shadows: the Old 'Un. "Perhaps," the Colonel thought, "perhaps it would ease my mind a bit if I came down before dinner. He may stay on my side." He withdrew his gaze from the Old 'Un to find, when he looked up at Jacob's Cottage, that Mr. Phinn, motionless, with his cat still on his shoulder, was looking at him through a pair of field-glasses.

"Ah hell!" muttered the Colonel. He crossed the bridge and passed out of sight of Jacob's Cottage and continued on his way home.

The path crossed a narrow meadow and climbed the lower reach of Watt's Hill. His own coppice and Commander Syce's spinney concealed from the Colonel the upper portions of the three demesnes. Someone was coming down the path at a heavy jog-trot. He actually heard the wheezing and puffing of this person and recognized the form of locomotion practised by Mr. Phinn before the latter appeared wearing an old Norfolk jacket and tweed hat which, in addition to being stuck with trout-fishing flies, had Mr. Phinn's reading spectacles thrust through the band like an Irishman's pipe. He was carrying his elaborate collection of fishing impedimenta. He had the air of having got himself together in a hurry and was attended by Mrs. Thomasina Twitchett, who, after the manner of her kind, suggested that their association was purely coincidental.

The path was narrow. It was essential that someone should give way and the Colonel, sick of rows with his neighbours, stood on one side. Mr. Phinn jogged glassily down upon him. The cat suddenly cantered ahead.

"Hullo, old girl," said the Colonel. He stopped down and snapped a finger and thumb at her. She stared briefly and passed him with a preoccupied air, twitching the tip of her tail.

The Colonel straightened up and found himself face-to-face with Mr. Phinn.

"Good evening," said the Colonel.

"Sir," said Mr. Phinn. He touched his dreadful hat with one finger, blew out his cheeks and advanced. "Thomasina," he added, "hold your body more seemly."

For Thomasina, waywardly taken with the Colonel, had returned and rolled on her back at his feet.

"Nice cat," said the Colonel and added, "Good fishing to you. The Old 'Un lies below the bridge on my side, by the way?"

"Indeed?"

"As no doubt you guessed," the Colonel added against his better judgment, "when you watched me through your field-glasses."

If Mr. Phinn had contemplated a conciliatory position, he at once abandoned it. He made a belligerent gesture with his net. "The landscape, so far as I am aware," he said, "is not under some optical interdict. It may be viewed, I believe. To the best of my knowledge, there are no squatter's rights over the distant prospect of the Chyne."

"None whatever. You can stare," said the Colonel, "at the Chyne, or me, or anything else you fancy till you are black in the face, for all I care. But if you realized...If you...." He scratched his head, a gesture that with the Colonel denoted profound emotional disturbance. "My dear Phinn..." he began again, "if you only knew...God bless my soul, what *does* it matter! Good evening to you."

He encircled Mr. Phinn and hurried up the path. "And for that grotesque," he thought resentfully, "for that impossible, that almost certifiable buffoon I have saddled myself with a responsibility that will make me wretchedly uncomfortable for the rest of my life."

He mended his pace and followed the path into the Hammer coppice. Whether summoned by maternal obligations or because she had taken an inscrutable cat's fancy to the Colonel, Thomasina Twitchett accompanied him, trilling occasionally and looking about for an evening bird. They came within view of the lawn, and there was Commander Syce, bow in hand, quiver at thigh and slightly unsteady on his feet, hunting about in the underbrush.

"Hullo, Cartarette," he said. "Lost a damned arrow. What a thing! Missed the damned target and away she went."

"Missed it by a dangerously wide margin, didn't you?" the Colonel rejoined rather testily. After all, people did use the path, he reflected, and he began to help in the search. Thomasina Twitchett, amused by the rustle of leaves, pretended to join in the hunt.

"I know," Commander Syce agreed; "rotten bad show, but I saw old Phinn and it put me off. Did you hear what happened about me and his cat? Damnedest thing you ever knew! Purest accident, but the old what-not wouldn't have it. Great grief, I told him, I *like* cats."

He thrust his hand into a heap of dead leaves. Thomasina Twitchett leapt merrily upon it and fleshed her claws in his wrist. "Perishing little bastard," said Commander Syce. He freed himself and aimed a spank at her which she easily avoided and being tired of their company, made for her home and kittens. The Colonel excused himself and turned up through the spinney into the open field below his own lawn.

His wife was in her hammock dangling a tightly encased black-velvet leg, a flame-colored sleeve and a pair of enormous ear-rings. The cocktail tray was already on her iron table.

"How late you are," she said, idly. "Dinner in half an hour. What have you been up to at Nunspardon?"

"I had to see George."

"What about?"

"Some business his father asked me to do."

"How illuminating." -

"It was very private, my dear."

"How *is* George?"

The Colonel remembered George's empurpled face and said, "Still rather upset."

"We must ask him to dinner. I'm learning to play golf with him tomorrow, by the way. He's giving me some clubs. Nice, isn't it?"

"When did you arrange that?"

"Just now. About twenty minutes ago," she said, watching him.

"Kitty, I'd rather you didn't."

"You don't by any chance suspect me of playing you false with George, do you?"

"Well," said the Colonel after a long pause, "are you?"

"No."

"I still think it might be better not to play golf with him tomorrow."

"Why on earth?"

"Kitty, what have you said to George about Mark and Rose?"

"Nothing you couldn't have seen for yourself, darling. Rose is obviously head over heels in love with Mark."

"I don't believe you."

"My good Maurice, you don't suppose the girl is going to spend the rest of her existence doting on Daddy, do you?"

"I wouldn't have it for the world. Not for the world."

"Well, then."

"But I . . . I didn't know . . . I still don't believe . . ."

"He turned up here five minutes ago looking all churned-up, and they're closeted together in the drawing-room. Go and see. I'll excuse your changing, if you like."

"Thank you, my dear," the Colonel said miserably and went indoors.

If he hadn't been so rattled and worried he would no doubt have given some sort of warning of his approach. As it was, he crossed the heavy carpet of the hall, opened the drawing-room door and discovered his daughter locked in Mark Lacklander's arms, from which embrace she was making but ineffectual attempts to escape.

# CHAPTER III

## The Valley of the Chyne

Rose and Mark behaved in the classic manner of surprised lovers. They released each other. Rose turned white and Mark red, and neither of them uttered a word.

The Colonel said, "I'm sorry, my dear. Forgive me," and made his daughter a little bow.

Rose, with a sort of agitated spontaneity, ran to him, linked her hands behind his head and cried, "It had to happen sometime, darling, didn't it?"

Mark said, "Sir, I want her to marry me."

"But I won't," Rose said, "I won't unless you can be happy about it. I've told him."

The Colonel, with great gentleness, freed himself and then put an arm round his daughter.

"Where have you come from, Mark?" he asked.

"From Chyning. It's my day at the hospital."

"Yes, I see." The Colonel looked from his daughter to her lover and thought how ardent and vulnerable they seemed. "Sit down, both of you," he said. "I've got to think what I'm going to say to you. Sit down."

They obeyed him with an air of bewilderment.

"When you go back to Nunspardon, Mark," he said, "you will find your father very much upset. That is because of a talk I've just had with him. I'm at liberty to repeat the substance of that talk to you, but I feel some hesitation in doing so. I think he should be allowed to break it to you himself."

"*Break* it to me?"

"It is not good news. You will find him entirely opposed to any thought of your marriage with Rose."

"I can't believe it," Mark said.

"You will, however. You may even find that you yourself (forgive me, Rose, my love, but it may be so) feel quite differently about..." the Colonel smiled faintly... "about contracting an alliance with a Cartarette."

"But, my poorest Daddy," Rose ejaculated, clinging to a note of irony, "what have you been up to?"

"The very devil and all, I'm afraid, my poppet," her father rejoined.

"Well, whatever it may be," Mark said and stood up, "I can assure you that blue murder wouldn't make me change my mind about Rose."

"O," the Colonel rejoined mildly, "this is not blue murder."

"Good." Mark turned to Rose. "Don't be fussed, darling," he said. "I'll go home and sort it out."

"By all means, go home," the Colonel agreed, "and try." He took Mark by the arm and led him to the door.

"You won't feel very friendly towards me tomorrow, Mark," he said. "Will you try to believe that the action I've been compelled to take is one that I detest taking?"

"Compelled?" Mark repeated. "Yes, well...yes, of course" He stuck out the Lacklander jaw and knitted the Lacklander brows. "Look here, sir," he said, "if my father welcomes our engagement...and I can't conceive of his doing anything else...will you have any objection? I'd better tell you now that no objection on either side will make the smallest difference."

"In that case," the Colonel said, "our question is academic. And now I'll leave you to have a word with Rose before you go home." He held out his hand. "Goodbye, Mark."

When the Colonel had gone, Mark turned to Rose and took her hands in his. "But how ridiculous," he said. "How in the world could these old boys cook up anything that would upset *us?*"

"I don't know. I don't know how they could, but it's serious. He's terribly worried, poor darling."

"Well," Mark said, "it's no good attempting a diagnosis before we've heard the history. I'll go home, see what's happened and ring you up in about fifteen minutes. The all-important, utterly bewildering and Heaven-sent joy is that you love me, Rose. Nothing," Mark continued with an air of coining a brand-new phrase, "nothing can alter that. Au revoir, darling."

He kissed Rose in a business-like manner and was gone.

She sat still for a time hugging to herself the knowledge of their feeling for each other. What had happened to all her scruples about leaving her father? She didn't even feel properly upset by her father's extraordinary behaviour, and when she realized this circumstance, she realized the extent of her exthrallment. She stood in the French window of the drawing-room and looked across the valley to Nunspardon. It was impossible to be anxious . . . her whole being ached with happiness. It was now and for the first time that Rose understood the completeness of love.

Time went by without her taking thought of it. The gong sounded for dinner and at the same moment the telephone rang. She flew to it.

"Rose," Mark said. "Say at once that you love me. At once."

"I love you."

"And on your most sacred word of honour that you'll marry me. Say it, Rose. Promise it. Solemnly promise."

"I solemnly promise."

"Good," said Mark. "I'll come back at nine."

"Do you know what's wrong?"

"Yes. It's damn' ticklish. Bless you, darling. Till nine."

"Till nine," Rose said and in a state of enthrallment went in to dinner.

*ii*

By eight o'clock the evening depression had begun to settle over Commander Syce. At about five o'clock, when the sun was over the yard-arm, he had a brandy and soda. This raised his spirits. With its successors, up to the third or fourth, they rose still further. During this period he saw himself taking a job and making a howling success of it. From that emotional eminence he fell away with each succeeding dram, and it was during his decline that he usually took to archery. It had been in such a state of almost suicidal depression that he had suddenly shot an arrow over his coppice into Mr. Danberry-Phinn's bottom meadow and slain the mother of Thomasina Twitchett.

To-night the onset of depression was more than usually severe. Perhaps his encounter with the Colonel, whom he liked, gave point to his own loneliness. Moreover, his married couple were on their annual holiday and he had not been bothered to do anything about an evening meal. He found his arrow and limped back to the archery lawn. He no longer wanted to shoot. His gammy leg ached, but he thought he'd take a turn up the drive.

When he arrived at the top, it was to discover Nurse Kettle seated by the roadside in gloomy contemplation of her bicycle, which stood upside down on its saddle and handlebars.

"Hullo, Commander," said Nurse Kettle, "I've got a puncture."

"Evening. Really? Bore for you," Syce shot out at her.

"I can't make up me great mind to push her the three miles to Chyning, so I'm going to have a shot at running repairs.

**42**

Pumping's no good," said Nurse Kettle.

She had opened a tool kit and was looking dubiously at its contents. Syce hung off and on and watched her make a pass with a lever at her tyre.

"Not like that," he shouted when he could no longer endure it. "Great grief, you'll get nowhere that fashion."

"I believe you."

"And in any case you'll want a bucket of water to find the puncture." She looked helplessly at him. "Here!" he mumbled. "Give it here."

He righted the bicycle and with a further, completely inaudible remark began to wheel it down his drive. Nurse Kettle gathered up her tool kit and followed. A look strangely compounded of compassion and amusement had settled on her face.

Commander Syce wheeled the bicycle into a gardener's shed and without the slightest attempt at any further conversation set about the removal of the tyre. Nurse Kettle hitched herself up on a bench and watched him. Presently she began to talk.

"I *am* obliged to you. I've had a bit of a day. Epidemic in the village, odd cases all over the place, and then this happens. There! Aren't you neat-fingered. I looked in at Nunspardon this evening," she continued. "Lady Lacklander's got a 'toe,' and Dr. Mark arranged for me to do the fomentations."

Commander Syce made an inarticulate noise.

"If you ask *me*, the new baronet's feeling his responsibilities. Came in just as I was leaving. Very bad colour and jumpy," Nurse Kettle gossiped cosily. She swung her short legs and interrupted herself from time to time to admire Syce's handiwork. "Pity!" she thought. "Shady hands. Alcoholic skin. Nice chap, too. Pity!"

He repaired the puncture and replaced the tube and tyre. When he had finished and made as if to stand up, he gave a sharp cry of pain, clapped his hand to the small of his back and sank down again on his knees.

"Hul—lo!" Nurse Kettle ejaculated. "What's all this? 'Bago?"

Commander Syce swore under his breath. Between clenched teeth he implored her to go away. "Most frightfully sorry," he groaned. "Ask you to excuse me. Ach!"

It was now that Nurse Kettle showed the quality that caused people to prefer her to grander and more up-to-date nurses. She exuded dependability, resourcefulness and authority. Even the common and pitilessly breezy flavour of her remarks was comfortable. To Commander Syce's conjurations to leave him alone, followed in the extremity of his pain by furious oaths, she paid no attention. She went down on all fours beside him, enticed and aided him towards the bench, encouraged him to use it and her own person as aids to rising, and finally had him, though almost bent double, on his feet. She helped him into his house and lowered him down on a sofa in a dismal drawing-room.

"Down-a-bumps," she said. Sweating and gasping, he reclined and glared at her. "Now, what are we going to do about *you*, I wonder? Did I or did I not see a rug in the hall? Wait a bit."

She went out and came back with a rug. She called him "dear" and, taking his pain seriously, covered him up, went out again and returned with a glass of water. "Making myself at home, I suppose you're thinking. Here's a couple of aspirins to go on with," said Nurse Kettle.

He took them without looking at her. "Please don't trouble," he groaned. "Thank you. Under my own steam." She gave him a look and went out again.

In her absence, he attempted to get up but was galvanized with a monstrous jab of lumbago and subsided in agony. He began to think she had gone for good and to wonder how he was to support life while the attack lasted, when he heard her moving about in some remote part of the house. In a moment she came in with two hot-water bags.

"At this stage," she said, "heat's the ticket."

"Where did you get those things?"

"Borrowed 'em from the Cartarettes."

"My God!"

She laid them against his back.

"Dr. Mark's coming to look at you," she said.

"My God!"

"He was at the Cartarettes and if you ask me, there's going to be some news from that quarter before any of us are much older. At least," Nurse Kettle added rather vexedly, "I *would* have said so, if it hadn't been for them all looking a bit put out." To his horror she began to take off his shoes.

"With a yo-heave-ho," said Nurse Kettle out of compliment to the navy. "Aspirin doing its stuff?"

"I...I think so. I *do beg*..."

"I suppose your bedroom's upstairs?"

"I do BEG..."

"We'll see what the doctor says, but I'd suggest you doss down in the housekeeper's room to save the stairs. I mean to say," Nurse Kettle added with a hearty laugh, "always provided there's no housekeeper."

She looked into his face so good-humouredly and with such an air of believing him to be glad of her help that he found himself accepting it.

"Like a cup of tea?" she asked.

"No thank you."

"Well, it won't be anything stronger unless the doctor says so."

He reddened, caught her eye and grinned.

"Come," she said, "that's better."

"I'm really ashamed to trouble you so much."

"I might have said the same about my bike, mightn't I? There's the doctor."

She bustled out again and came back with Mark Lacklander.

Mark, who was a good deal paler than his patient, took a crisp line with Syce's expostulations.

"All right," he said. "I daresay I'm entirely extraneous. This isn't a professional visit if you'd rather not."

"Great grief, my dear chap, I don't mean that. Only too grateful but...I mean...busy man...right itself..."

"Well, suppose I take a look-see," Mark suggested. "We won't move you."

The examination was brief. "If the lumbago doesn't clear up, we can do something a bit more drastic," Mark said, "but in the meantime Nurse Kettle'll get you to bed..."

"Good God!"

"...and look in again to-morrow morning. So will I. You'll need one or two things; I'll ring up the hospital and get them sent out at once. All right?"

"Thank you. Thank you. You don't," said Syce, to his own surprise, "look terribly fit yourself. Sorry to have dragged you in."

"That's all right. We'll bring your bed in here and put it near the telephone. Ring up if you're in difficulties. By the way, Mrs. Cartarette offered..."

"NO!" shouted Commander Syce and turned purple.

"...to send in meals," Mark added. "But of course you may be up and about again to-morrow. In the meantime I think we can safely leave you to Nurse Kettle. Good-night."

When he had gone, Nurse Kettle said cheerfully, "You'll have to put up with me, it seems, if you don't want lovely ladies all round you. Now we'll get you washed up and settled for the night."

Half an hour later when he was propped up in bed with a cup of hot milk and a plate of bread and butter and the lamp within easy reach, Nurse Kettle looked down at him with her quizzical air.

"Well," she said, "I shall now, as they say, love you and leave you. Be good and if you can't be good, be careful."

"Thank you," gabbled Commander Syce, nervously. "Thank you, thank you, thank you."

She had plodded over to the door before his voice arrested her. "I...ah...I don't suppose," he said, "that you are familiar with Aubrey's *Brief Lives*, are you?"

"No," she said. "Who was *he* when he was at home?"

"He wrote a 'brief life' of a man called Sir Jonas Moore. It begins: 'Sciatica he cured it, by boyling his buttocks.' I'm glad, at least, you don't propose to try that remedy."

"Well!" cried Nurse Kettle delightedly. "You *are* coming out of your shell, to be sure. Nighty-bye."

*iii*

During the next three days Nurse Kettle, pedalling about her duties, had occasion to notice, and she was sharp in such matters, that something untoward was going on in the district. Wherever she went, whether it was to attend upon Lady Lacklander's toe, or upon the abscess of the gardener's child at Hammer, or upon Commander Syce's strangely persistent lumbago, she felt a kind of heightened tension in the behaviour of her patients and also in the behaviour of young Dr. Mark Lacklander. Rose Cartarette, when she encountered her in the garden, was white and jumpy; the Colonel looked strained and Mrs. Cartarette singularly excited.

"Kettle," Lady Lacklander said, on Wednesday, wincing a little as she endured the approach of a fomentation to her toe, "have you got the cure for a bad conscience?"

Nurse Kettle did not resent being addressed in this restoration-comedy fashion by Lady Lacklander, who had known her for some twenty years and used the form with an intimate and even an affectionate air much prized by Nurse Kettle.

"Ah," said the latter, "there's no mixture-as-before for *that* sort of trouble."

"No. How long," Lady Lacklander went on, "have you been looking after us in Swevenings, Kettle?"

"Thirty years if you count five in the hospital at Chyning."

"Twenty-five years of fomentations, enemas, slappings, and thumpings," mused Lady Lacklander. "And I suppose you've learnt quite a lot about us in that time. There's nothing like a love affair," she added unexpectedly, "to disguise it. This is agony," she ended mildly, referring to the fomentation.

"Stick it if you can, dear," Nurse Kettle advised, and Lady Lacklander for her part did not object to being addressed as "dear" by Nurse Kettle, who continued, "How do you mean, I wonder, about love disguising character?"

"When people are in love," Lady Lacklander said with a little scream as a new fomentation was applied, "they instinctively present themselves to each other in their most favourable light. They assume pleasing characteristics as unconsciously as a cock pheasant puts on his spring plumage. They display such virtues as magnanimity, charitableness and modesty and wait for them to be admired. They develop a positive genius for suppressing their least attractive points. They can't help it, you know, Kettle. It's just the behaviourism of courtship."

"Fancy."

"Now don't pretend you don't know what I'm talking about, because you most certainly do. You think straight and that's more than anybody else seems to be capable of doing in Swevenings. You're a gossip, of course," Lady Lacklander added, "but I don't think you're a malicious gossip, are you?"

"Certainly not. The idea!"

"No. Tell me, now, without any frills, what do you think of *us*?"

"Meaning, I take it," Nurse Kettle returned, "the aristocracy?"

"Meaning exactly that. Do you," asked Lady Lacklander with relish, "find us effete, ineffectual, vicious, obsolete and altogether extraneous?"

"No," said Nurse Kettle stoutly, "I don't."

"Some of are, you know."

Nurse Kettle squatted back on her haunches retaining a firm grip on Lady Lacklander's little heel. "It's not the people so much as the idea," she said.

"Ah," said Lady Lacklander, "you're an Elizabethan, Kettle. You *believe* in degree. You're a female Ulysses, old girl. But degree is now dependent upon behaviour, I'd have you know."

Nurse Kettle gave a jolly laugh and said she didn't know what that meant. Lady Lacklander rejoined that, among other things, it meant that if people fall below something called a certain standard, they are asking for trouble. "I mean," Lady Lacklander went on, scowling with physical pain and mental concentration, "I mean we'd better behave ourselves in the admittedly few jobs that by right of heritage used to be ours. I mean, finally, that whether they think we're rubbish or whether they think we're not, people still expect that in certain situations we will give certain reactions. Don't they, Kettle?"

Nurse Kettle said she supposed they did.

"Not," Lady Lacklander said, "that I give a damn what they think. But still . . ."

She remained wrapped in moody contemplation while Nurse Kettle completed her treatment and bandaged the toe.

"In short," her formidable patient at last delcaimed, "we can allow ourselves to be almost anything but shabbily behaved. That we'd better avoid. I'm extremely worried, Kettle." Nurse Kettle looked up enquiringly. "Tell me, is there any gossip in the village about my grandson? Romantic gossip?"

"A bit," Nurse Kettle said and after a pause added, "It'd be lovely, wouldn't it? She's a sweet girl. *And* an heiress into the bargain."

"Umph."

"Which is not to be sneezed at nowadays, I suppose. They tell me everything goes to the daughter."

"Entailed," Lady Lacklander said. "Mark, of course, gets nothing until he succeeds. But it's not that that bothers me."

"Whatever it is, if I were you, I should consult Dr. Mark, Lady Lacklander. An old head on young shoulders if ever I saw one."

"My dear soul, my grandson is, as you have observed, in love. He is, therefore, as I have tried to point out, extremely likely to take up a high-falutin' attitude. Besides, he's involved. No, I must take matters into my own hands, Kettle. Into my own hands. You go past Hammer on your way home, don't you?"

Nurse Kettle said she did.

"I've written a note to Colonel Cartarette. Drop it there like a good creature, will you?"

Nurse Kettle said she would and fetched it from Lady Lacklander's writing desk.

"It's a pity," Lady Lacklander muttered, as Nurse Kettle was about to leave. "It's a pity poor George is such an ass."

*iv*

She considered that George gave only too clear a demonstration of being an ass when she caught a glimpse of him on the following evening. He was playing a round of golf with Mrs. Cartarette. George, having attained the tricky age for Lacklanders, had fallen into a muddled, excited dotage upon Kitty Cartarette. She made him feel dangerous, and this sensation enchanted him. She told him repeatedly how chivalrous he was and so cast a glow of knight-errantry over impulses that are not usually seen in that light. She allowed him only the most meagre rewards, doling out the lesser stimulants of courtship in positively homeopathic doses. Thus on the Nunspardon golf course, he was allowed to watch, criticize and correct her swing. If his interest in this exercise was far from being purely athletic, Mrs. Cartarette gave only the slightest hint that she was aware of the fact and industriously swung and swung again while he fell back to observe, and advanced to adjust, her technique.

Lady Lacklander, tramping down River Path in the cool of the evening with a footman in attendance to carry her sketching impedimenta and her shooting-stick, observed her son and his pupil as it were in pantomime on the second tee. She noticed how George rocked on his feet, with his head on one side, while Mrs. Cartarette swung, as Lady Lacklander angrily noticed, everything that a woman could swing. Lady Lacklander looked at the two figures with distaste tempered by speculation. "Can George," she wondered, "have some notion of employing the strategy of indirect attack upon Maurice? But no, poor boy, he hasn't got the brains."

The two figures disappeared over the crest of the hill, and Lady Lacklander plodded heavily on in great distress of mind. Because of her ulcerated toe she wore a pair of her late husband's shooting boots. On her head was a battered solar topee of immense antiquity which she found convenient as an eye-shade. For the rest, her vast person was clad in baggy tweeds and a tent-like blouse. Her hands, as always, were encrusted with diamonds.

She and the footman reached Bottom Bridge, turned left and came to a halt before a group of elders and the prospect of a bend in the stream. The footman, under Lady Lacklander's direction, set up her easel, filled her water-jar at the stream, placed her camp stool and put her shooting-stick beside it. When she fell back from her work in order to observe it as a whole, Lady Lacklander was in the habit of supporting her bulk upon the shooting-stick.

The footman left her. She would reappear in her own time at Nunspardon and change for dinner at nine o'clock. The footman would return and collect her impedimenta. She fixed her spectacles on her nose, directed at her subject the sort of glance Nurse Kettle often bestowed on a recalcitrant patient, and set to work, massive and purposeful before her easel.

It was at half past six that she established herself there, in the meadow on the left bank of the Chyne not far below Bottom Bridge.

At seven, Mr. Danberry-Phinn, having assembled his paraphernalia for fishing, set off down Watt's Hill. He did not continue to Bottom Bridge but turned left, and made for the upper reaches of the Chyne.

At seven, Mark Lacklander, having looked in on a patient in the village, set off on foot along Watt's lane. He carried his case of instruments, as he wished to lance the abscess of the gardener's child at Hammer, and his racket and shoes, as he proposed to play tennis with Rose Cartarette. He also hoped to have an extremely serious talk with her father.

At seven, Nurse Kettle, having delivered Lady Lacklander's note at Hammer, turned in at Commander Syce's drive and free-wheeled to his front door.

At seven, Sir George Lacklander, finding himself favourably situated in a sheltered position behind a group of trees, embraced Mrs. Cartarette with determination, fervour and an ulterior motive.

It was at this hour that the hopes, passions and fears that had slowly mounted in intensity since the death of Sir Harold Lacklander began to gather an emotional momentum and slide towards each other like so many downhill streams, influenced in their courses by accidents and detail, but destined for a common and profound agitation.

At Hammer, Rose and her father sat in his study and gazed at each other in dismay.

"When did Mark tell you?" Colonel Cartarette asked.

"On that same night . . . after you came in and . . . and found us. He went to Nunspardon and his father told him and then he came back here and told me. Of course," Rose said looking at her father with eyes as blue as periwinkles behind their black lashes, "of course it wouldn't have been any good for Mark to pretend nothing had happened. It's quite extraordinary how each of us seems to know exactly what the other one's thinking."

The Colonel leant his head on his hand and half smiled at this expression of what he regarded as one of the major fallacies of love. "My poor darling," he murmured.

"Daddy, you do understand, don't you, that theoretically Mark is absolutely on your side? Because . . . well, because the facts of any case always should be demonstrated. I mean, that's the scientific point of view."

The Colonel's half-smile twisted, but he said nothing.

"And I agree, too, absolutely," Rose said, "other things being equal."

"Ah!" said the Colonel.

"But they're not, darling," Rose cried out, "they're nothing like equal. In terms of human happiness, they're all cockeyed. Mark says his grandmother's so desperately worried that with all this coming on top of Sir Harold's death and everything she may crack up altogether."

The Colonel's study commanded a view of his own spinney and of that part of the valley that the spinney did not mask: Bottom Bridge and a small area below it on the right bank of the Chyne. Rose went to the window and looked down. "She's down there somewhere," she said, "sketching in Bottom Meadow on the far side. She only sketches when she's fussed."

"She's sent me a chit. She wants me to go down and talk to her at eight o'clock when I suppose she'll have done a sketch and hopes to feel less fussed. Damned inconvenient hour but there you are. I'll cut dinner, darling, and try the evening rise. Ask them to leave supper for me, will you, and apologies to Kitty."

"O.K.," Rose said with forced airiness. "And, of course," she added, "there's the further difficulty of Mark's papa."

"George."

"Yes, indeed, George. Well, we know he's not exactly as bright as sixpence, don't we, but all the same he *is* Mark's papa, and he's cutting up most awfully rough and..."

Rose caught back her breath, her lips trembled, and her eyes filled with tears. She launched herself into her father's arms and burst into a flood of tears. "What's the use," poor Rose sobbed, "of being a brave little woman? I'm not in the least brave. When Mark asked me to marry him, I said I wouldn't because of you and there I was, so miserable that when he asked me again I said I would. And now, when we're so desperately in love, this happens. We have to do them this really frightful injury. Mark says of course they must take it and it won't make any difference to *us*, but of course it *will*, and how can I bear to be married to Mark and know how his people feel about you when next to Mark, my darling, darling Daddy, I love you best in the world? And *his* father," Rose wept, "his father says that if Mark marries me, he'll never forgive him and that they'll do a sort of Montague and Capulet thing to us and, darling, it wouldn't be much fun for Mark and me, would it, to be star-crossed lovers?"

"My poor baby," murmured the agitated and sentimental Colonel, "my poor baby!" And he administered a number of unintentionally hard thumps between his daughter's shoulder blades.

"It's so many people's business," Rose sobbed. "It's all of us."

Her father dabbed at her eyes with his own handkerchief, kissed her and put her aside. In his turn he went over to the window and looked down at Bottom Bridge and up at the roofs of Nunspardon. There were no figures in view on the golf course.

"You know, Rose," the Colonel said in a changed voice, "I don't carry the whole responsibility. There is a final decision to be made, and mine must rest upon it. Don't hold out too many hopes, my darling, but I suppose there is a chance. I've time to get it over before I talk to Lady Lacklander, and indeed I suppose I should. There's nothing to be gained by any further delay. I'll go now."

He went to his desk, unlocked a drawer and took out an envelope.

Rose said, "Does Kitty...?"

"Oh, yes," the Colonel said. "She knows."

"Did you tell her, Daddy?"

The Colonel had already gone to the door. Without turning his head and with an air too casual to be convincing, he said, "O, no. No. She arranged to play a round of golf with George, and I imagine he elected to tell her. He's a fearful old gas-bag is George."

"She's playing now, isn't she?"

"Is she? Yes," said the Colonel, "I believe she is. He came to fetch her, I think. It's good for her to get out."

"Yes, rather," Rose agreed.

Her father went out to call on Mr. Octavius Danberry-Phinn. He took his fishing gear with him as he intended to go straight on to his meeting with Lady Lacklander and to ease his troubled mind afterwards with the evening rise. He also took his spaniel Skip, who was trained to good behaviour when he accompanied his master to the trout stream.

*v*

Lady Lacklander consulted the diamond-encrusted watch which was pinned to her tremendous bosom and discovered that it was now seven o'clock. She had been painting for half an hour and an all-too-familiar phenomenon had emerged from her efforts.

"It's a curious thing," she meditated, "that a woman of my character and determination should produce such a puny affair. However, it's got me in better trim for Maurice Cartarette, and that's a damn' good thing. An hour to go if he's punctual, and he's sure to be that."

She tilted her sketch and ran a faint green wash over the foreground. When it was partly dry, she rose from her stool, tramped some distance away to the crest of a hillock, seated herself on her shooting-stick and contemplated her work through a lorgnette tricked out with diamonds. The shooting-stick sank beneath her in the soft meadowland so that the disk which was designed to check its descent was itself imbedded to the depth of several inches. When Lady Lacklander returned to her easel, she merely abandoned her shooting-stick, which remained in a vertical position and from a distance looked a little like a giant fungoid growth. Sticking up above intervening hillocks and rushes, it was observed over the top of his glasses by the longsighted Mr. Phinn when, accompanied by Thomasina Twitchett, he came nearer to Bottom Bridge. Keeping on the right bank, he began to cast his fly in a somewhat mannered but adroit fashion over the waters most often frequented by the Old 'Un. Lady Lacklander, whose ears were as sharp as his, heard the whirr of his reel and, remaining invisible, was perfectly able to deduce the identity and movements of the angler. At the same time, far above them on Watt's Hill, Colonel Cartarette, finding nobody but seven cats at home at Jacob's Cottage, walked round the house and looking down into the little valley at once spotted both Lady Lacklander and Mr. Phinn, like figures in Nurse Kettle's imaginary map, the one squatting on her camp stool, the other in slow motion near Bottom Bridge.

"I've time to speak to him before I see her," thought the Colonel. "But I'll leave it here in case we don't meet." He posted his long envelope in Mr. Phinn's front door, and then greatly troubled in spirit, he made for the river path and went down into the valley, the old spaniel, Skip, walking at his heels.

Nurse Kettle, looking through the drawing-room window at Uplands, caught sight of the Colonel before he disappeared beyond Commander Syce's spinney. She administered a final tattoo with the edges of her muscular hands on Commander Syce's lumbar muscles and said, "There goes the Colonel for the evening rise. You wouldn't have stood *that* amount of punishment two days ago, would you?"

"No," a submerged voice said, "I suppose not."

"Well! So that's all I get for my trouble."

"No, no! Look here, look here!" he gabbled, twisting his head in an attempt to see her. "Good heavens! What are you saying?"

"All right. I know. I was only pulling your leg. There!" she said. "That's all for to-day and I fancy it won't be long before I wash my hands of you altogether."

"Of course I can't expect to impose on your kindness any longer."

Nurse Kettle was clearing up. She appeared not to hear this remark and presently bustled away to wash her hands. When she returned, Syce was sitting on the edge of his improvised bed. He wore slacks, a shirt, a scarf and a dressing gown.

"Jolly D.," said Nurse Kettle. "Done it all yourself."

"I hope you will give me the pleasure of joining me for a drink before you go."

"On duty?"

"Isn't it off duty, now?"

"Well," said Nurse Kettle, "I'll have a drink with you, but I hope it won't mean that when I've gone on me way rejoicing, you're going to have half a dozen more with yourself."

Commander Syce turned red and muttered something about a fellah having nothing better to do.

"Get along," said Nurse Kettle, "find something better. The idea!"

They had their drinks, looking at each other with an air of comradeship. Commander Syce, using a walking-stick and holding himself at an unusual angle, got out an album of photographs taken when he was on the active list in the navy. Nurse Kettle adored photographs and was genuinely interested in a long sequence of naval vessels, odd groups of officers and views of seaports. Presently she turned a page and discovered quite a dashing water-colour of a corvette and then an illustrated menu with lively little caricatures in the margin. These she greatly admired and observing a terrified and defiant expression on the face of her host, ejaculated, "You never did these yourself! You *did!* Well, aren't you the clever one!"

Without answering, he produced a small portfolio, which he silently thrust at her. It contained many more sketches. Although Nurse Kettle knew nothing about pictures, she did, she maintained, know what she liked. And she liked these very much indeed. They were direct statements of facts, and she awarded them direct statements of approval and was about to shut the portfolio when a sketch that had faced the wrong way round caught her attention. She turned it over. It was of a woman lying on a chaise-longue smoking a cigarette in a jade holder. A bougainvillea flowered in the background.

"Why," Nurse Kettle ejaculated. "Why, that's Mrs. Cartarette!"

If Syce had made some kind of movement to snatch the sketch from her, he checked himself before it was completed. He said very rapidly, "Party. Met her Far East. Shore Leave. Forgotten all about it."

"That would be before they were married, wouldn't it?" Nurse Kettle remarked with perfect simplicity. She shut the portfolio, said, "You know I believe you could make my picture-map of Swevenings," and told him of her great desire for one. When she got up and collected her belongings, he too rose, but with an ejaculation of distress.

"I see I haven't made a job of you yet," she remarked.

"Same time to-morrow suit you?"

"Admirably," he said. "Thank you, thank you, thank you."
He gave her one of his rare painful smiles and watched her as
she walked down the path towards his spinney. It was now a
quarter to nine.

Nurse Kettle had left her bicycle in the village, where she
was spending the evening with the Women's Institute. She
therefore took the river path. Dusk had fallen over the valley
of the Chyne, and as she descended into it, her own footfall
sounded unnaturally loud on the firm turf. Thump, thump,
thump she went, down the hillside. Once, she stopped dead,
tilted her head and listened. From behind her at Uplands
came the not unfamiliar sound of a twang followed by a sharp
penetrating blow. She smiled to herself and walked on. Only
desultory rural sounds disturbed the quiet of nightfall. She
could actually hear the cool voice of the stream.

She did not cross Bottom Bridge but followed a rough path
along the right bank of the Chyne, past a group of elders and
another of willows. This second group, extending in a
sickle-shaped mass from the water's edge into Bottom
Meadow, rose up vapourishly in the dusk. She could smell
willow leaves and wet soil. As sometimes happens when we
are solitary, she had the sensation of being observed, but she
was not a fanciful woman and soon dismissed this feeling.

"It's turned much cooler," she thought.

A cry of mourning, intolerably loud, rose from beyond the
willows and hung on the night air. A thrust whirred out of the
thicket close to her face, and the cry broke and wavered
again. It was the howl of a dog.

She pushed through the thicket into an opening by the river
and found the body of Colonel Cartarette with his spaniel
Skip beside it, mourning him.

# CHAPTER **IV**

## Bottom Meadow

Nurse Kettle was acquainted with death. She did not need Skip's lament to tell her that the curled figure resting its head on a turf of river grass was dead. She knelt beside it and pushed her hand under the tweed jacket and silk shirt. "Cooling," she thought. A tweed hat with fisherman's flies in the band lay over the face. Someone, she thought, might almost have dropped it here. She lifted it and remained quite still with it suspended in her hand. The Colonel's temple had been broken as if his head had come under a waxworker's hammer. The spaniel threw back its head and howled again.

"O, do be quiet!" Nurse Kettle ejaculated. She replaced the hat and stood up, knocking her head against a branch. The birds that spent the night in the willows stirred again and some of them flew out with a sharp whirring sound. The Chyne gurgled and plopped and somewhere up in Nunspardon woods an owl hooted. "He has been murdered," thought Nurse Kettle.

Through her mind hurtled all the axioms of police procedure as laid down in her chosen form of escape-literature. One must, she recollected, not touch the body, and she had touched it. One must send at once for the police, but she had nobody to send. She thought there was also something about not leaving the body, yet to telephone or to fetch Mr. Oliphant, the police-sergeant at Chyning, she would have to leave the body, and while she was away, the spaniel she supposed, would sit beside it and howl. It was now quite darkish and the moon not yet up. She could see, however, not far from the Colonel's hands, the glint of a trout's scales in the grass and of a knife blade nearby. His rod was laid out on the lip of the bank, less than a pace from where he lay. None of these things, of course, must be disturbed. Suddenly Nurse Kettle thought of Commander Syce, whose Christian name she had discovered was Geoffrey, and wished with all her heart that he was at hand to advise her. The discovery in herself of this impulse astonished her and, in a sort of flurry, she swapped Geoffrey Syce for Mark Lacklander. "I'll find the doctor," she thought.

She patted Skip. He whimpered and scratched at her knees with his paws. "Don't howl, doggy," she said in a trembling voice. "Good boy! Don't howl." She took up her bag and turned away.

As she made her way out of the willow grove, she wondered for the first time about the identity of the being who had reduced Colonel Cartarette to the status of a broken waxwork. A twig snapped. "Suppose," she thought, "he's still about! Help, what a notion!" And as she hurried back along the path to Bottom Bridge, she tried not to think of the dense shadows and dark hollows that lay about her. Up on Watt's Hill the three houses—Jacob's Cottage, Uplands and Hammer—all had lighted windows and drawn blinds. They looked very far off to Nurse Kettle.

She crossed Bottom Bridge and climbed the zigzag path that skirted the golf course, coming finally to the Nunspardon

Home Spinney. Only now did she remember that her flashlamp was in her bag. She got it out and found that she was breathless. "Too quick up the hill," she thought. "Keep your shirt on, Kettle." River Path proper ran past the spinney to the main road, but a by-path led up through the trees into the grounds of Nunspardon. This she took and presently came out into the open gardens with the impressive Georgian facade straight ahead of her.

The footman who answered the front door bell was well enough known to her. "Yes, it's me again, William," she said. "Is the doctor at home?"

"He came in about an hour ago, miss."

"I want to see him. It's urgent."

"The family's in the library, miss. I'll ascertain . . ."

"Don't bother," said Nurse Kettle. "Or, yes. Ascertain if you like, but I'll be hard on your heels. Ask him if he'll come out here and speak to me."

He looked dubiously at her, but something in her face must have impressed him. He crossed the great hall and opened the library door. He left it open and Nurse Kettle heard him say, "Miss Kettle to see Dr. Lacklander, my lady."

"Me?" said Mark's voice. "O Lord! All right, I'll come."

"Bring her in here," said Lady Lacklander's voice commanded. "Talk to her in here, Mark. I want to see Kettle." Hearing this, Nurse Kettle, without waiting to be summoned, walked quickly into the library. The three Lacklanders had turned in their chairs. George and Mark got up. Mark looked sharply at her and came quickly towards her. Lady Lacklander said, "Kettle! What's happened to *you!*"

Nurse Kettle said, "Good evening, Lady Lacklander. Good evening, Sir George." She put her hands behind her back and looked full at Mark. "May I speak to you, sir?" she said. "There's been an accident."

"All right, Nurse," Mark said. "To whom?"

"To Colonel Cartarette, sir."

The expression of enquiry seemed to freeze on their faces. It was as if they retired behind newly assumed masks.

"What sort of accident?" Mark said.

He stood behind Nurse Kettle and his grandmother and father. She shaped the word "killed" with her lips and tongue.

"Come out here," he muttered and took her by the arm.

"Not at all," his grandmother said. She heaved herself out of her chair and bore down upon them. "Not at all, Mark. What has happened to Maurice Cartarette? Don't keep things from me; I am probably in better trim to meet an emergency than anyone else in this house. What has happened to Maurice?"

Mark, still holding Nurse Kettle by the arm, said, "Very well, Gar. Nurse Kettle will tell us what has happened."

"Let's have it, then. And in case it's as bad as you look, Kettle, I suggest we all sit down. What did you say, George?"

Her son had made in indeterminate noise. He now said galvanically, "Yes, of course, Mama, by all means."

Mark pushed a chair forward for Nurse Kettle, and she took it thankfully. Her knees, she discovered, were wobbling.

"Now, then, out with it," said Lady Lacklander. "He's dead, isn't he, Kettle?"

"Yes, Lady Lacklander."

"Where?" Sir George demanded. Nurse Kettle told him.

"When," Lady Lacklander said, "did you discover him?"

"I've come straight up here, Lady Lacklander."

"But why here, Kettle? Why not to Uplands?"

"I must break it to Kitty," said George.

"I must go to Rose," said Mark simultaneously.

"Kettle," said Lady Lacklander, "you used the word accident. What accident?"

"He has been murdered, Lady Lacklander," said Nurse Kettle.

The thought that crossed her mind after she had made this announcement was that the three Lacklanders were, in their several generations, superficially very much alike but that whereas in Lady Lacklander and Mark the distance between the eyes and the width of mouth suggested a certain generosity, in Sir George they seemed merely to denote the naive. Sir George's jaw dropped, and handsome though he undoubtedly was, he gaped unhandsomely. As none of them spoke, she added, "So I thought I'd better report to you, sir."

"Do you mean," Sir George said loudly, "that he's lying there in my bottom meadow, murdered?"

"Yes, Sir George," Nurse Kettle said, "I do."

"How?" Mark said.

"Injuries to the head."

"You made quite sure, of course?"

"Quite sure."

Mark looked at his father. "We must ring the Chief Constable," he said. "Would you do that, Father? I'll go down with Nurse Kettle. One of us had better stay there till the police come. If you can't get the C.C., would you ring Sergeant Oliphant at Chyning?"

Sir George's hand went to his moustache. "I think," he said, "you may take it, Mark, that I understand my responsibilities."

Lady Lacklander said, "Don't be an ass, George. The boy's quite right," and her son, scarlet in the face, went off to the telephone. "Now," Lady Lacklander continued, "what are we going to do about Rose and that wife of his?"

"Gar..." Mark began, but his grandmother raised a fat glittering hand.

"Yes, yes," she said. "No doubt you want to break it to Rose, Mark, but in my opinion you will do better to let me see both of them first. I shall stay there until you appear. Order the car."

Mark rang the bell. "And you needn't wait," she added. "Take Miss Kettle with you." It was characteristic of Lady Lacklander that she restricted her use of the more peremptory form of address to the second person. She now used it. "Kettle," she said, "we're grateful to you and mustn't impose. Would you rather come with me or go back with my grandson. Which is best, do you think?"

"I'll go with the doctor, thank you, Lady Lacklander. I suppose," Nurse Kettle added composedly, "that as I found the body, I'll be required to make a statement."

She had moved with Mark to the door when Lady Lacklander's voice checked her.

"And I suppose," the elderly voice said, "that as I may have been the last person to speak to him, I shall be required to make one, too."

## ii

In the drawing-room at Hammer there was an incongruous company assembled. Kitty Cartarette, Mark Lacklander and Nurse Kettle waited there while Lady Lacklander sat with Rose in the Colonel's study. She had arrived first at Hammer, having been driven round in her great car while Mark and Nurse Kettle waited in the valley and George rang up the police station at Chyning. George had remembered he was a Justice of the Peace and was believed to be in telephonic conference with his brethren of the bench.

So it had fallen to Lady Lacklander to break the news to Kitty, whom she had found, wearing her black-velvet tights and flame-coloured top in the drawing-room. Lady Lacklander in the course of a long life spent in many embassies had encountered every kind of eccentricity in female attire and was pretty well informed as to the predatory tactics of women whom, in the Far East, she had been wont to describe as "light cruisers." She had made up her mind about Kitty Cartarette but had seemed to be prepared to concede her certain qualities if she showed any signs of possessing them.

She had said, "My dear, I'm the bearer of bad tidings," and noticing that Kitty at once looked very frightened, had remarked to herself, "She thinks I mean to tackle her about George."

"Are you?" Kitty had said. "What sort of tidings, please?"

"About Maurice." Lady Lacklander had waited for a moment, added, "I'm afraid it's the worst kind of news," and had then told her. Kitty stared at her. "Dead?" she said. "Maurice dead? I don't believe you. How can he be dead? He's been fishing down below there and I daresay he's looked in at the pub." Her hands with their long painted nails began to tremble. "How can he be dead?" she repeated.

Lady Lacklander became more specific, and presently

Kitty broke into a harsh strangulated sobbing, twisting her fingers together and turning her head aside. She walked about the room, still, Lady Lacklander noticed, swaying her hips. Presently she fetched up by a grog tray on a small table and shakily poured herself a drink.

"That's a sensible idea," Lady Lacklander said as the neck of the decanter chattered against the glass. Kitty awkwardly offered her a drink, which she declined with perfect equanimity. "Her manner," she thought to herself, "is really too dreadful. What shall I do if George marries her?"

It was at this juncture that Nurse Kettle and Mark had appeared outside the French windows. Lady Lacklander signalled to them. "Here are my grandson and Nurse Kettle," she said to Kitty. "Shall they come in? I think it would be a good idea, don't you?"

Kitty said shakily, "Yes, please. Yes, if you like." Lady Lacklander heaved her bulk out of her chair and let them in.

"Sergeant Oliphant's there," Mark murmured. They're going to ring Scotland Yard. Does Rose . . . ?"

"Not yet. She's out in the garden, somewhere."

Mark went across to Kitty and spoke to her with a quiet authority that his grandmother instantly approved. She noticed how Kitty steadied under it, how Mark, without fussing, got her into a chair. Nurse Kettle, as a matter of course, came forward and took the glass when Kitty had emptied it. A light and charming voice sang in the hall:

"Come away, come away, death . . ." and Mark turned sharply.

"I'll go," his grandmother said, "and I'll fetch you when she asks for you."

With a swifter movement than either her size or her age would have seemed to allow she had gone into the hall. The little song of death stopped, and the door shut behind Lady Lacklander.

Kitty Cartarette was quieter but still caught her breath now and again in a harsh sob.

"Sorry," she said looking from Nurse Kettle to Mark. "Thanks. It's just the shock."

"Yes, of course, dear," Nurse Kettle said.

"I sort of can't believe it. You know?"

"Yes, of course," Mark said.

"It seems so queer...Maurice!" She looked at Mark. "What was that," she said, "about somebody doing it? Is it true?"

"I'm afraid it looks very much like it."

"I'd forgotten," she muttered vaguely. "You've seen him, haven't you, and you're a doctor, of course." Her mouth trembled. She wiped the back of her hand over it. A trail of red was dragged across her cheek. It was a sufficient indication of her state of mind that she seemed to be unaware of it. She said, "No, it's no good, I can't believe it. We saw him down there, fishing." And then she suddenly demanded, "Where's George?"

Nurse Kettle saw Mark's back stiffen. "My father?" he asked.

"O, yes, of course, I'd forgotten," she said again, shaking her head. "He's your father. Silly of me."

"He's looking after one or two things that must be done. You see, the police have had to be told at once."

"Is George getting the police?"

"He's rung them up. He will, I think, come here as soon as he can."

"Yes," she said. "I expect he will."

Nurse Kettle saw George's son compress his lips. At that moment George himself walked in and the party became even less happily assorted.

Nurse Kettle had acquired a talent for retiring into whatever background presented itself, and this talent she now exercised. She moved through the open French window onto the terrace, shut the door after her and sat on a garden seat within view of the drawing-room but facing across the now completely dark valley. Mark, who would perhaps have liked to follow her, stood his ground. His father, looking extraordinarily handsome and not a little self-conscious, went straight to Kitty. She used the gesture that Mark had found embarrassing and extended her left hand to Sir George, who kissed it with an air nicely compounded of embarrassment, deference, distress and devotion.

"My dear Kitty," said Sir George in a special voice, "I'm so terribly, terribly sorry. What can one say! What can one do!"

He apparently had already said and done more than any of the others to assuage Kitty's distress, for it began perceptibly to take on a more becoming guise. She looked into his eyes and said, "How terribly good of you to come." He sat down beside her, began to pat her hand, noticed his son and said, "I'll have a word with you in a moment, old boy."

Mark was about to retire to the terrace when the door opened and his grandmother looked in. "Mark?" she said. He went quickly into the hall. "In the study," Lady Lacklander said, and in a moment he was there with Rose sobbing bitterly in his arms.

"You need pay no attention to me," Lady Lacklander said. "I am about to telephone New Scotland Yard. Your father tells me they have been called in, and I propose to send for Helena Alleyn's boy."

Mark, who was kissing Rose's hair, left off abruptly to say, "Can you mean Chief Inspector Alleyn, Gar?"

"I don't know what his rank is, but he used to be a nice boy twenty-five years ago before he left the Service to become a constable. Central? This is Hermione, Lady Lacklander. I want New Scotland Yard, London. The call is extremely urgent as it is concerned with murder. Yes, murder. You will oblige me by putting it through at once. Thank you." She glanced at Mark. "In the circumstances," she said, "I prefer to deal with a gent."

Mark had drawn Rose to a chair and was kneeling beside her, gently wiping away her tears.

"Hullo!" Lady Lacklander said after an extremely short delay. "New Scotland Yard. This is Hermione, Lady Lacklander, speaking. I wish to speak to Mr. Roderick Alleyn. If he is not on your premises, you will no doubt know where he is to be found. I don't know his rank..."

Her voice, aristocratic, cool, sure of itself, went steadily on. Mark dabbed at Rose's eyes. His father, alone with Kitty in the drawing-room muttered agitatedly, "... I'm sorry it's hit you so hard, Kit."

Kitty looked wanly at him. "I suppose it's the shock," she

said, and added without rancour, "I'm not as tough as you all think." He protested chaotically. "O," she said quite gently, "I know what they'll say about me. Not you, p'raps, but the others. They'll say it's cupboard-sorrow. 'That's what's upsetting the widow,' they'll say. I'm the outsider, George."

"Don't, Kit. Kit, listen..." He began to plead with her. "There's something I must ask you—if you'd just have a look for—you know—that thing—I mean—if it was found—"

She listened to him distractedly. "It's awful," George said. "I know it's awful to talk like this now, Kitty, but all the same—all the same—with so much at stake. I know you'll understand." Kitty said, "Yes. All right. Yes. But let me *think*."

Nurse Kettle out on the terrace was disturbed by the spatter of a few giant rain drops.

"There's going to be a storm," she said to herself. "A summer storm."

And since she would have been out of place in the drawing-room and in the study, she took shelter in the hall. She had no sooner done so than the storm broke in a downpour over the valley of the Chyne.

*iii*

Alleyn and Fox had worked late, tidying up the last phase of a tedious case of embezzlement. At twelve minutes to ten they had finished. Alleyn shut the file with a slap of his hand.

"Dreary fellow," he said. "I hope they give him the maximum. Damn' good riddance. Come back with me and have a drink, Br'er Fox. I'm a grass-widower and hating it. Troy and Ricky are in the country. What do you say?"

Fox drew his hand across the lower part of his face. "Well, now, Mr. Alleyn, that sounds very pleasant," he said. "I say yes and thank you."

"Good." Alleyn looked round the familiar walls of the Chief Inspector's room at New Scotland Yard. "There are occasions," he said, "when one suddenly sees one's natural habitat as if for the first time. It is a terrifying sensation. Come on. Let's go while the going's good."

They went half-way to the door when the telephone rang. Fox said, "Ah, hell!" without any particular animosity and went back to answer it.

"Chief Inspector's room," he said heavily. "Well, yes, he's here. Just." He listened for a moment, gazing blandly at his superior. "Say I'm dead," Alleyn suggested moodily. Fox laid his great palm over the receiver. "They make out it's a Lady Lacklander on call from somewhere called Swevenings," he said.

"Lady *Lacklander*? Good lord! That's old Sir Harold Lacklander's widow," Alleyn ejaculated. "What's up with her, I wonder."

"Chief Inspector Alleyn will take the call," Fox said and held out the receiver.

Alleyn sat on his desk and put the receiver to his ear. An incisive elderly voice was saying "... I don't know his rank and I don't know whether he's on your premises or not, but you'll be good enough if you please to find Mr. Roderick Alleyn for me. It is Hermione, Lady Lacklander, speaking. Is that New Scotland Yard and have you heard me? I wish to speak to ..."

Alleyn announced himself cautiously into the receiver. "Indeed!" the voice rejoined. "Why on earth couldn't you say so in the first instance? Hermione Lacklander speaking. I won't waste time reminding you about myself. You're Helena Alleyn's boy and I want an assurance from you. A friend of mine has just been murdered," the voice continued, "and I hear the local police are calling in your people. I would greatly prefer you, personally, to take charge of the whole thing. That can be arranged, I imagine?"

Alleyn, controlling his astonishment, said, "I'm afraid only if the Assistant Commissioner happens to give me the job."

"Who's he?"

Alleyn told her.

"Put me through to him," the voice commanded.

A second telephone began to ring. Fox answered it and in a moment held up a warning hand.

"Will you wait one second, Lady Lacklander?" Alleyn asked. Her voice, however, went incisively on, and he stifled it against his chest. "What the hell is it, Fox?" he asked irritably.

"Central office, sir. Orders for Swevenings. Homicide."

"Blistered apes! Us?"

"Us," said Fox stolidly.

Alleyn spoke into his own receiver. "Lady Lacklander? I *am* taking this case, it appears."

"Glad to hear it," said Lady Lacklander. "I suggest you look pretty sharp about it. Au revoir," she added with unexpected modishness, and rang off.

Fox, in the meantime, had noted down instructions. "I'll inform Mr. Alleyn," he was saying. "Yes, very good, I'll inform him. Thank you." He hung up his receiver. "It's a Colonel Cartarette," he said. "We go to a place called Chyning in Barfordshire, where the local sergeant will meet us. Matter of two hours. Everything's laid on down below."

Alleyn had already collected his hat, coat and professional case. Fox followed his example. They went out together through the never-sleeping corridors.

It was a still, hot night. Sheet-lightning played fretfully over the East End. The air smelt of petrol and dust. "Why don't we join the River Police?" Alleyn grumbled. "One long water carnival."

A car waited for them with detective-Sergeants Bailey and Thompson and their gear already on board. As they drove out of the Yard, Big Ben struck ten.

"That's a remarkable woman, Fox," Alleyn said. "She's got a brain like a turbine and a body like a tun. My mother, who has her share of guts, was always terrified of Hermione Lacklander."

"Is that so, Mr. Alleyn? Her husband died only the other day, didn't he?"

"That's right. A quarter of a century ago he was one of my great white chiefs in the D.S. Solemn chap . . . just missed being brilliant. She was a force to be reckoned with even then. What's she doing in this party? What's the story, by the way?"

"A Colonel Cartarette found dead with head injuries by a fishing-stream. The C.C. down there says they're all tied up with the Royal Visit at Siminster and are understaffed, anyway, so they've called us in."

"Who found him?"

"A district nurse. About an hour ago."

"Fancy," said Alleyn mildly, and after a pause, "I wonder just why that old lady has come plunging in after me."

"I daresay," Fox said with great simplicity, "she has a fancy for someone of her own class."

Alleyn replied absently, "Do you, now?" and it said something for their friendship that neither of them felt the smallest embarrassment. Alleyn continued to ruminate on the Lacklanders. "Before the war," he said, "the old boy was Chargé d'Affaires at Zlomce. The Special Branch got involved for a time, I remember. There was a very nasty bit of leakage: a decoded message followed by the suicide of the chap concerned. He was said to have been in cahoots with known agents. I was with the Special Branch at that time and had quite a bit to do with it. Perhaps the dowager wishes to revive old memories or something. Or perhaps she merely runs the village of Swevenings, murdered colonels and all, with the same virtuosity she brought to her husband's public life. Do you know Swevenings, Br'er Fox?"

"Can't say I do, sir."

"I do. Troy did a week's painting there a summer or two ago. It's superficially pretty and fundamentally beautiful," Alleyn said. "Quaint as hell, but take a walk after dusk and you wouldn't be surprised at anything you met. It's one of the oldest in England. 'Swevenings,' meaning Dreams. There was some near-prehistoric set-to in the valley, I forget what, and another during Bolingbroke's rebellion and yet another in the Civil Wars. This Colonel's blood is not the first soldier's, by a long chalk, to be spilt at Swevenings."

"They *will* do it," Fox said cryptically and with resignation. For a long time they drove on in a silence broken at long intervals by the desultory conversation of old friends.

"We're running into a summer storm," Alleyn said

presently. Giant drops appeared on the windscreen and were followed in seconds by a blinding downpour.

"Nice set-up for field-work," Fox grumbled.

"It may be local. Although . . . no, by gum, we're nearly there. This is Chyning. Chyning: meaning, I fancy, a yawn or yawning."

"Yawns and dreams," Fox said. "Funny sort of district! What language would that be, Mr. Alleyn?"

"Chaucerian English, only don't depend on me. The whole district is called the Vale of Traunce, or brown-study. It all sounds hellishly quaint, but that's how it goes. There's the blue lamp."

The air smelt fresher when they got out. Rain drummed on roofs and flagstones and cascaded down the sides of houses. Alleyn led the way into a typical county police-station and was greeted by a tall sandy-haired sergeant.

"Chief Inspector Alleyn, sir? Sergeant Oliphant. Very glad to see you, sir."

"Inspector Fox," Alleyn said, introducing him. There followed a solemn shaking of hands and a lament that has become increasingly common of late years in the police force. "We're that short of chaps in the county," Sergeant Oliphant said, "we don't know which way to turn if anything of this nature crops up. The Chief Constable said to me, "Can we do it, Oliphant? Suppose we call on Siminster, can we do it? And look, Mr. Alleyn, I had to say no, we can't.""

Fox said, "T'ch."

"Well, exactly, Mr. Fox," Oliphant said. "If you haven't got the chaps, it's no good blundering in, is it? I've left my one P.C. in charge of the body, and that reduces my staff to me. Shall we move off, Mr. Alleyn? You'll find it wettish."

Alleyn and Fox accompanied the sergeant in his car while Bailey, Thompson and the Yard driver followed their lead. On the way Sergeant Oliphant gave a business-like report. Sir George Lacklander had rung up Sir James Punston, the Chief Constable, who in turn had rung Oliphant at a quarter to nine. Oliphant and his constable had then gone to Bottom Meadow and had found Dr. Mark Lacklander, Nurse Kettle and the body of Colonel Cartarette. They had taken a brief statement from Nurse Kettle and asked her to remain handy. Dr. Lacklander, who, in Oliphant's presence, made a very brief examination of the body, had then gone to break the news to the relatives of the deceased, taking Nurse Kettle with him. The sergeant had returned to Chyning and reported to the Chief Constable, who decided to call in the Yard. The constable had remained on guard by the body with Colonel Cartarette's spaniel, the latter having strenuously resisted all attempts to remove him.

"Did you form any opinion at all, Oliphant?" Alleyn asked. This is the most tactful remark a C.I.D. man can make to a county officer, and Oliphant coruscated under its influence.

"Not to say opinion, sir," he said. "Not to say that. One thing I did make sure of was not to disturb anything. He's lying on a patch of shingle screened in by a half-circle of willows and cut off on the open side by the stream. He's lying on his right side, kind of curled up as if he'd been bowled over from a kneeling position, like. His hat was over his face. Nurse Kettle moved it when she found him, and Dr. Lacklander moved it again when he examined the wound which is in the left temple. A dirty great puncture," the sergeant continued, easing off his official manner a point or two, "with what the doctor calls extensive fractures all round it. Quite turned my chap's stomach, drunks-in-charge and disorderly behaviour being the full extent of his experience."

Alleyn and Fox having chuckled in the right place, the sergeant continued. "No sign of the weapon, so far as we could make out, flashing our torches round. I was particular not to go hoofing over the ground.

"Admirable," said Alleyn.

"Well," said Sergeant Oliphant, "it's what we're told, sir, isn't it?"

"Notice anything at all out of the way?" Alleyn asked. The question was inspired more by kindliness than curiosity, and the sergeant's reaction surprised him. Oliphant brought his two freckled hams of hands down on the driving-wheel and made a complicated snorting noise. "Out of the way!" he shouted. "Ah, my God, I'll say we did. Out of the way! Tell me, now, sir, are you a fly-fisherman?"

"Only fair to middling to worse. I do when I get the chance. Why?"

"Now listen," Sergeant Oliphant said, quite abandoning his official position. "There's a dirty great fish in this Chyne here would turn your guts over for you. Pounds if he's an ounce, he is. Old in cunning, he is, wary and sullen and that lordly in his lurkings and slinkings he'd break your heart. Sometimes he'll rise like a monster," said Sergeant Oliphant, urging his car up Watt's hill, "and snap, he's took it, though that's only three times. Once being the deceased's doing a matter of a fortnight ago, which he left his cast in his jaws, he being a mighty fighter. And once the late squire Sir Harold Lacklander, which he lost him through being, as the man himself frankly admitted, overzealous in the playing of him, and NOW," the sergeant shouted, "NOW, for the last and final cast, hooked, played and landed by the poor Colonel, sir, and lying there by his dead body, or I can't tell a five-pound trout from a stickleback. Well, if he had to die, he couldn't have had a more glorious end. The Colonel, I mean, Mr. Alleyn, not the Old 'Un," said Sergeant Oliphant.

They had followed Watt's Lane down into the valley and up the slope through blinking rain to the village. Oliphant pulled up at a spot opposite the Boy and Donkey. A figure in a mackintosh and tweed hat stood in the lighted doorway.

"The Chief Constable, sir," said Oliphant. "Sir James Punston. He said he'd drive over and meet you."

"I'll have a word with him, before we go on. Wait a moment."

Alleyn crossed the road and introduced himself. The Chief Constable was a weather-beaten, tough-looking man who had been a Chief Commissioner of Police in India.

"Thought I'd better come over," Sir James said, "and take a look at this show. Damn' bad show it is. Damn' nice fellow, Cartarette. Can't imagine who'd want to set about him, but no doubt you'll be able to tell us. I'll come down with you. Filthy night, isn't it?"

The Yard car had drawn up behind Oliphant's. Bailey, Thompson and the driver got out and unloaded their gear with the economic movements of long usage and a stubborn disregard of the rain. The two parties joined up and led by the Chief Constable climbed a stile and followed a rough path down a drenched hillside. Their torches flashed on rods of rain and dripping furze bushes.

"They call this River Path," the Chief Constable said. "It's a right-of-way through the Nunspardon estate and comes out at Bottom Bridge, which we have to cross. I hear the dowager rang you up."

"She did indeed," Alleyn said.

"Lucky they decided it was your pigeon anyway. She'd have raised hell if they hadn't."

"I don't see where she fits in."

"She doesn't in any ordinary sense of the phrase. She's merely taken it upon herself ever since she came to Nunspardon to run Chyning and Swevenings. For some reason they seem to like it. Survival of the feudal instinct, you might think. It does survive, you know, in isolated pockets. Swevenings is an isolated pocket and Hermione, Lady Lacklander, has got it pretty well where she wants it." Sir James continued in this local strain as they slid and squelched down the muddy hillside. He gave Alleyn an account of the Cartarette family and their neighbours with a particularly racy profile of Lady Lacklander herself.

"There's the local gossip for you," he said. "Everybody knows everybody and has done so for centuries. There have been no stockbroking overflows into Swevenings. The Lacklanders, the Phinns, the Syces and the Cartarettes have lived in their respective houses for a great many generations. They're all on terms of intimacy, except that of late years there's been, I fancy, a little coolness between the Lacklanders and old Occy Phinn. And now I come to think of it, I fancy Maurice Cartarette fell out with Phinn over fishing or something. But then old Occy is really a bit mad. Rows with everybody. Cartarette, on the other hand, was a very pleasant, nice chap. Oddly formal and devilishly polite, though, especially with people he didn't like or had fallen out with. Not that he was a quarrelsome chap. Far from it. I have heard, by the way," Sir James gossiped, "that there's been some sort of coolness between Cartarette and that ass George Lacklander. However! And after all that, here's the bridge."

As they crossed it, they could hear the sound of rain beating on the surface of the stream. On the far side their feet sank into mud. They turned left on the rough path. Alleyn's shoes filled with water and water poured off the brim of his hat.

"Hell of a thing to happen, this bloody rain," said the Chief Constable. "Ruin the terrain."

A wet branch of willow slapped Alleyn's face. On the hill to their right they could see the lighted windows of three houses. As they walked on, however, distant groups of trees intervened and the windows were shut off.

"Can the people up there see into the actual area?" Alleyn asked.

Sergeant Oliphant said, "No, sir. Their own trees as well as this belt of willows screen it. They can see the stretch on the far side above the bridge, and a wee way below it."

"That's Mr. Danberry-Phinn's preserve, isn't it?" asked the Chief Constable. "Above the bridge?"

"Mr. *Danberry*-Phinn?" Alleyn said, sharply.

"Mr. Octavius Danberry-Phinn, to give you the complete works. The 'Danberry' isn't insisted upon. He's the local eccentric I told you about. He lives in the top house up there. We don't have a village idiot in Swevenings; we have a bloody-minded old gentleman. It's more classy," said Sir James, acidly.

"Danberry-Phinn," Alleyn repeated. "Isn't there some connection there with the Lacklanders?"

Sir James said shortly, "Both Swevenings men, of course." His voice faded uncertainly as he floundered into a patch of reeds. Somewhere close at hand a dog howled dismally and a deep voice apostrophized it, "Ah, stow it, will you." A light bobbed up ahead of them.

"Here we are," Sir James said. "That you, Gripper?"

"Yes, sir," said the deep voice. The mackintosh cape of

a uniformed constable shone in the torchlight.

"Dog still at it seemingly," said the sergeant.

"That's right, Mr. Oliphant. I've got him tethered here." A torch flashed on Skip, tied by a handkerchief to a willow branch.

"Hullo, old fellow," Alleyn said.

They all waited for him to go through the thicket. The constable shoved back a dripping willow branch for him.

"You'll need to stoop a little, sir."

Alleyn pushed through the thicket. His torchlight darted about in the rain and settled almost at once on a glistening mound.

"We got some groundsheets down and covered him," the sergeant said, "when it looked like rain."

"Good."

"And we've covered up the area round the corpse as best we could. Bricks and one or two planks from the old boatshed yonder. But I daresay the water's got under just the same."

Alleyn said, "Fair enough. We couldn't ask for better. I think before we go any nearer we'll get photographs. Come through, Bailey. Do the best you can. As it stands and then uncovered, with all the details you can get, in case it washes out before morning. By Jove, though, I believe it's lifting."

They all listened. The thicket was loud with the sound of dripping foliage, but the heavy drumming of rain had stopped, and by the time Bailey had set up his camera, a waxing moon had ridden out over the valley.

When Bailey had taken his last flash-photograph of the area and the covered body, he took away the ground sheet and photographed the body again from many angles, first with the tweed hat over the face and then without it. He put his camera close to Colonel Cartarette's face and it flashed out in the night with raised eyebrows and pursed lips. Only when all this had been done, did Alleyn, walking delicately, go closer, stoop over the head and shine his torch full on the wound.

"Sharp instrument?" said Fox.

"Yes," Alleyn said, "yes, a great puncture, certainly. But

**77**

could a sharp instrument do all that, Br'er Fox? No use speculating till we know what it was." His torchlight moved away from the face and found a silver glint on a patch of grass near Colonel Cartarette's hands and almost on the brink of the stream. "And this is the Old 'Un?" he murmured.

The Chief Constable and Sergeant Oliphant both broke into excited sounds of confirmation. The light moved to the hands, lying close together. One of them was clenched about a wisp of green.

"Cut grass," Alleyn said. "He was going to wrap his trout in it. There's the knife, and there's the creel beside him."

"What we reckoned, sir," said the sergeant in agreement.

"Woundy great fish, isn't it?" said the Chief Constable, and there was an involuntary note of envy in his voice.

Alleyn said, "What was the surface like before it rained?"

"Well, sir," the sergeant volunteered, "as you see, it's partly gravel. There was nothing to see in the willows where the ground was dry as a chip. There was what we reckoned were the deceased's footprints on the bank where it was soft and where he'd been fishing and one or two on the earthy bits near where he fell, but I couldn't make out anything else and we didn't try, for fear of messing up what little there was."

"Quite right. Will it rain again before morning?"

The three local men moved back into the meadow and looked up at the sky.

"All over, I reckon, sir," said the sergeant.

"Set fine," said the deep-voiced constable.

"Clearing," said Sir James Punston.

"Cover everything up again, Sergeant, and set a watch till morning. Have we any tips of any sort about times? Anybody known to have come this way?"

"Nurse Kettle, sir, who found him. Young Dr. Lacklander came back with her to look at him, and *he* says he came through the valley and over the bridge earlier in the evening. We haven't spoken to anyone else, sir."

"How deep," Alleyn asked, "is the stream just here?"

"About five foot," said Sergeant Oliphant.

"Really? And he lies on his right side roughly parallel with the stream and facing it. Not more than two feet from the brink. Head pointing down-stream, feet towards the bridge. The fish lies right on the brink by the strand of grass he was cutting to wrap it in. And the wound's in the left temple. I take it he was squatting on his heels within two feet of the brink and just about to bed his catch down in the grass. Now, if, as the heelmarks near his feet seem to indicate, he kneeled straight over into the position the body still holds, one of two things must have happened, wouldn't you say, Br'er Fox?"

"Either," Fox said stolidly, "he was coshed by a left-handed person standing behind him or by a right-handed person standing in front of him and at least three feet away."

"Which would place the assailant," said Alleyn, "about twelve inches out on the surface of the stream. Which is not as absurd as it sounds when you put it that way. All right. Let's move on. What comes next?"

The Chief Constable, who had listened to all this in silence, now said, "I gather there's a cry of possible witnesses waiting for you up at Hammer. That's Cartarette's house up here on Watt's Hill. If you'll forgive me, Alleyn, I won't go up with you. Serve no useful purpose. If you want me, I'm five miles away at Tourets. Anything I can do, delighted, but sure you'd rather be left in peace. I would be in my day. By the way, I've told them at the Boy and Donkey that you'll probably want beds for what's left of the night. You'll find a room at the head of the stairs. They'll give you an early breakfast if you leave a note. Good-night."

He was gone before Alleyn could thank him.

With the sergeant as guide, Alleyn and Fox prepared to set out for Hammer. Alleyn had succeeded in persuading the spaniel Skip to accept them, and after one or two false starts and whimperings he followed at their heels. They used torches in order to make their way with as little blundering as possible through the grove. Oliphant, who was in the lead, suddenly uttered a violent oath.

"What is it?" Alleyn asked, startled.

"*Gawd!*" Oliphant said. "I thought someone was looking at me. *Gawd, d'you see that!*"

His wavering torchlight flickered on wet willow leaves. A pair of luminous disks stared out at them from the level of a short man's eyes.

"Touches of surrealism," Alleyn muttered, "in Bottom Meadow." He advanced his own torch, and they saw a pair of spectacles caught up in a broken twig.

"We'll pluck this fruit with grateful care," he said and gathered the spectacles into his handkerchief.

The moon now shone on Bottom Meadow, turning the bridge and the inky shadow it cast over the broken-down boatshed and punt into a subject for a wood engraving. A group of tall reeds showed up romantically in its light, and the Chyne took on an air of enchantment.

They climbed the river path up Watt's Hill. Skip began to whine and to wag his tail. In a moment the cause of his excitement came into view, a large tabby cat sitting on the path in the bright moonlight washing her whiskers. Skip dropped on his haunches and made a ridiculous sound in his throat. Thomasina Twitchett, for it was she, threw him an inimical glance, rolled on her back at Alleyn's feet and trilled beguilement. Alleyn liked cats. He stooped down and found that she was in the mood to be carried. He picked her up. She kneaded his chest and advanced her nose towards his.

"My good woman," Alleyn said, "you've been eating fish."

Though he was unaware of it at the time, this was an immensely significant discovery.

# CHAPTER V

## Hammer Farm

When they approached Hammer Farm, Alleyn saw that the three desmesnes on Watt's Hill ended in spinneys that separated them from the lower slopes and, as the sergeant had observed, screened them from the reaches of the Chyne below Bottom Bridge. The river path ran upwards through the trees and was met by three private paths serving the three houses. The sergeant led the way up the first of these. Thomasina Twitchett leapt from Alleyn's embrace and with an ambiguous remark darted into the shadows.

"That'll be one of Mr. Phinn's creatures, no doubt," said Sergeant Oliphant. "He's crackers on cats, is Mr. Phinn."

"Indeed," Alleyn said, sniffing at his fingers.

They emerged in full view of Hammer Farm house with its row of French windows lit behind their curtains.

"Not," said the sergeant, "that it's been a farm or anything like it, for I don't know how long. The present lady's had it done up considerable."

Skip gave a short bark and darted ahead. One of the curtains was pulled open, and Mark Lacklander came through to the terrace, followed by Rose.

"Skip?" Rose said. "Skip?"

He whined and flung himself at her. She sank to her knees crying and holding him in her arms. "Don't, darling darling," Mark said, "don't. He's wet and muddy. Don't."

Alleyn, Fox and Sergeant Oliphant had halted. Mark and Rose looked across the lawn and saw them standing in the moonlight with their wet clothes shining and their faces shadowed by their hatbrims. For a moment neither group moved or spoke, and then Alleyn crossed the lawn and came towards them, bareheaded. Rose stood up. The skirts of her linen house-coat were bedabbled with muddy paw marks.

"Miss Cartarette?" Alleyn said. "We are from the C.I.D. My name is Alleyn."

Rose was a well-mannered girl with more than her share of natural dignity. She shook hands with him and introduced him to Mark. Fox was summoned and Sergeant Oliphant eased up the path in an anonymous manner and waited at the end of the terrace.

"Will you come in?" Rose said, and Mark added, "My grandmother is here, Mr. Alleyn, and my father, who informed the local police."

"And Nurse Kettle, I hope?"

"And Nurse Kettle."

"Splendid. Shall we go in, Miss Cartarette?"

Alleyn and Fox took off their wet mackintoshes and hats and left them on a garden seat.

Rose led the way through the French window into the drawing-room, where Alleyn found an out-of-drawing conversation piece established. Lady Lacklander, a vast black bulk, completely filled an arm chair. Alleyn noticed that upon one of her remarkably small feet she wore a buckled velvet shoe and upon the other, a man's bath slipper. Kitty Cartarette was extended on a sofa with one black-velvet leg dangling, a cigarette in her holder, a glass in her hand and an ash tray with butts at her elbow. It was obvious that she had wept, but repairs had been effected in her make-up, and though her hands were still shaky, she was tolerably composed. Between the two oddly assorted women, poised on the hearthrug with a whiskey-and-soda, looking exquisitely uncomfortable and good-looking, was Sir George Lacklander. And at a remove in a small chair perfectly at her ease sat Nurse Kettle, reclaimed from her isolation in the hall.

"Hullo," said Lady Lacklander, picking her lorgnette off her bosom and flicking it open. "Good evening to you. You're Roderick Alleyn, aren't you? We haven't met since you left the Foreign Service, and that's not yesterday nor the day before that. How many years is it? And how's your mama?"

"More than I care to remind you of and very well considering," Alleyn said, taking a hand like a pin-cushion in his.

"Considering what? Her age? She's five years my junior, and there's nothing but fat amiss with me. Kitty, this is Roderick Alleyn; Mrs. Cartarette. My son George."

"Hah—yoo?" George intervened coldly.

". . . and over there is Miss Kettle, our district nurse. Good evening," Lady Lacklander continued, looking at Fox.

"Good evening, my lady," said Fox placidly.

"Inspector Fox," Alleyn said.

"Now, what do you propose to do with us all? Take your time," she added kindly.

Alleyn thought to himself, "Not only must I take my time, but I must also take control. This old lady is up to something."

He turned to Kitty Cartarette. "I'm sorry," he said, "to come so hard on the heels of what must have been an appalling shock. I'm afraid that in these cases police enquiries are not the easiest ordeals to put up with. If I may, Mrs. Cartarette, I'll begin by asking you" . . . he glanced briefly round the room . . . "indeed, all of you, if you've formed any opinion at all about this affair."

There was a pause. He looked at Kitty Cartarette and then steadily, for a moment, at Rose, who was standing at the far end of the room with Mark.

Kitty said, "Somehow, I can't sort of get it. It seems so . . . so *unlikely*."

"And you, Miss Cartarette?"

"No," Rose said. "No. It's unthinkable that anyone who knew him should want to hurt him."

George Lacklander cleared his throat. Alleyn glanced at him. "I . . . ah . . ." George said, "I . . . ah . . . personally believe it must have been some tramp or other. Trespassing or something. There's nobody in the district, I mean. I mean, it's quite incredible."

"I see," Alleyn said. "The next point is: do we know of anybody who was near Colonel Cartarette within, let us say, two hours of the time . . . I believe it was five minutes to nine . . . when you, Miss Kettle, found him?"

"Exactly what," Lady Lacklander said, "do you mean by 'near'?"

"Let us say within sight of hearing of him."

"I was," said Lady Lacklander. "I made an appointment with him for eight, which he kept twenty minutes early. Our meeting took place on the river bank opposite the willow grove where I understand he was found."

Fox, unobtrusively stationed by the piano, had begun to take notes. Although her back was turned towards him, Lady Lacklander appeared to sense this activity. She shifted massively in her chair and looked at him without comment.

"Come," Alleyn said, "that's a starting point, at least. We'll return to it later if we may. Does anyone know anything about Colonel Cartarette's movements after this meeting which lasted . . . how long do you think, Lady Lacklander?"

"About ten minutes. I remember looking at my watch after Maurice Cartarette left me. He re-crossed Bottom Bridge, turned left and disappeared behind the willow grove. It was then nine minutes to eight. I packed up my things and let them to be collected and went home. I'd been sketching."

"About nine minutes to eight?" Alleyn repeated.

Kitty said, "I didn't see him, but...I must have been somewhere near him, I suppose, when I came back from the golf course. I got home at five past eight—I remember."

"The golf course?"

"At Nunspardon," George Lacklander said. "Mrs. Cartarette and I played a round of golf there this evening."

"Ah, yes. The course is above the stream, isn't it, and on the opposite side of the valley from where we are now?"

"Yes, but the greater part is over the crest of the hill."

"The second tee," Mark said, "overlooks the valley."

"I see. You came home by the bottom bridge, Mrs. Cartarette?"

"Yes. The river path."

"On the far side wouldn't you overlook the willow grove?"

Kitty pressed the palms of her hands against her head.

"Yes, I suppose you would. I don't think he could have been there. I'm sure I'd have seen him if he had been there. As a matter of fact," Kitty said, "I wasn't looking much in that direction. I was looking, actually, at the upper reaches to see..." she glanced at George Lacklander..."well, to see if I could spot Mr. Phinn," she said.

In the silence that followed, Alleyn was quite certain that the Lacklander wariness had been screwed up to its highest tension. All three had made slight movements that were instantly checked.

"Mr. Danberry-Phinn?" Alleyn said. "And did you see him?"

"Not then. No. He must have either gone home or moved beyond the upper bend."

"Fishing?"

"Yes."

"Poaching!" George Lacklander ejaculated. "Yes, by God, poaching!"

There were subdued ejaculations from Mark and his grandmother.

"Indeed?" Alleyn asked. "What makes you think so?"

"We saw him. No, Mama, I insist on saying so. We saw him from the second tee. He rents the upper reaches above the

bridge from me, by God, and Maurice Cartarette rents . . . I'm
sorry, Kitty . . . rented the lower. And there . . . damndest thing
you ever saw . . . there he was on his own ground on the right
bank above the bridge, casting above the bridge and letting
the stream carry his cast under the bridge and below it into
Cartarette's waters."

Lady Lacklander gave a short bark of laughter. George
cast an incredulous and scandalized glance at her. Mark said,
"Honestly! How he dared!"

"Most blackguardly thing I ever saw," George continued.
"Deliberate. And the cast, damme, was carried over that hole
above the punt where the Old 'Un lurks. I saw it with my own
eyes! Didn't I, Kitty? Fellow like that deserves no consideration at all. *None*," he repeated with a violence that made
Alleyn prick up his ears and seemed to rebound (to his
embarrassment) upon George himself.

"When did this nefarious bit of trickery occur?" Alleyn
asked.

"I don't know when."

"When did you begin your round?"

"At six-thirty. No!" shouted George in a hurry and turning
purple. "No! Later. About seven."

"It wouldn't be later than seven-fifteen then, when you
reached the second tee?"

"About then, I daresay."

"Would you say so, Mrs. Cartarette?"

Kitty said, "I should think, about then."

"Did Mr. Phinn see you?"

"Not he. Too damned taken up with his poaching," said
George.

"Why didn't you tackle him?" Lady Lacklander enquired.

"I would have for tuppence, Mama, but Kitty thought
better not. We walked away," George said virtuously, "in
disgust."

"I saw you walking away," said Lady Lacklander, "but
from where I was, you didn't look particularly disgusted,
George."

Kitty opened her mouth and shut it again, and George remained empurpled.

"Of course," Alleyn said, "you were sketching, Lady Lacklander, weren't you? Whereabouts?"

"In a hollow about the length of this room below the bridge on the left bank."

"Near a clump of alders?"

"You're a sharpish observant fellow, it appears. Exactly." Lady Lacklander said rather grimly, "through the alders."

"But you couldn't see Mr. Phinn poaching?"

"I couldn't," Lady Lacklander said, "but somebody else could and did."

"Who was that, I wonder?"

"None other," said Lady Lacklander, "than poor Maurice Cartarette himself. He saw it and the devil of a row they had over it, I may tell you."

If the Lacklanders had been different sort of people, Alleyn thought, they would have more clearly betrayed the emotion that he suspected had visited them all. It was, he felt sure from one or two slight manifestations, one of relief rather than surprise on Mark's part and of both elements on his father's. Rose looked troubled and Kitty merely stared. It was, surprisingly, Nurse Kettle who made the first comment.

"That old fish," she said. "Such a lot of fuss!"

Alleyn looked at her and liked what he saw. "I'll talk to her first," he thought, "when I get round to solo interviews."

He said, "How do you know, Lady Lacklander, that they had this row?"

"A: because I heard 'em, and B: because Maurice came straight to me when they parted company. That's how, my dear man."

"What happened, exactly?"

"I gathered that Maurice Cartarette came down intending to try the evening rise when I'd done with him. He came out of his own spinney and saw Occy Phinn up to no good down by the bridge. Maurice crept up behind him. He caught Occy red-handed, having just landed the Old 'Un. They didn't see me," Lady Lacklander went on, "because I was down in my hollow on the other bank. Upon my soul, I doubt if they'd have bridled their tongues if they had. They sounded as if they'd come to blows. I heard them tramping about on the bridge. I was debating whether I should rise up like some rather oversized deity and settle them when Occy bawled out that Maurice could have his so-and-so fish and Maurice said he wouldn't be seen dead with it." A look of absolute horror appeared for one second in Lady Lacklander's eyes. It was as if they had all shouted at her, "But he *was* seen dead with it, you know." She made a sharp movement with her hands and hurried on. "There was a thump, as if someone had thrown something wet and heavy on the ground. Maurice said he'd make a county business of it, and Occy said if he did, he, Occy, would have Maurice's dog empounded for chasing his, Occy's, cats. On that note they parted. Maurice came fuming over the hillock and saw me. Occy, as far as I know, stormed back up the hill to Jacob's Cottage."

"Had Colonel Cartarette got the fish in his hands, then?"

"Not he. I told you, he refused to touch it. He left it there, on the bridge. I saw it when I went home. For all I know, it's still lying there on the bridge."

"It's lying by Colonel Cartarette," Alleyn said, "and the question seems to be, doesn't it, who put it there?"

*ii*

This time the silence was long and completely blank.

"He must have come back and taken it, after all," Mark said dubiously.

"No," Rose said strongly. They all turned to her. Rose's face was dimmed with tears and her voice uncertain. Since Alleyn's arrival she had scarcely spoken, and he wondered if she was so much shocked that she did not even try to listen to them.

"No?" he said gently.

"He wouldn't have done that," she said. "It's not at all the sort of thing he'd do."

"That's right," Kitty agreed. "He wasn't like that," and she caught her breath in a sob.

"I'm sorry," Mark said at once. "Stupid of me. Of course, you're right. The Colonel wasn't like that."

Rose gave him a look that told Alleyn as much as he wanted to know about their relationship. "So they're in love," he thought. "And unless I'm growing purblind, his father's got more than half an eye on her stepmother. What a very compact little party, to be sure."

He said to Lady Lacklander, "Did you stay there long after he left you?"

"No. We talked for about ten minutes and then Maurice re-crossed the bridge, as I told you, and disappeared behind the willows on the right bank."

"Which way did you go home?"

"Up through the Home Spinney to Nunspardon."

"Could you see into the willow grove at all?"

"Certainly. When I was half-way up I stopped to pant, and I looked down and there he was, casting into the willow-grove reach."

"That would be about eight."

"About eight, yes."

"I think you said you left your painting gear to be collected, didn't you?"

"I did."

"Who collected it, please?"

"One of the servants. William, the footman, probably."

"No," Mark said. "No, Gar. I did."

"You?" his grandmother said. "What were you doing..." and stopped short.

Mark said rapidly that after making a professional call in the village he had gone in to play tennis at Hammer and had stayed there until about ten minutes past eight. He had returned home by the river path and as he approached Bottom Bridge had seen his grandmother's shooting-stick, stool and painting gear in a deserted group on a hillock. He

carried them back to Nunspardon and was just in time to
prevent the footman from going down to collect them. Alleyn
asked him if he had noticed a large trout lying on Bottom
Bridge. Mark said that he hadn't done so, but at the same
moment his grandmother gave one of her short ejaculations.

"You must have seen it, Mark," she said. "Great gaping
thing lying there where Octavius Phinn must have chucked it
down. On the bridge, my dear boy. You must have practically
stepped over it."

"It wasn't there," Mark said. "Sorry, Gar, but it wasn't,
when I went home."

"Mrs. Cartarette," Alleyn said, "you must have crossed
Bottoms Bridge a few minutes after Lady Lacklander had
gone home, mustn't you?"

"That's right," Kitty said. "We saw her going into the
Nunspardon Home Spinney as we came over the hill by the
second tee."

"And Sir George, then, in his turn, went home through the
Home Spinney, and you came down the hill by the river
path?"

"That's right," she said drearily.

"Did you see the fabulous trout lying on Bottom Bridge?"

"Not a sign of it, I'm afraid."

"So that between about ten to eight and ten past eight the
trout was removed by somebody and subsequently left in the
willow grove. Are you all of the opinion that Colonel
Cartarette would have been unlikely to change his mind and
go back for it?" Alleyn asked.

George looked huffy and said he didn't know, he was sure,
and Lady Lacklander said that judging by what Colonel
Cartarette had said to her, she was persuaded that wild horses
wouldn't have induced him to touch the trout. Alleyn thought
to himself, "If he was disinclined to touch it, still less would he
feel like wrapping it up in grass in order to stow it away in his
creel, which apparently was what he had been doing when he
died."

"I suppose there's no doubt about this fish being the classic
Old 'Un?" Alleyn asked.

"None," Mark said. "There's not such another in the Chyne. No question."

"By the way, did you look down at the willow grove as you climbed up the hill to the Home Spinney?"

"I don't remember doing so. I was hung about with my grandmother's sketching gear and I didn't..."

It was at this moment that Kitty Cartarette screamed.

She did not scream very loudly; the sound was checked almost as soon as it was born, but she had half risen from her sofa and was staring at something beyond and behind Alleyn. She had clapped her hands over her mouth. Her eyes were wide open beneath their raised brows. He noticed that they were inclined to be prominent.

They all turned to discover what it was that Kitty stared at but found only an uncovered French window reflecting the lighted room and the ghosts of their own startled faces.

"There's someone out there!" Kitty whispered. "A man looked in at the window. George!"

"My dear girl," Lady Lacklander said, "you saw George's reflection. There's nobody there."

"There is."

"It's probably Sergeant Oliphant," Alleyn said. "We left him outside. Fox?"

Fox was already on his way, but before he reached the French window, the figure of a man appeared beyond its reflected images. The figure moved uncertainly, coming in from the side and halting when it was some way from the glass. Kitty made a slight retching sound. Fox's hand was on the knob of the French window when beyond it the beam of Sergeant Oliphant's torchlight shot across the dark and the man's face was illuminated. It was crowned by a tasselled smoking cap and was deadly pale.

Fox opened the French windows.

"Pray forgive an unwarrantable intrusion," said Mr. Danberry-Phinn. "I am in quest of a fish."

### iii

Mr. Phinn's behaviour was singular. The light from the room seemed to dazzle him. He screwed up his eyes and nose, and this gave him a supercilious look greatly at variance with his extreme pallor and unsteady hands. He squinted at Fox and then beyond him at the company in the drawing-room.

"I fear I have called at an inconvenient moment," he said. "I had no idea...I had hoped to see..." his Adam's apple bobbed furiously... "to see," he repeated, "in point of fact, Colonel Cartarette." He disclosed his teeth, clamped together in the oddest kind of smile.

Kitty made an indeterminate sound, and Lady Lacklander began, "My dear Octavius..." but before either of them could get any further, Alleyn moved in front of Mr. Phinn. "Did you say, sir," Alleyn asked, "that you are looking for a fish?"

Mr. Phinn said, "Forgive me, I don't *think* I have the pleasure...?" and peered up into Alleyn's face "*Have* I the pleasure?" he asked. He blinked away from Alleyn towards Fox. Fox was one of those, nowadays rather rare, detectives who look very much like their job. He was a large, grizzled man with extremely bright eyes.

"And in this case," Mr. Phinn continued with a breathless little laugh, "I indubitably have *not* the pleasure."

"We are police officers," Alleyn said. "Colonel Cartarette has been murdered, Mr. Phinn. You are Mr. Octavius Danberry-Phinn, I think, aren't you?"

"But how perfectly terrible!" said Mr. Phinn. "My dear Mrs. Cartarette! My dear Miss Rose! I am appalled. APPALLED!" Mr. Phinn repeated, opening his eyes as wide as they could go.

"You'd better come in, Occy," Lady Lacklander said. "They'll want to talk to you."

"To *me!*" he ejaculated. He came in and Fox shut the French window behind him.

Alleyn said, "I shall want to have a word with you, sir. In fact, I think it is time that we saw some of you individually rather than together, but before we do that, I should like Mr. Phinn to tell us about the fish he is looking for." He raised his hand. If any of his audience had felt like interrupting, they now thought better of the impulse. "If you please, Mr. Phinn?" Alleyn said.

"I'm so confused, indeed so horrified at what you have told me . . ."

"Dreadful," Alleyn said, "Isn't it? About the fish?"

"The fish? The fish, my dear sir, is or was a magnificent trout. The fish is a fish of great fame. It is the trout to end all trout. A piscine emperor. And I, let me tell you, I caught him."

"Where?" Lady Lacklander demanded.

Mr. Phinn blinked twice. "Above Bottom Bridge, my dear Lady L.," he said. "Above Bottom Bridge."

"You *are* an old humbug, Occy," she said.

George suddenly roared out, "That's a bloody lie, Octavius. You poached him. You were fishing under the bridge. We saw you from the second tee."

"Dear me, George," said Mr. Phinn going white to the lips. "What a noise you do make, to be sure."

Fox had stepped unobtrusively aside and was busy with his notebook.

"To talk like that!" Mr. Phinn continued with two half bows in the direction of Kitty and Rose. "In a house of mourning! Really, George, I must say!"

"By God . . . !" George began, but Alleyn intervened.

"What," he asked Mr. Phinn, "happened to your catch?"

Mr. Phinn sucked in a deep breath and began to speak very quickly indeed. "Flushed," he said in a voice that was quite steady, "with triumph, I resolved to try the upper reaches of the Chyne. I therefore laid my captive to rest on the very field of his defeat, *id est*, the upper, repeat upper, approach to Bottom Bridge. When I returned, much later, I cannot tell you *how* much later for I did not carry a watch, but much, *much* later, I went to the exact spot where my Prince of Piscines should have rested and . . ." he made a wide gesture during the execution of which it was apparent that his hands were tremulous . . . "Gone! Vanished! Not a sign! Lost!" he said.

"Now, look here, Occy..." Lady Lacklander in her turn began, and in her turn was checked by Alleyn.

"Please, Lady Lacklander," Alleyn interjected. She glared at him. "Do you mind?" he said.

She clasped her plump hands together and rested the entire system of her chins upon them. "Well," she said, "I called you in, after all. Go on."

"What did you do," Alleyn asked Mr. Phinn, "when you discovered your loss?"

Mr. Phinn looked very fixedly at him. "Do?" he repeated. "What should I do? It was growing dark. I looked about in the precincts of the bridge but to no avail. The trout was gone. I returned home, a bitterly chagrined man."

"And there you remained, it seems, for about four hours. It's now five minutes past one in the morning. Why, at such an hour, are you paying this visit, Mr. Phinn?"

Looking at Mr. Phinn, Alleyn thought, "He was ready for that one."

"Why!" Mr. Phinn exclaimed spreading his unsteady hands. "My dear sir, I will tell you why. Rendered almost suicidal by the loss of this Homeric catch, I was unable to contemplate my couch with any prospect of repose. Misery and frustration would have been my bedfellows, I assume you, had I sought it. I attempted to read, to commune with the persons of my house (I refer to my cats, sir), to listen to an indescribably tedious piece of buffoonery upon the wireless. All, I regret to say, was of no avail: my mind was wholly occupied by The Great Fish. Some three quarters of an hour or so ago, I sought the relief of fresh air and took a turn down the river path. On emerging from the ruffian Syce's spinney, I observed lights behind these windows. I heard voices. Knowing," he said with a singular gulp, "knowing that poor Cartarette's interest as a fellow angler would be aroused, I...my dear Lady L., why *are* you looking at me in this most disconcerting fashion?"

"Occy!" Lady Lacklander said. "Yard or no Yard, I can't contain my information for another second. I was within a stone's throw of you when you had your row with Maurice

Cartarette. What's more a few minutes earlier his wife and George both saw you poaching under the bridge. I heard you or Maurice throw down the trout on the bridge and I heard you part company in a high rage. What's more Maurice came hot-foot to where I was painting and I had the whole story all over again from him. Now, my dear Roderick Alleyn, you may be as cross with me as you please, but I really could not allow this nonsensical tarradiddle to meander on for another second."

Mr. Phinn blinked and peered and fumbled with his lips. 'It used to be quite a little joke between my dear wife and me," he said at least, "that one must never contradict a Lacklander."

Only Alleyn and Fox looked at him.

"Mr. Phinn," Alleyn said, "you normally wear spectacles, I think, don't you?"

Mr. Phinn made a strange little gesture with his thumb and forefinger as if he actually adjusted his glasses. Thus, momentarily, he hid the red groove across the top of his nose and the flush that had begun to spread across his face. "Not all the time," he said. "Only for reading."

Lady Lacklander suddenly clapped the palms of her hands down on the arms of her chair. "So there we are," she said. "And having said my say, George, I should like you, if you please, to take me home."

She put out her right arm and as George was a little slow in coming, Alleyn took her hand, braced himself and hauled.

"'Up she rises,'" Lady Lacklander quoted self-derisively, and up she rose. She stared for a moment at Mr. Phinn, who gaped back at her and mouthed something undistinguishable. She looked straight into Alleyn's eyes. "Do you, after all," she said, "propose to let me go home?"

Alleyn raised an eyebrow. "I shall feel a good deal safer," he said, "with you there than here, Lady Lacklander."

"Take me to my car. I have to shuffle a bit because of my damn' toe. It's no better, Kettle. George, you may join me in five minutes. I want to have a word with Roderick Alleyn."

She said goodbye to Rose, holding her for a moment in her arms. Rose clung to her and gave a shuddering sob. Lady

Lacklander said, "My poor child, my poor little Rose; you must come to us as soon as possible. Get Mark to give you something to make you sleep."

Kitty had risen. "It was awfully kind of you to come," she said and held out her hand. Lady Lacklander took it and after a scarcely perceptible pause let it be known that Kitty was expected to kiss her. This Kitty did with caution.

"Come and see me to-morrow, Kettle," said Lady Lacklander, "unless they lock you up."

"Let 'em try," said Nurse Kettle, who had been entirely silent ever since Mr. Phinn's arrival. Lady Lacklander gave a short laugh. She paid no attention to Mr. Phinn but nodded to Alleyn. He hastened to open the door and followed her through a large and charmingly shaped hall to the main entrance. Outside this a vast elderly car waited.

"I'll sit in the back," she said. "George will drive. I find him an irritating companion in time of trouble."

Alleyn opened the door and switched on a light in the car.

"Now tell me," she said, after she had heaved herself in, "tell me, not as a policeman to an octogenarian dowager but as a man of discretion to one of your your mother's oldest friends, what did you think of Occy Phinn's behaviour just now?"

Alleyn said, "Octogenarian dowagers, even if they are my mother's oldest friend, shouldn't lure me out of doors at night and make improper suggestions."

"Ah," she said, "so you're not going to respond."

"Tell me, did Mr. Phinn have a son called Ludovic? Ludovic Danberry-Phinn?"

In the not very bright light he watched her face harden as if, behind its mask of fat, she had set her jaw. "Yes," she said. "Why?"

"It could hardly not be, could it, with those names?"

"I wouldn't mention the boy if I were you. He was in the Foreign Service and blotted his copybook, as I daresay you know. It was quite a tragedy. It's never mentioned."

"Is it not? What sort of a man was Colonel Cartarette?"

"Pigheaded, quixotic fellow. Obstinate as a mule. One of

those pathetically conscientious people who aim so high they get a permanent crick in their conscience."

"Are you thinking of any particular incident?"

"No," Lady Lacklander said firmly, "I am not."

"Do you mind telling me what you and Colonel Cartarette talked about?"

"We talked," Lady Lacklander said coolly, "about Occy poaching and about a domestic matter that is for the moment private and can have no bearing whatever on Maurice's death. Good-night to you, Roderick. I suppose I call you Roderick, don't I?"

"When we're alone together."

"Impudent fellow!" she said and aimed a sort of dab at him. "Go back and bully those poor things in there. and tell George to hurry."

"Can you remember exactly what Mr. Phinn and Colonel Cartarette said to each other when they had their row?"

She looked hard at him, folded her jewelled hands together and said, "Not word for word. They had a row over the fish. Occy rows with everybody."

"Did they talk about anything else?"

Lady Lacklander continued to look at him and said, "No," very coolly indeed.

Alleyn made her a little bow. "Good-night," he said. "If you remember specifically anything that they said to each other, would you be terribly kind and write it down?"

"Roderick," Lady Lacklander said, "Occy Phinn is no murderer."

"Is he not?" Alleyn said. "Well, that's something to know, isn't it? Good-night."

He shut the door. The light in the car went out

*iv*

As he turned back to the house, Alleyn met George Lacklander. It struck him that George was remarkably ill at ease in his company and would greatly have preferred to deal exclusively with Fox.

"Oh... ah, hullo," George said. "I... ah... I wonder, may I have a word with you? I don't suppose you remember, by the way, but we have met a thousand years ago, ha, ha, when, I think, you were one of my father's bright young men, weren't you?"

Alleyn's twenty-five-year-old recollection of George rested solely on the late Sir Harold Lacklander's scorching comments on his son's limitations. "No damn' use expecting anything of George," Sir Harold had once confided. "Let him strike attitudes at Nunspardon and in the ripeness of time become a J.P. That is George's form." It occurred to Alleyn that this prophecy had probably been fulfilled.

He answered George's question and blandly disregarded its sequel. "Please do," he said.

"Fact is," George said, "I'm wondering just what the drill is. I am, by the way, and not that it makes any real difference, a Beak. So I suppose I may be said to fill my humble pigeon-hole in the maintenance of the Queen's peace, what?"

"And why not?" Alleyn infuriatingly replied.

"Yes," George continued, goggling at him in the dark. "Yes. Well, now, I wanted to ask you what exactly will be the drill about poor Maurice Cartarette's—ah—about the—ah—the body. I mean, one is concerned for Kitty's sake. For their sake, I mean. His wife and daughter. One can perhaps help with the arrangements for the funeral and all that. What?"

"Yes, of course," Alleyn agreed. "Colonel Cartarette's body will remain where it is under guard until to-morrow morning. It will then be taken to the nearest mortuary and a police surgeon will make an examination and possibly an extensive autopsy. We will, of course, let Mrs. Cartarette know as soon as possible when the funeral may be held. I think we shall probably be ready to hand over in three days, but it doesn't do to be positive about these things."

"O, quite!" George said. "Quite. Quite. Quite."

Alleyn said, "Simply for the record—I shall have to put this sort of question to everybody who was in Colonel Cartarette's landscape last evening—you and Mrs. Cartarette began your round of golf, I think you said, at seven?"

"I didn't notice the exact time," George said in a hurry.

"Perhaps Mrs. Cartarette will remember. Did she meet you on the course?"

"Ah—no. No, I—ah—I called for her in the car. On my way back from Chyning."

"But you didn't drive her back?"

"No. Shorter to walk, we thought. From where we were."

"Yes, I see. . . . And Mrs. Cartarette says she arrived here at about five past eight. Perhaps you played golf, roughly, for an hour. How many holes?"

"We didn't go round the course. Mrs. Cartarette is learning. It was her first—ah—attempt. She asked me to give her a little coaching. We—ah—we only played a couple of holes. We spent the rest of the time practising some of her shots," George said, haughtily.

"Ah, yes. And you parted company at about ten to eight. Where?"

"At the top of the river path," he said and added, "as far as I remember."

"From there would you see Lady Lacklander coming up towards you? She began her ascent at ten to eight."

"I didn't look down. I didn't notice."

"Then you won't have noticed Colonel Cartarette either. Lady Lacklander says he was fishing in the willow grove at the time and that the willow grove is visible from the river path."

"I didn't look down. I . . . ah . . . I merely saw Mrs. Cartarette to the river path and went on through the Home Spinney to Nunspardon. My mother arrived a few minutes later. And now," George said, "if you'll excuse me, I really must drive my mama home. By the way, I do hope you'll make use of us. I mean, you may need a headquarters and so on. Anything one can do."

"How very kind," Alleyn rejoined. "Yes, I think we may let you go now. Afraid I shall have to ask you to stay in Swevenings for the time being."

He saw George's jaw drop.

"Of course," he added, "if you have important business elsewhere, it will be quite in order to come and tell me about it and we'll see what can be done. I shall be at the Boy and Donkey."

"Good God, my dear Alleyn . . ."

"Damn' nuisance, I know," Alleyn said, "but there you are. If they *will* turn on homicide in your bottom meadow. Good-night to you."

He circumnavigated George and returned to the drawing-room, where he found Rose, Mark and Kitty uneasily silent, Mr. Phinn biting his fingers, and Inspector Fox in brisk conversation with Nurse Kettle on the subject of learning French conversation by means of Gramophone records. "I don't," Mr. Fox was saying, "make the headway I'd like to."

"I picked up more on a cycling tour in Brittany when I *had* to than I ever got out of *my* records."

"That's what they all tell me, but in our line what chance do you get?"

"You must get a holiday some time, for Heaven's sake."

"True," Fox said, sighing. "That's a fact. You do. But somehow I've never got round to spending it anywhere but Birchington. Excuse me, Miss Kettle, here's the Chief."

Alleyn gave a Fox a look both of them understood very well, and the latter rose blandly to his feet. Alleyn addressed himself to Kitty Cartarette.

"If I may," he said, "I should like to have a very short talk with Miss Kettle. Is there perhaps another room we may use? I saw one, I think, as I came across the hall. A study perhaps."

He had the feeling that Mrs. Cartarette was not overanxious for him to use the study. She hesitated, but Rose said, "Yes, of course. I'll show you."

Fox had gone to the French window and had made a majestical signal to the sergeant, who now came into the drawing-room.

"You all know Sergeant Oliphant, of course," Alleyn said. "He will be in charge of the local arrangements, Mrs. Cartarette, and I thought perhaps you would like to have a word with him. I would be grateful if you would give him the names of your husband's solicitor and bank and also of any relations who should be informed. Mr. Phinn, I will ask you to repeat the substance of your account to Sergeant Oliphant, who will take it down and get you to sign it if it is correct."

Mr. Phinn blinked at him. "I cannot," he said, with a show of spirit, "of course, be compelled."

"Of course not. But I'm afraid we shall have to trouble all of you to give us signed statements, if you are willing to do so. If you do yours first, it will leave you free to go home. I hope," Alleyn concluded, "that you will not find it too difficult without your glasses. And now, Miss Cartarette, may we indeed use the study?"

Rose led the way across the hall into the room where eight hours ago she had talked to her father about her love for Mark. Alleyn and Fox followed her. She waited for a moment and stared, as it seemed to Alleyn, with a kind of wonder at the familiar chairs and desk. Perhaps she saw a look of compassion in his face. She said, "He seems to be here, you know. The room can't go on without him, one would think. This was his place more than anywhere else." She faltered for a moment and then said, "Mr. Alleyn, he was such a darling, my father. He was as much like my child as my father, he depended on me so completely. I don't know why I'm saying this to you."

"It's sometimes a good idea to say things like that to strangers. They make uncomplicated confidants."

"Yes," she said and her voice was surprised, "that's quite true. I'm glad I told you."

Alleyn saw that she suffered from the kind of nervous ricochet that often follows a severe shock. Under its impetus the guard that people normally set over their lightest remarks is lowered and they speak spontaneously of the most surprising matters, as now when Rose suddenly added, "Mark says he couldn't have felt anything. I'm sure he's not just saying that to comfort me, because being a doctor, he wouldn't. So I suppose in a way it's what people call a release. From everything."

Alleyn asked quietly, "Was he worried about anything in particular?"

"Yes," Rose said sombrely, "he was indeed. But I can't tell

you about that. It's private, and even if it wasn't, it couldn't possibly be of any use."

"You never know," he said lightly.

"You do in this case."

"When did you see him last?"

"This evening. I mean last evening, don't I? He went out soon after seven. I think it was about ten past seven."

"Where did he go?"

She hesitated and then said, "I believe to call on Mr. Phinn. He took his rod and told me he would go on down to the Chyne for the evening rise. He said he wouldn't come in for dinner, and I asked for something to be left out for him."

"Do you know why he called on Mr. Phinn?"

Rose waited for a long time and then said, "I think it had something to do with . . . with the publishing business."

"The *publishing* business?"

She pushed a strand of hair back and pressed the heels of her hands against her eyes. "*I* don't know who could do such a thing to him," she said. Her voice was drained of all its colour. "She's exhausted," Alleyn thought and, against his inclination, decided to keep her a little longer.

"Can you tell me, very briefly, what sort of pattern his life has taken over the last twenty years?"

Rose sat on the arm of her father's chair. Her right arm was hooked over its back and she smoothed and re-smoothed the place where his bald head had rested. She was quite calm and told Alleyn in a flat voice of the Colonel's appointments as military attache at various embassies, of his job at Whitehall during the war, of his appointment as military secretary to a post-war commission that had been set up in Hong Kong and finally, after his second marriage, of his retirement and absorption in a history he had planned to write of his own regiment. He was a great reader, it seemed, particularly of the Elizabethan dramatists, an interest that his daughter had ardently shared. His only recreation apart from his books had been fishing. Rose's eyes, fatigued by tears, looked for a moment at a table against the wall where a tray of threads, scraps of feathers and a number of casts was set out.

"I always tied the flies. We made up a fly he nearly always fished with. I tied this one this afternoon."

Her voice trembled and trailed away and she yawned suddenly like a child.

The door opened and Mark Lacklander came in looking angry.

"Ah, there you are!" he said. He walked straight over to her and put his fingers on her wrist. "You're going to bed at once," he said. "I've asked Nurse Kettle to make a hot drink for you. She's waiting for you now. I'll come and see you later and give you a nembutal. I'll have to run into Chyning for it. You don't want me again, I imagine?" he said to Alleyn.

"I do for a few minutes, I'm afraid."

"Oh!" Mark said, and after a pause, "well, yes, of course, I suppose you do. Stupid of me."

"I don't want any dope, Mark, honestly," Rose said.

"We'll see about that when you're tucked up. Go to bed now." He glared at Alleyn. "Miss Cartarette is my patient," he said, "and those are my instructions."

"They sound altogether admirable," Alleyn rejoined. "Good-night, Miss Cartarette. We'll try to worry you as little as possible."

"You don't worry me at all," Rose said politely and gave him her hand.

"I wonder," Alleyn said to Mark, "if we may see Nurse Kettle as soon as she is free. And you, a little later, if you please, Dr. Lacklander."

"Certainly, sir," Mark said stiffly and taking Rose's arm, led her out of the room.

"And I also wonder, Br'er Fox," Alleyn said "apart from bloody murder, what it is that's biting all these people."

"I've got a funny sort of notion," Fox said, "and mind, it's only a notion so far, that the whole thing will turn out to hang on that fish."

"And I've got a funny sort of notion you're right."

# CHAPTER **VI**

## The Willow Grove

Nurse Kettle sat tidily on an armless chair with her feet crossed at the ankles and her hands at the wrists. Her apron was turned up in the regulation manner under her uniform coat, and her regulation hat was on her head. She had just given Alleyn a neat account of her finding of Colonel Cartarette's body, and Fox, who had taken the notes, was gazing at her with an expression of the liveliest approval.

"That's all, really," she said, "except that I had a jolly strong feeling I was being watched. There now!"

Her statement hitherto had been so positively one of fact that they both stared at her in surprise. "And now," she said, "you'll think I'm a silly hysterical female because although I thought once that I heard a twig snap and fancied that when a bird flew out of the thicket it was not me who'd disturbed it, I didn't *see* anything at all. Not a thing. And yet I thought I was watched. You get it on night duty in a ward. A patient lying awake and staring at you. You always know before you look. Now laugh that away if you like."

"Who's laughing?" Alleyn rejoined. "We're not are we, Fox?"

"On no account," Fox said. "I've had the same sensation many a time on night beat in the old days, and it always turned out there was a party in a dark doorway having a look at you."

"Well, fancy!" said the gratified Nurse Kettle.

"I suppose," Alleyn said, "you know all these people pretty well, don't you, Miss Kettle? I always think in country districts the Queen's Nurses are rather like liaison officers."

Nurse Kettle looked pleased. "Well now," she said, "we do get to know people. Of course, our duties take us mostly to the ordinary folk, although with the present shortage we find ourselves doing quite a lot for the other sort. They pay the full fee and that helps the Association, so, as long as it's not depriving the ones who can't afford it, we take the odd upper-class case. Like me and Lady Lacklander's toe, for instance."

"Ah, yes," Alleyn said, "there's the toe." He observed with surprise the expression of enraptured interest in his colleague's elderly face.

"Septic," Nurse Kettle said cosily.

"'T, 't, 't," said Fox.

"And then again, for example," Nurse Kettle went on, "I night-nursed the old gentleman. With him when he died, actually. Well, so was the family. And the Colonel, too, as it happens."

"Colonel Cartarette?" Alleyn asked without laying much stress on it.

"That's right. Or wait a minute. I'm telling stories. The Colonel didn't come back into the room. He stayed on the landing with the papers."

"The papers?"

"The old gentleman's memoirs they were. The Colonel was to see about publishing them, I fancy, but I don't really know. The old gentleman was very troubled about them. He couldn't be content to say goodbye and give up until he'd seen the Colonel. Mind you, Sir Harold was a great man in his day, and his memoirs'll be very important affairs, no doubt."

"No doubt. He was a distinguished ambassador."

"That's right. Not many of that sort left, I always say. Everything kept up. Quite feudal."

"Well," Alleyn said, "there aren't many families left who can afford to be feudal. Don't they call them the Lucky Lacklanders?"

"That's right. Mind, there are some who think the old gentleman overdid it."

"Indeed?" Alleyn said, keeping his mental fingers crossed. "How?"

"Well, not leaving the grandson anything. Because of him taking up medicine instead of going into the army. Of course, it'll all come to him in the end, but in the meantime, he has to make do with what he earns, though of course—but listen to me gossiping. Where was I now. Oh, the old gentleman and the memoirs. Well, no sooner had he handed them over than he took much worse and the Colonel gave the alarm. We all went in. I gave brandy. Doctor Mark gave an injection, but it was all over in a minute. 'Vic,' he said, 'Vic, Vic,' and that was all." Alleyn repeated, "Vic?" and then was silent for so long that Nurse Kettle had begun to say. "Well, if that's all I can do . . ." when he interrupted her.

"I was going to ask you," he said, "who lives in the house between this one and Mr. Phinn's?"

Nurse Kettle smiled all over her good-humoured face. "At Uplands?" she said. "Commander Syce, to be sure. He's another of my victims," she added and unaccountably turned rather pink. "Down with a bad go of 'bago, poor chap."

"Out of the picture, then, from our point of view?"

"Yes, if you're looking for . . . oh, my gracious," Nurse Kettle suddenly ejaculated, "here we are at goodness knows what hour of the morning talking away as pleasant as you please and all the time you're wondering where you're going to find a murderer. Isn't that frightful?"

"Don't let it worry you," Fox begged her.

Alleyn stared at him.

"Well, of course I'm worried. Even suppose it turns out to have been a tramp. Tramps are people just like other people," Nurse Kettle said vigorously.

"Is Mr. Phinn one of your patients?" Alleyn asked.

"Not to say patient. I nursed a carbuncle for him years ago. I wouldn't be getting ideas about him if I were you."

"In our job," Alleyn rejoined, "we have to get ideas about everybody."

"Not about *me*, I hope and trust."

Fox made a complicated soothing and scandalized noise in his throat.

Alleyn said, "Miss Kettle, you liked Colonel Cartarette, didn't you? It was clear from your manner, I thought, that you liked him very much indeed."

"Well, I did," she said emphatically. "He was one of the nicest and gentlest souls: a gentleman if ever I saw one. Devoted father. Never said an unkind word about anybody."

"Not even about Mr. Phinn?"

"Now *look* here," she began, then caught herself up. "Listen," she said; "Mr. Phinn's eccentric. No use my pretending otherwise for you've seen him for yourselves and you'll hear what others say about him. But there's no malice. No, perhaps I wouldn't say there's no *malice* exactly, but there's no real harm in him. Not a scrap. He's had this tragedy in his life, poor man, and in my opinion he's never been the same since it happened. Before the war, it was. His only son did away with himself. Shocking thing."

"Wasn't the son in the Foreign Service?"

"That's right. Ludovic was his name, poor chap. Ludovic! I ask you! Nice boy and very clever. He was in some foreign place when it happened. Broke his mother's heart, they always say, but she was a cardiac, anyway, poor thing. Mr. Phinn never really got over it. You never know, do you?"

"Never. I remember hearing about it," Alleyn said vaguely. "Wasn't he one of Sir Harold Lacklander's young men?"

"That's right. The old gentleman was a real squire. You know: the old Swevenings families and all that. I think he asked for young Phinn to be sent out to him, and I know he was very cut up when it happened. I daresay he felt responsible."

"You never know," Alleyn repeated. "So the Swevenings families," he added, "tend to gravitate towards foreign parts?"

Nurse Kettle said that they certainly seemed to do so. Apart from young Viccy Danberry-Phinn getting a job in Sir Harold's embassy, there was Commander Syce, whose ship had been based on Singapore, and the Colonel himself, who had been attached to a number of missions in the Far East, including one at Singapore. Nurse Kettle added, after a pause, that she believed he had met his second wife there.

"Really?" Alleyn said with no display of interest. "At the time when Syce was out there, do you mean?" It was the merest shot in the dark, but it found its mark. Nurse Kettle became pink in the face and said with excessive brightness that she believed that "the Commander and the second Mrs. C." had known each other out in the East. She added, with an air of cramming herself over some emotional hurdle, that she had seen a very pretty drawing that the Commander had made of Mrs. Cartarette. "You'd pick it out for her at once," she said. "Speaking likeness, really, with tropical flowers behind and all."

"Did you know the first Mrs. Cartarette?"

"Well, not to say *know*. They were only married eighteen months when she died giving birth to Miss Rose. She was an heiress, you know. The whole fortune goes to Miss Rose. It's well known. The Colonel was quite hard up, but he's never touched a penny of his first wife's money. It's well known," Nurse Kettle repeated, "so I'm not talking gossip."

Alleyn skated dexterously on towards Mark Lacklander, and it was obvious that Nurse Kettle was delighted to sing Mark's praises. Fox, respectfully staring at her, said there was a bit of romance going on there, seemingly, and she at once replied that *that* was as plain as the noses on all their faces and a splendid thing, too. A real Swevenings romance, she added.

Alleyn said, "You *do* like to keep yourselves to yourselves in this district, don't you?"

"Well," Nurse Kettle chuckled, "I daresay we do. As I was

saying to a gentleman patient of mine, we're rather like one of those picture-maps. Little world of our own, if you know what I mean. I was suggesting . . ." Nurse Kettle turned bright pink and primmed up her lips. "Personally," she added rather obscurely, "I'm all for the old families and the old ways of looking at things."

"Now, it strikes me," Fox said, raising his brows in bland surprise, "and mind, I may be wrong, very likely I am, but it strikes *me* that the present Mrs. Cartarette belongs to quite a different world. Much more *mondaine*, if you'll overlook the faulty accent, Miss Kettle."

Miss Kettle muttered something that sounded like "demi-mondaine" and hurried on. "Well, I daresay we're a bit stodgy in our ways in the Vale," she said, "and she's been used to lots of gaiety and there you are." She stood up. "If there's nothing more," she said, "I'll just have a word with the doctor and see if there's anything I can do for Miss Rose or her stepmother before they settle down."

"There's nothing more here. We'll ask you to sign a statement about finding the body, and, of course, you'll be called at the inquest."

"I suppose so." She got up and the two men also rose. Alleyn opened the door. She looked from one to the other.

"It won't be a Vale man," she said. "We're not a murderous lot in the Vale. You may depend upon it."

*ii*

Alleyn and Fox contemplated each other with the absent-minded habit of long association.

"Before we see Dr. Lacklander," Alleyn said, "let's take stock, Br'er Fox. What are you thinking about?" he added.

"I was thinking," Fox said with his customary simplicity, "about Miss Kettle. A very nice woman."

Alleyn stared at him. "You are not by any chance transfixed by Dan Cupid's dart?"

"Ah," Fox said complacently, "that would be the day, wouldn't it, Mr. Alleyn? I like a nice compact woman," he added.

Drag your fancy away from thoughts of Nurse Kettle's contours, compact or centrifugal, and consider. Colonel Cartarette left this house about ten past seven to call on Octavius Danberry-Phinn. Presumably there was no one at home, because the next we hear of him he's having a violent row with Phinn down by the bottom bridge. That's at about half past seven. At twenty to eight he and Phinn part company. The Colonel crosses the bridge and at twenty minutes to eight is having an interview with Lady Lacklander, who is sketching in a hollow on the left bank almost opposite the willow grove on the right bank. Apparently this alfresco meeting was by arrangement. It lasted about ten minutes. At ten to eight Cartarette left Lady Lacklander, re-crosssed the bridge, turned left and evidently went straight into the willow grove because she saw him there as she herself panted up the hill to Nunspardon. Soon after eight Mrs. Cartarette said goodbye to that prize ass George Lacklander and came down the hill. At about a quarter past seven she and he had seen old Phinn poaching, and as she tripped down the path, she looked along his fishing to see if she could spot him anywhere. She must have just missed Lady Lacklander, who, one supposes, had by that time plunged into this Nunspardon Home Spinney they talk so much about. Kitty . . ."

Fox said, "Who?"

"Her name's Kitty, Kitty Cartarette. She came hipping and thighing down the hill with her eye on the upper reaches of the Chyne, where she expected to see Mr. Phinn. She didn't notice her husband in the willow grove, but that tells us nothing until we get a look at the landscape, and anyway, her attention, she says, was elsewhere. She continued across the bridge and so home. She saw nothing unusual on the bridge. Now Lady Lacklander saw a woundy great trout lying on the bridge where, according to Lady L., Mr. Phinn had furiously chucked it when he had his row, thirty-five minutes earlier, with Colonel Cartarette. The next thing that happens is that

Mark Lacklander (who has been engaged in tennis and, one supposes, rather solemn dalliance with that charming girl Rose Cartarette) leaves this house round about the time Mrs. Cartarette returns to it and goes down to the bottom bridge, where he does *not* find a woundy great trout and is certain that there was no trout to find. He does however, find his grandmother's sketching gear on the left bank of the Chyne and like a kind young bloke carries it back to Nunspardon, thus saving the footman a trip. He disappears into the spinney, and as far as we know, this darkling valley is left to itself until a quarter to nine when Nurse Kettle, who has been slapping Commander Syce's lumbago next door, descends into Bottom Meadow, turns off to the right, hears the dog howling and discovers the body. Those are the facts, if they are fact, arising out of the information received up to date. What emerges?"

Fox dragged his palm across his jaw. "For a secluded district," he said, "there seems to have been quite a bit of traffic in the valley of the Chyne."

"Doesn't there? Down this hill. Over the bridge. Up the other hill and t'other way round. None of them meeting except the murdered man and old Phinn at half past seven and the murdered man and Lady Lacklander ten minutes later. Otherwise it seems to have been a series of near misses on all hands. I can't remember the layout of the valley with any accuracy, but it appears that from the houses on this side only the upper reaches of the Chyne and a few yards below the bridge on the right bank are visible. We'll have to do an elaborate check as soon as it's light, which is hellish soon, by the way. Unless we find signs of angry locals hiding in the underbrush or of mysterious coloured gentlemen from the East lurking in the village, it's going to look a bit like a small field of suspects."

"Meaning this lot," Fox said with a wag of his head in the direction of the drawing-room.

"There's not a damn' one among them except the nurse who isn't holding something back; I'll swear there isn't. Let's have a word with young Lacklander, shall we? Fetch him in, Foxkin, and while you're there, see how Mr. Phinn's getting on with his statement to the sergeant. I wanted an ear left in that room, the sergeant's was the only one available and the statement seemed the best excuse for planting him there. We'll have to go for dabs on those spectacles we picked up, and I swear they'll be Mr. Phinn's. If he's got off his chest as much as he's decided to tell us, let him go home. Ask him to remain on tap, though, until further notice. Away you go."

While Fox was away, Alleyn looked more closely at Colonel Cartarette's study. He thought he found in it a number of interesting divergences from the accepted convention. True, there were leather saddleback chairs, a pipe-rack and a regimental photograph, but instead of sporting prints the Colonel had chosen half a dozen Chinese drawings, and the books that lined two of his walls, although they included army lists and military biographies, were for the greater part well-worn copies of Elizabethan and Jacobean dramatists and poets with one or two very rare items on angling. With these Alleyn was interested to find a sizable book with the title *The Scaly Breed* by Maurice Cartarette. It was a work on the habits and characteristics of fresh-water trout. On his desk was a photograph of Rose, looking shy and misty, and one of Kitty looking like an imitation of something it would be difficult to define.

Alleyn's gaze travelled over the surface of the desk and down the front. He tried the drawers. The top pair were unlocked and contained only writing paper and envelopes and a few notes written in a distinguished hand, evidently by the Colonel himself. The centre pairs on each side were locked. The bottom left-hand drawer pulled out. It was empty. His attention was sharpened. He had stooped down to look more closely at it when he heard Fox's voice in the hall. He pushed the drawer to and stood away from the desk.

Mark Lacklander came in with Fox.

Alleyn said, "I shan't keep you long; indeed I have only asked you to come in to clear up one small point and to help us with another, not so small. The first question is this: when you went home at quarter past eight last evening, did you hear a dog howling in Bottom Meadow?"

"No," Mark said. "No, I'm sure I didn't."

"Did Skip really stick close to the Colonel?"

"Not when he was fishing," Mark said at once. "The Colonel had trained him to keep a respectful distance away "

"But you didn't see Skip?"

"I didn't see or hear a dog but I remember meeting a tabby cat. One of Occy Phinn's menagerie, I imagine, on an evening stroll."

"Where was she?"

"This side of the bridge," said Mark, looking bored.

"Right. Now, you'd been playing tennis here, hadn't you, with Miss Cartarette, and you returned to Nunspardon by the bottom bridge and river path. You collected your grandmother's sketching gear on the way, didn't you?"

"I did."

"Were you carrying anything else?"

"Only my tennis things. Why?"

"I'm only trying to get a picture. Collecting these things must have taken a few moments. Did you hear or see anything at all out of the ordinary?"

"Nothing. I don't think I looked across the river at all."

"Right. And now will you tell us, as a medical man, what you make of the injuries to the head?"

Mark said very readily, "Yes, of course, for what my opinion's worth on a superficial examination."

"I gather," Alleyn said, "that you went down with Miss Kettle after she gave the alarm and that with exemplary economy you lifted up the tweed hat, looked at the injury, satisfied yourself that he was dead, replaced the hat and waited for the arrival of the police. That it?"

"Yes. I had a torch and I made as fair an examination as I could without touching him. As a matter of fact, I was able to look pretty closely at the injuries."

"Injuries," Alleyn repeated, stressing the plural. "Then you would agree that he was hit more than once?"

"I'd like to look again before giving an opinion. It seemed to me he had been hit on the temple with one instrument before he was stabbed through it with another. Although—I don't know—a sharp object striking the temple could of itself produce very complex results. It's useless to speculate. Your man will no doubt make a complete examination and what he finds may explain the appearances that to me are rather puzzling."

"But on what you saw your first reaction was to wonder if he'd been stunned before he was stabbed? Is that right?"

"Yes," Mark said readily. "That's right."

"As I saw it," Alleyn said, "there seemed to be an irregular bruised area roughly about three by two inches and inside that a circular welt that might have been made by a very big hammer with a concave striking surface, if such a thing exists. And inside that again is the actual puncture, a hole that, it seemed to me, must have been made by a sharply pointed instrument."

"Yes," Mark said, "that's an accurate description of the superficial appearance. But, of course, the queerest appearances can follow cranial injuries."

"The autopsy may clear up the ambiguities," Alleyn said. He glanced at Mark's intelligent and strikingly handsome face. He decided to take a risk.

"Look here," he said, "it's no good us trying to look as if we're uninterested in Mr. Danberry-Phinn. He and Colonel Cartarette had a flaming row less than an hour, probably, before Cartarette was murdered. What do you feel about that? I don't have to tell you this is entirely off the record. What sort of a chap is Mr. Phinn? You must know him pretty well."

Mark thrust his hands into his pockets and scowled at the floor. "I don't know him as well as all that," he said. "I mean. I've known him all my life, of course, but he's old enough to be my father and not likely to be much interested in a medical student or a young practitioner."

"Your father would know him better, I suppose."

"As a Swevenings man and my father's elder contemporary, yes, but they hadn't much in common."

"You knew his son, Ludovic, of course?"

"Oh, yes," Mark said composedly. "Not well," he added:

"he was at Eton and I'm at Wykehamist. He trained for the Diplomatic, and I left Oxford for the outer darkness of the dissecting rooms at Thomas's. Completely *declasse*. I dare say," Mark added, with a grin, "that my grandfather thought much the same about you, sir. Didn't you desert him and the Diplomatic for Lord Trenchard and the lonely beat?"

"If you like to put it that way, which is a good deal more flattering to me than it is to either of my great white chiefs. Young Phinn, by the way, was at your grandfather's embassy in Zlomce, wasn't he?"

"He was," Mark said, and as if he realized that this reply sounded uncomfortably short, he added, "My grandfather was a terrific 'Vale Man,' as we say in these parts. He liked to go all feudal and surround himself with local people. When Viccy Phinn went into the service, I fancy grandfather asked if he could have have him with the idea of making one corner of a Zlomcefield forever Swevenings. My God," Mark added, "I didn't mean to put it like that, I mean . . ."

"You've remembered, perhaps, that young Phinn blew out his brains in one corner of a Zlomce field."

"You knew about that?"

"It must have been a great shock to your grandfather."

Mark compressed his lips and turned away. "Naturally," he said. He pulled out a case and still with his back to Alleyn lit himself a cigarette. The match scraped and Fox cleared his throat.

"I believe," Alleyn said, "that Sir Harold's autobiography is to be published."

Mark said, "Did Phinn tell you that?"

"Now, why in the wide world," Alleyn asked, "should Mr. Octavius Phinn tell me?"

There was a long silence broken by Mark.

"I'm sorry, sir," Mark said. "I must decline absolutely to answer any more questions."

"You are perfectly within your rights. It's not so certain that you are wise to do so."

"After all," Mark said. "I must judge of that for myself. Is there any objection now to my driving to the dispensary?"

Alleyn hesitated for the fraction of a second. "No objection in the world," he said. "Good morning to you, Dr. Lacklander."

Mark repeated, "I'm sorry," and with a troubled look at both of them went out of the room.

"Br'er Fox," Alleyn said, "we shall snatch a couple of hours sleep at the Boy and Donkey, but before we do so, will you drag your fancy away from thoughts of District Nurses and bend it upon the bottom drawer on the left-hand side of Colonel Cartarette's desk?"

Fox raised his eyebrows, stationed himself before the desk, bent his knees, placed his spectacles across his nose and did as he was bidden.

"Forced," he said. "Recent. Chipped."

"Quite so. The chip's on the floor. The paper knife on the desk is also chipped and the missing bit is in the otherwise empty drawer. The job's been done unhandily by an amateur in a hurry. We'll seal this room and to-morrow we'll put in the camera-and-dabs boys. Miss Kettle's, Mr. Phinn's and Dr. Lacklander's prints'll be on their statements. Lacklander's and Mrs. Cartarette's grog glasses had better be rescued and locked up in here. If we want dabs from the others, we'll pick them up in the morning." He took a folded handkerchief from his pocket, put it on the desk and opened it up. A pair of cheap spectacles was revealed. "And before we go to bed," he said, "we'll discover if Mr. Danberry-Phinn has left his dabs on his reach-me-down specs. And in the morning, Foxkin, if you are a good boy, you shall be told the sad and cautionary story of Master Ludovic Phinn."

*iii*

Kitty Cartarette lay in a great Jacobean bed. She had asked, when she was first married to have it done over in quilted and buttoned peach velvet, but had seen at once that this would be considered an error in taste. Anxious at that time to establish her position, she had given up this idea, but the dressing-table and chairs and lamp had all been her own choice. She stared miserably at them now, and a fanciful observer might have found something valedictory in her glance. By shifting across the bed, she was able to see herself in her long glass. The pink silk sheet billowed up round her puffed and tear-stained face. "I do look a sight," she muttered. She may have then remembered that she lay in her husband's place, and if a coldness came over her at this recollection, nobody in Swevenings would have suggested that it was because she had ever really loved him. Lady Lacklander had remarked, indeed, that Kitty was one of those rare women who seem to get through life without forming a deep attachment to anybody, and Lady Lacklander would have found it difficult to say why Kitty had been weeping. It would not have occurred to her to suppose that Kitty was lonelier than she had ever been before, but merely that she suffered from shock, which, of course, was true.

There was a tap on the door and this startled Kitty. Maurice, with his queer old-fashioned delicacy, had always tapped.

"Hullo?" she said.

The door opened and Rose came in. In her muslin dressing-gown and with her hair drawn into a plait she looked like a school-girl. Her eyelids, like Kitty's, were swollen and pink, but even this disfigurement, Kitty noticed with vague resentment, didn't altogether blot out Rose's charm. Kitty supposed she ought to have done a bit more about Rose. "But I can't think of everything," she told herself distractedly.

Rose said, "Kitty, I hope you don't mind my coming in. I couldn't get to sleep and I came out and saw the light under your door. Mark's fetching me some sleeping things from Chyning and I wondered if you'd like one."

"I've got some things of my own, thanks all the same. Has everybody gone?"

"Lady Lacklander and George have and, I think, Occy Phinn. Would you like Mark to look in?"

"What for?"

"You might find him sort of helpful," Rose said in a shady voice. "I do."

"I daresay," Kitty rejoined dryly. She saw Rose blush faintly. "It was nice of you to think of it, but I'm all right. What about the police? Are they still making themselves at home in your father's study?" Kitty asked.

"I think they must have gone. They're behaving awfully well, really. Kitty. I mean it *is* a help, Mr. Alleyn being a gent."

"I daresay," Kitty said again. "OK., Rose," she added. "Don't worry. I know."

Her manner was good-naturedly dismissive, but Rose still hesitated. After a pause she said, "Kitty, while I've been waiting—for Mark to come back, you know—I've been thinking. About the future."

"The *future?*" Kitty repeated and stared at her. "I should have thought the present was enough!"

"I can't think about that," Rose said quickly. "Not yet. Not about Daddy. But it came into my mind that it was going to be hard on you. Perhaps you don't realize—I don't know if he told you, but—well—"

"Oh, yes," Kitty said wearily, "I know. He did tell me. He was awfully scrupulous about anything to do with money, wasn't he?" She looked up at Rose. "O.K., Rose," she said. "Not to fuss. I'll make out. I wasn't expecting anything. My sort," she added obscurely, "don't."

"But I wanted to tell you; you needn't worry. Not from any financial point of view. I mean—it's hard to say and perhaps I should wait till we're more used to what's happened, but I *want* to help," Rose stammered. She began to speak rapidly. It was almost as if she had reached that point of emotional exhaustion that is akin to drunkenness. Her native restraint seemed to have forsaken her and to have been replaced by an urge to pour out some kind of sentiment upon somebody. She appeared scarcely to notice her stepmother as an individual. "You see," she was saying, weaving her fingers together, "I might as well tell you. I shan't need Hammer for very long. Mark and I are going to be engaged."

Kitty looked up at her, hesitated, and then said, "Well, that's fine, isn't it? I do hope you'll be awfully happy. Of course, I'm not exactly surprised."

"No," Rose agreed. "I expect we've been terribly transparent." Her voice trembled and her eyes filled with reiterant tears. "Daddy knew," she said.

"Yes," Kitty agreed with a half-smile. "I told him."

"*You* did?"

It was as if Rose was for the first time positively aware of her stepmother.

"You needn't mind," Kitty said. "It was natural enough. I couldn't help noticing."

"We told him ourselves," Rose muttered.

"Was he pleased? Look, Rose," Kitty said, still in that half-exhausted, half-good-natured manner, "don't let's bother to hedge. I know about the business over Old Man Lacklander's memoirs."

Rose made a slight distasteful movement. "I hadn't thought of it," she said. "It doesn't make any difference."

"No," Kitty agreed, "in a way, I suppose it doesn't—now. What's the matter?"

Rose's chin had gone up. "I think I hear Mark," she said. She went to the door.

"Rose," Kitty said strongly, and Rose stopped short. "I know it's none of my business but—you're all over the place now. We all are. I wouldn't rush anything! 'Don't rush your fences,' that's what your father would have said, isn't it?"

Rose looked at Kitty with an air of dawning astonishment. "I don't know what you mean," she said. "What fences?"

She had opened the door. A well-kept hand came round it and closed over hers.

"Hallo?" Mark's voice said. "May I come in?"

Rose looked at Kitty, who again hesitated. "Why, yes," she said. "Of course. Come in, Mark."

He was really a *very* handsome young man: tall, dark and with enough emphasis in his mouth and jaw to give him the masterful air that is supposed to be so irresistible to women. He stood looking down at Kitty with Rose's hand drawn through his arm. They made what used to be known as a striking couple.

"I heard your voices," he said, "and thought I'd look in. Is there anything I can do at all? I've bought some things for Rose to help her get to sleep; if you'd like to take one it might be quite an idea."

"I'll see," she said. "I've got something, actually, somewhere."

"Shall we leave one in case?" Mark suggested. He shook a couple of capsules from a packet onto her bedside table and fetched a glass of water. "One is enough," he said.

He was standing above Kitty and between her and Rose, who had not moved from the door at the far end of the room. Kitty looked up into his face and said loudly, "You were the first there, weren't you?"

Mark made a slight admonitory gesture and turned towards Rose. "Not actually the first," he said quietly. "Miss Kettle—"

"Oh—old Kettle," Kitty said irritably, dismissing her. "What I want to know—after all, I am his wife—what *happened?*"

"Rose," Mark said. "You run along to bed."

"No, Mark darling," Rose said, turning deadly white. "I want to know, too. Please. It's worse not to."

"Yes, much worse," Kitty agreed. "Always."

Mark waited for an appreciable time and then said quickly, "Well first of all—there's no disfigurement to his face—"

Kitty made a sharp grimace and Rose put her hands to her eyes.

"—and I don't think he felt anything at all," Mark said. He lifted a finger. "All right. It was a blow. Here. On the temple."

"That—?" Rose said. "Just that?"

"It's a very vulnerable part, darling."

"Then—might it be some sort of accident?"

"Well—no, I'm afraid not."

"O, Mark, why not?"

"It's out of the question, Rose darling."

"But why?"

"The nature of the injuries."

"More that one?" she said. He went quickly to her and took her hands in his.

"Well—yes."

"But you said—" Rose began.

"You see, there are several injuries all in that one small area. It wouldn't do any good if I let you think they might have been caused accidentally, because the—the pathologist will certainly find that they were not."

Kitty, unnoticed, said, "I see," and added abruptly, "I'm sorry, but I don't think I can take any more tonight. D'you mind?"

Mark looked at her with sharpened interest. "You should try to settle down." He lifted her wrist professionally.

"No, no," she said and drew it away. "That's unnecessary, thanks all the same. But I do think Rose ought to go to bed before she drops in her tracks."

"I quite agree," Mark said again, rather coldly, and opened the door. Rose said, "Yes, I'm going; I hope you do manage to sleep, Kitty," and went out. Mark followed her to her own door.

"Mark, darling, good-night," Rose said. She freed herself gently.

"To-morrow," he said, "I'm going to carry you off to Nunspardon."

"Oh," she said, "no—I don't think we can quite do that, do you? Why Nunspardon?"

"Because I want to look after you and because, making all due allowances, I don't think your stepmother's particularly sympathetic or congenial company for you," Mark Lacklander said, frowning.

"It's all right," Rose said. "It doesn't matter. I've learned not to notice."

*iv*

Fox was duly acquainted with the story of Ludovic Phinn over a breakfast of ham and eggs in the parlour of the Boy and Donkey shortly after dawn. Bailey and Thompson, who had also spent the tag end of the night at the pub, were already afoot in Bottom Meadow with the tools of their trade, and the Home Office pathologist was expected from London. The day promised to be fine and warm.

"I know about young Phinn," Alleyn said, "because his debacle occurred when I was doing a spell in the Special Branch in 1937. At that time the late Sir Harold Lacklander was our Ambassador at Zlomce, and Master Danberry-Phinn was his personal secretary. It was known that the German Government was embarked on a leisurely and elaborate party with the local government over railway concessions. We picked up information to the effect that the German boys were prepared to sign an important and, to us, disastrous undertaking in the fairly distant future. Lacklander was instructed to throw a spanner in the works. He was empowered to offer the Zlomce boys certain delectable concessions, and it was fully expected that they would play. The Germans, however, learnt of his little plot and immediately pressed on their own negotiations to a successful and greatly accelerated conclusion. Our government wanted to know why. Lacklander realized that there had been a leakage of information and, since there was nobody else in a position to let the leakage occur, he tackled young Phinn, who at once broke down and admitted that it was his doing. It seems that he had not been able to assimilate his Zlomce oats too well. It's an old and regrettable story. He arrived with his alma mater's milk wet on his lips, full of sophisticated backchat and unsophisticated thinking. He made some very dubious Zlomce chums, among whom was a young gent whom we afterwards found to be a German agent of a particularly persuasive sort. He was said to have fastened on young Phinn, who became completely sold on the Nazi formula and agreed to act for the Germans. As usual, our sources of information were in themselves dubious. Phinn was judged on results, and undoubtedly he behaved like a traitor. On the night after a crucial cable had come through for his chief, he went off to the gypsies or somewhere with his Nazi friend. The decoding of the cable had been entrusted to him. It developed that he presented his Zlomce chums with the whole story. It was said afterwards that he'd taken bribes. Lacklander gave him bottled hell, and he went away and blew his brains out. We were told that he'd had a kind of hero-fixation on Lacklander, and we always thought it odd that he should have behaved as he did. But he was, I believe, a brilliant but unbalanced boy, an only child whose father, the Octavius we saw last night, expected him to retrieve the fortunes of their old and rather reduced family. His mother died a few months afterwards, I believe."

"Sad," said Mr. Fox.

"It was indeed."

"Would you say, Mr. Alleyn, now, that this Mr. Phinn, Sr., was slightly round the bend?"

"Dotty?"

"Well—eccentric."

"His behaviour in the watches of last night was certainly oddish. He was a frightened man, Fox, if I ever saw one. What do you think?"

"The *opportunity* was there," Fox said, going straight to the first principle of police investigation.

"It was. And by the way, Bailey's done his dab-drill. The spectacles *are* Mr. Danberry-Phinn's."

"There now!" Fox ejaculated with the utmost satisfaction.

"It's not conclusive, you know. He might have lost them down there earlier in the day. He'd still be very chary of owning to them."

"Well . . ." Fox said sceptically.

"I quite agree. I've got my own idea about when and how they got there, which is this."

He propounded his idea. Fox listened with raised brows.

"And as for opportunity, Fox," Alleyn went on, "as far as we've got, it was also there for his wife, all three Lacklanders and, for a matter of that, Nurse Kettle herself."

Fox opened his mouth, caught a derisive glint in his senior's eye and shut it again.

"Of course," Alleyn said, "we can't exclude the tramps or even the dark-skinned stranger from the Far East. But there's one item that emerged last night which I don't think we can afford to disregard, Fox. It seems that Colonel Cartarette was entrusted by Sir Harold Lacklander, then on his deathbed, with the Lacklander memoirs. He was to supervise their publication."

"Well, now," Fox began, "I can't say . . ."

"This item may be of no significance whatever," Alleyn rejoined. "On the other hand, isn't it just possible that it may be a link between the Lacklanders on the one hand and Mr. Octavius Phinn on the other, that link being provided by Colonel Cartarette with the memoirs in his hands."

"I take it," Fox said in his deliberate way, "that you're wondering if there's a full account of young Phinn's offence in the memoirs and if his father's got to know of it and made up his mind to stop publication."

"It sounds hellish thin when you put it like that, doesn't it? Where does such a theory land us? Cartarette goes down the hill at twenty past seven, sees Phinn poaching, and, overheard by Lady Lacklander, has a flaming row with him. They part company. Cartarette moves on to talk to Lady Lacklander, stays with her for ten minutes and then goes to the willow grove to fish. Lady L. returns home and Phinn comes back and murders Cartarette because Cartarette is going to publish old Lacklander's memoirs to the discredit of young Phinn's name. But Lady L. doesn't say a word about this to me. She doesn't say she heard them quarrel *about the memoirs,* although, if they did, there's no reason that I can see why she wouldn't. She merely says that they had a row about poaching and that Cartarette talked about this to her. She adds that he and she also discussed a private and domestic business which had nothing to do with Cartarette's death. This, of course, is as it may be. Could the private and domestic business by any chance be anything to do with the publication of the memoirs? If so, why should she refuse to discuss it with me?"

"Have we any reason to think it might be about these memoirs, though?"

"No. I'm doing what I always say you shouldn't do. I'm speculating. But it was clear, wasn't it, that young Lacklander didn't like the memoirs being mentioned. He shut up like a trap over them. They crop up, Br'er Fox. They occur. They link the Cartarettes with the Lacklanders, and they may well link Mr. Phinn with both. They provide, so far, the only connecting theme in this group of apparently very conventional people."

"I wouldn't call her ladyship conventional," Fox observed.

"She's unconventional along orthodox lines, believe me. There's a car pulling up. It'll be Dr. Curtis. Let's return to the bottom field and to the question of opportunity and evidence."

But before he led the way out, he stood rubbing his nose and staring at his colleague.

"Don't forget," he said, "that old Lacklander died with what sounds like an uneasy conscience and the word 'Vic' on his lips."

"Ah. Vic."

"Yes. And Mark Lacklander referred to young Phinn as Viccy! Makes you think, don't it? Come on."

*v*

By mid-summer morning light, Colonel Cartarette looked incongruous in the willow grove. His coverings had been taken away and there, close to the river's brink, he was: curled up, empty of thought and motion, wearing the badge of violence upon his temple...a much photographed corpse. Bailey and Thompson had repeated the work of the previous night but without, Alleyn thought, a great deal of success.

Water had flooded under duck boards, seeped up through earthy places, soaked into Colonel Cartarette's Harris tweeds and had collected in a pool in the palm of his right hand.

Dr. Curtis completed a superficial examination and stood up.

"That's all I want here, Alleyn," he said. "I've given Oliphant the contents of the pockets. A bundle of keys, tobacco, pipe, lighter. Fly case. Handkerchief. Pocket book with a few notes and a photograph of his daughter. That's all. As for general appearances: rigor is well established and is, I think, about to go off. I understand you've found out that he was alive up to quarter past eight and that he was found dead at nine. I won't get any closer in time than that."

"The injuries?"

"I'd say, tentatively, two weapons, or possibly one weapon used in two ways. There's a clean puncture with deep penetration, there's a circular indentation with the puncture as its centre, and there's been a heavy blow over the same area that has apparently caused extensive fracturing and a lot of extravasation. It might have been made by one of those stonebreaker's hammers or even by a flat oval-shaped stone itself. I think it was the first injury he got. It would almost certainly have knocked him right out. Might have killed him. In any case it would have left him wide open to the second attack."

Alleyn had moved round the body to the edge of the steam.

"And no prints?" he said looking at Bailey.

"There's prints from the people that found him," Bailey said, "clear enough. Man and woman. Overlapping and straight forward ... walk towards, squat down, stand, walk away. And there's his own heel marks, Mr. Alleyn, as you noticed last night. Half filled with surface drainage they were then, but you can see how he was, clear enough."

"Yes," Alleyn said. "Squatting on a bit of soft ground. Facing the stream. He'd cut several handfuls of grass with his knife and was about to wrap up that trout. There's the knife, there's the grass in his hands, and there's the trout! A whopper if ever there was one. Sergeant Oliphant says the Colonel himself hooked and lost him some days ago."

He stooped and slipped an exploratory finger into the trout's maw. "Ah, yes," he said, "it's still there. We'd better have a look at it."

His long fingers were busy for a minute. Presently they emerged from the jaws of the Old 'Un with a broken cast. "That's not a standard commercial fly," he said. "It's a beautiful home-made one. Scraps of red feather and gold cloth bound with bronze hair, and I think I've seen its mates in the Colonel's study. Rose Cartarette tied the flies for her father, and I fancy this is the one he lost when he hooked the Old 'Un on the afternoon before Sir Harold Lacklander's death."

Alleyn looked at the Colonel's broken head and blankly acquiescent face. "But you didn't hook him this time," he said, "and why in the world should you shout, at half past seven, that you wouldn't be seen dead with him, and be found dead with him at nine?"

He turned towards the stream. The willow grove sheltered a sort of miniature harbour with its curved bank going sheer down to the depth of about five feet at the top end of the little bay and running out in a stony shelf at the lower end. The stream poured into this bay with swirling movement, turning back upon its course.

Alleyn pointed to the margin of the lower bank of the bay. It carried an indented scar running horizontally below the lip.

"Look here, Fox," Alleyn said, "and here, above it." He nodded at a group of tall daisies, strung along the edge of the bank up-stream from where the Colonel lay and perhaps a yard from his feet. They were in flower. Alleyn pointed to three leggy stems, taller than their fellows, from which the blooms had been cut away.

"You can move him," he said. "But don't tramp over the ground more than you can help. We *may* want another peer at it. And, by the way, Fox, have you noticed that inside the willow grove, near the point of entry, there's a flattened patch of grass and several broken and bent twigs? Remember that Nurse Kettle thought she was observed. Go ahead. Oliphant."

Sergeant Oliphant and P. C. Gripper came forward with a stretcher. They put it down some distance from the body, which they now raised. As they did so, a daisy head, crumpled and sodden, dropped from the coat.

"Pick it up, tenderly," Alleyn said as he did so, "and treat it with care. We must find the other two if we can. This murderer said it with flowers." He put it away in his case. Oliphant and Gripper laid the body on the stretcher and waited.

Alleyn found a second daisy on the bank below the point where Colonel Cartarette's head had lain. "The third," he said, "may have gone down-stream, but we'll see."

He now looked at Colonel Cartarette's rod, squatting beside it where it rested on the bank, its point overhanging the stream. Alleyn lifted the cast, letting it dangle from his long fingers. "The fellow of the one that the Old 'Un broke for him," he said.

He looked more closely at the cast and sniffed at it.

"He hooked a fish yesterday," he said; "there's a flake of flesh on the barb. Where, then, is this trout he caught? Too small? Did he chuck it back? Or what? Damn this ruined ground." He separated the cast from the line and put it away in his case. He sniffed into the dead curved hands. "Yes," he said, "he's handled a fish. We'll go over the hands, fingernails and clothes for any more traces. Keep that tuft of grass that's in his hand. Where's the rest of it?"

He turned back to the riverbank and gathered up every blade of grass that was scattered where the Colonel had cut it. He examined the Colonel's pocket knife and found that, in addition to having traces of grass, it smelt of fish. Then he very cautiously lifted the Old 'Un and examined the patch of stones where the great fish had lain all night.

"Traces there, all right," he said. "And they all off this one fish, however? Look, there's a sharp flinty bit of stone with a flap of fish skin on it. Now let's see."

He turned the great trout over and searched its clamminess for a sign of a missing piece of skin and could find none. "This looks more like business," he muttered and took out his pocket lens. His subordinates coughed and shifted their feet. Fox watched him with calm approval.

"Well," Alleyn said at last, "we'll have to get an expert's opinion and it may be crucial. But it's pretty clear that he made a catch of his own, that it lay on this patch, that a bit of its skin was torn off on this stone, that the fish itself was subsequently removed and the Old 'Un put in its place. It doesn't look as if it was chucked back in the stream, does it? In that case he would have taken it off his hook and thrown it back at once. He wouldn't have laid it down on the bank. And why was a flap of its skin scraped off on the stone? And why was the Old 'Un laid over the trace of the other fish? And by whom? And when?"

Fox said, "As for when: before the rain at all events. The ground shows that."

"That doesn't help, since he was killed before the rain and found before the rain. But consider, Br'er Fox, he was killed with a tuft of cut grass in his hand. Isn't it at least possible that he was cutting his grass to wrap up his own catch? He had refused to touch the Old 'Un and had left it lying on the bridge. The people who knew him best all agree he'd stick to his word. All right. Somebody kills him. Is it that 'somebody' who takes the Colonel's fish and replaces it with the Old 'Un?"

"You'd think so, Mr. Alleyn, wouldn't you?"

"And why did he do it?"

"Gawd knows!" said Oliphant in disgust. Sergeants Bailey and Thompson and P. C. Gripper made sympathetic noises. Dr. Curtis, squatting by the stretcher, grinned to himself.

"What was the actual position of the killer at the time of the blow or blows?" Alleyn continued. "As I read it, and you'll correct me here, Curtis, Colonel Cartarette was squatting on his heels facing the stream with the cut grass in his hands. The heel marks and subsequent position suggest that when he was struck on the left temple he keeled over, away from the blow, and fell in the position in which Nurse Kettle found him. Now, he was either belted from behind by a left-hander or rammed by a sort of crouching charge from his left side or struck from the front by a swinging right-hand swipe . . . Yes, Oliphant?"

Sergeant Oliphant said, "Well, pardon me, sir, I was only going to remark, would it be, for example, something like the sort of blow a quarryman gives a wedge that is sticking out from a rock-face at the level of his knee?"

"Ah!" said P. C. Gripper appreciatively. "Or an underhand serve, like tennis."

"That kind of thing," Alleyn said, exchanging a look with Fox. "Now there wasn't enough room between the Colonel and the brink for such a blow to be delivered; which is why I suggested his assailant would have had to be three feet out on the surface of the stream. Now, take a look up-stream towards the bridge, Br'er Fox. Go roundabout, because we'll still keep the immediate vicinity unmucked up, and then come out here."

Fox joined Alleyn on the lower bank of the little bay at the point where it jutted farthest out into the stream. They looked up the Chyne past the willow grove, which hid the near end of the bridge, to the far end, which was just visible about forty feet away with the old punt moored in the hole beneath it.

Alleyn said, "Charming, isn't it? Like a lead-pencil vignette in a Victorian album. I wonder if Lady Lacklander ever sketches from this point. Have you read *The Rape of Lucrece*, Br'er Fox?"

"I can't say I have, unless it's on the police list, which it sounds as if it might be. Or would it be Shakespeare?"

"The latter. There's a bit about the eccentricities of river currents. The poem really refers to the Avon at Clopton Bridge, but it might have been written about the Chyne at this very point. Something about the stream that, coming through an arch, "yet in the eddy boundeth in his pride back to the strait that forced him on." Look at that twig sailing towards us now. It's got into just such a current, do you see, and instead of passing down the main stream is coming into this bay. Here it comes. Round it swirls in the eddy and back it goes towards the bridge. It's a strong and quite considerable sort of counter-current. Stay where you are, Fox, for a moment, will you. Get down on your sinful old hunkers and bow your head over an imaginary fish. Imitate the action of the angler. Don't look up and don't move till I tell you."

"Ah, what's all this, I do wonder," Mr. Fox speculated and squatted calmly at the water's edge with his great hands between his feet.

Alleyn skirted round the crucial area and disappeared into the willow grove.

"What's he up to?" Curtis asked of no one in particular and added a rude professional joke about Mr. Fox's posture. Sergeant Oliphant and P. C. Gripper exchanged scandalized glances. Bailey and Thompson grinned. They all heard Alleyn walk briskly across the Bottom Bridge, though only Fox, who faithfully kept his gaze on the ground, was in a position to see him. The others waited, expecting him for some reason of his own to appear on the opposite bank.

It was quite a shock to Dr. Curtis, Bailey, Thompson, Oliphant and Gripper when round the upstream point of the willow-grove bay the old punt came sliding with Alleyn standing in it, a wilted daisy head in his hand.

The punt was carried transversely by the current away from the far bank and across the main stream into the little willow-grove harbour. It glided silently to rest, its square prow fitting neatly into the scar Alleyn had pointed out in the down-stream bank. At the same time its bottom grated on the gravel spit and it became motionless.

"I suppose," Alleyn said, "you heard that, didn't you?"

Fox looked up.

"I heard it," he said. "But I saw and heard nothing until then."

"Cartarette must have heard it too," Alleyn said. "Which accounts, I fancy, for the daisies. Br'er Fox, do we think we know whodunit?"

Fox said, "If I take your meaning, Mr. Alleyn, I think you think *you* do."

# CHAPTER **VII**
## Watt's Hill

"Things to be borne in mind," Alleyn said, still speaking from the punt. "Point one: I found the daisy head in the prow. That is to say, on the same line with the other two heads but a bit further from the point of impact. Point two: this old crock has got a spare mooring line about thirty feet long. It's still made fast at the other end and I've only got to haul myself back. I imagine the arrangement is for the convenience of Lady Lacklander, who, judging by splashes of old water-colour and a squashed tube, occasionally paints from the punt. It's a sobering thought. I should like to see her, resembling one of the more obese female deities, seated in the prow of the punt, hauling herself back to harbourage. There is also, by the way, a pale-yellow giant hairpin in close association with two or three cigarette butts, some with lipstick and some not. Been there for some considerable time,

I should say, so that's another story."

"Sir G.," Fox ruminated, "and the girl-friend?"

"Trust you," Alleyn said, "for clamping down on the sex-story. To return. Point three: remember that the punt-journey would be hidden from the dwellers on Watt's Hill. Only this end of the bridge and the small area between it and the willow grove is visible to them. You can take him away now, Gripper."

Dr. Curtis covered the body with the groundsheet. P. C. Gripper and the constable-driver of the Yard car, assisted by Bailey and Tompson, carried Colonel Cartarette out of the willow grove and along the banks of his private fishing to Watt's Lane, where the Swevenings hospital van awaited him.

"He was a very pleasant gentleman," said Sergeant Oliphant. "I hope we get this chap, sir."

"Oh, we'll *get* him," Fox remarked and looked composedly at his principal.

"I suggest," Alleyn said, "that the killer saw Cartarette from the other bank, squatting over his catch. I suggest that the killer, familiar with the punt, slipped into it, let go the painter and was carried by what I'd like to call Shakespeare's current across the stream and into this bay, where the punt grounded and left the scar of its prow in the bank there. I suggest that this person was well enough acquainted with the Colonel for him merely to look up when he heard the punt grate on the gravel and not rise. You can see the punt's quite firmly grounded. Now if I stand about here, rather aft of amidships, I'm opposite the place where Cartarette squatted over his task and within striking distance of him if the blow was of the kind I think it was."

"If," said Fox.

"Yes, I know, 'if.' If you know of a better damn' theory, you can damn' well go to it," Alleyn said cheerfully.

"O.K." Fox said. "I don't, sir. So far."

"What may at first look tiresome," Alleyn went on, "is the position of the three decapitated daisy stalks and their heads. It's true that one swipe of a suitable instrument might have beheaded all three and landed one daisy on the Colonel, a second on the bank and a third in the punt. Fair enough. But the same swipe couldn't have reached the Colonel himself."

Oliphant started pointedly at the pole lying in the punt.

"No, Oliphant," Alleyn said. "You try standing in this punt, whirling that thing round your head, swishing it through the daisies and catching a squatting man neatly on the temple with the end. What do you think our killer is ... a caber-tosser from Braemar?"

"Do you reckon then," Fox said, "that the daisies were beheaded by a second blow or earlier in the day? Or something?"

Sergeant Oliphant suddenly remarked, "Pardon me, but did the daisies neces*sair*ily have anything to do with the crime?"

"I think there's probably a connection," Alleyn rejoined, giving the sergeant his full attention. "The three heads are fresh enough to suggest it. One was in the Colonel's coat and one was in the punt."

"Well, pardon me, sir," the emboldened sergeant continued with a slight modulation of his theme, "but did the punt neces*sair*ily have any bearing on the crime?"

"Unless we find a left-handed suspect, I think we must accept the punt as a working hypothesis. Have a look at the area between the punt and the place where the body lay and the patch of stones between the tuft from which the grass was cut and the place where the fish lay. It would be possible to step from the punt onto that patch of stones, and you would then be standing close to the position of Colonel Cartarette's head. You would leave little or no trace of your presence. Now, on the willow-grove side of the body the ground is soft and earthy. The Colonel himself, Nurse Kettle and Dr. Lacklander have all left recognizable prints there. But there are no traces of a fourth visitor. Accept for the moment the theory that, after the Colonel had been knocked out, our assailant did step ashore onto the stony patch to deliver the final injury, or perhaps merely to make sure the victim was already dead. How would such a theory fit in with the missing trout, the punt and the daisies?"

Alleyn looked from Oliphant to Fox. The former had assumed that air of portentousness that so often waits upon utter bewilderment. The latter merely looked mildly astonished. This expression indicated that Mr. Fox had caught on.

Alleyn elaborated his theory of the trout, the punt and the daisies, building up a complete and detailed picture of one way in which Colonel Cartarette might have been murdered. "I realize," he said, "that it's all as full of 'ifs' as a passport to paradise. Produce any other theory that fits the facts and I'll embrace it with fervour."

Fox said dubiously, "Funny business if it works out that way. About the punt, now . . ."

"About the punt, yes. There are several pieces of cut grass in the bottom of the punt, and they smell of fish."

"Do they now?" said Fox appreciatively and added, "So what we're meant to believe in is a murderer who sails up to his victim in a punt and lays him out. Not satisfied in his own mind that the man's dead, he steps ashore and has another go with another instrument. Then for reasons you've made out to sound O.K., Mr. Alleyn, though there's not much solid evidence, he swaps the Colonel's fish for the Old 'Un. To do this he has to tootle back in the punt and fetch it. And by way of a change at some time or another he swipes the heads off daisies. Where he gets his weapons and what he does with the first fish is a great big secret. Is that the story, Mr. Alleyn?"

"It is and I'm sticking to it. Moreover, I'm leaving orders, Oliphant, for a number one search for the missing fish. And meet me," Alleyn said to Fox, "on the other bank. I've something to show you."

He gathered up the long tow-rope, pulled himself easily into the counter-current and so back across forty feet of water to the boatshed. When Fox, having come round by the bridge, joined him there, he was shaking his head.

"Oliphant and his boy have been over the ground like a herd of rhinos," he said. "Getting their planks last night. Pity. Still . . . have a look here, Fox."

He led the way into a deep hollow on the left bank. Here

the rain had not obliterated the characteristic scars left by Lady Lacklander's sketching stool and easel. Alleyn pointed to them. "But the really interesting exhibit is up here on the hillock. Come and see."

Fox followed him over grass that carried faint signs of having been trampled. In a moment they stood looking down at a scarcely preceptible hold in the turf. It still held water. The grass nearby showed traces of pressure.

"If you examine that hole closely," Alleyn said, "you'll see it's surrounded by a circular indentation."

"Yes," Fox said after a long pause, "yes, by God, so it is. Same as the injury, by God."

"It's the mark of the second weapon," Alleyn said. "It's the mark of a shooting-stick, Br'er Fox."


## ii

"Attractive house," Alleyn said as they emerged from the Home Coppice into full view of Nunspardon, "attractive house, Fox, isn't it?"

"Very find residence," Fox said. "Georgian, would it be?"

"It would. Built on the site of the former house, which was a nunnery. Hence Nunspardon. Presented (as usual, by Henry VIII) to the Lacklanders. We'll have to go cautiously here, Br'er Fox, by gum, we shall. They'll have just about finished their breakfast. I wonder if Lady Lacklander has it downstairs or in her room. She has it downstairs," he added as Lady Lacklander herself came out of the house with half a dozen dogs at her heels.

"She's wearing men's boots!" Fox observed.

"That may be because of her ulcerated toe."

"Ah, to be sure. Lord love us!" Fox ejaculated. "She's *got* a shooting-stick on her arm."

"So she has. It may not be the one. And then again," Alleyn muttered as he removed his hat and gaily lifted it on high to the distant figure, "it may."

"Here she comes. No, she doesn't."

"Hell's boots, she's going to sit on it."

Lady Lacklander had in fact begun to tramp towards them but had evidently changed her mind. She answered Alleyn's salute by waving a heavy gardening glove at him. Then she halted, opened her shooting-stick and, with alarming empiricism, let herself down on it.

"With her weight," Alleyn said crossly, "she'll bloody well bury it. Come on."

As soon as they were within hailing distance, Lady Lacklander shouted, "Good morning to you." She then remained perfectly still and stared at them as they approached. Alleyn thought, "Old basilisk! She's being deliberately embarrassing, damn her," and he returned the stare with inoffensive interest, smiling vaguely.

"Have you been up all night?" she asked when they were at an appropriate distance. "Not that you look like it, I must say."

Alleyn said, "We're sorry to begin plaguing you so early but we're in a bit of a jam."

"Baffled?"

"Jolly nearly. Do you mind," Alleyn went on with what his wife would have called sheer rude charm, "do you mind having your brains picked at nine o'clock in the morning?"

"What do *you* want with other people's brains, I should like to know," she said. Her eyes, screwed in between swags of flesh, glittered at him.

Alleyn embarked on a careful tarradiddle. "We begin to wonder," he said, "if Cartarette's murderer may have been lying doggo in the vicinity for some time before the assault."

"Do you?"

"Yes."

"*I* didn't see him."

"I mean really doggo. And as far as we know, which is not as far as we'd like, there's no telling exactly where the hiding place could have been. We think it might have been somewhere that commanded at any rate a partial view of the bridge and the willow grove. We also think that it may have overlooked your sketching hollow."

"You've discovered where that is, have you?"

"Simplicity itself, I promise you. You used an easel and a sketching stool."

"And with my weight to sustain," she said rocking, to his dismay, backwards and forwards on the shooting-stick, "the latter no doubt left its mark."

"The thing is," Alleyn said, "we think this person in hiding may have waited until he saw you go before coming out of cover. Did you stay down in your hollow all the time?"

"No. I had a look at my sketch several times from a distance. Anaemic beast it turned out, in the end."

"Where exactly did you stand when you looked at it?"

"On the rise betwen the hollow and the bridge. You can't have gone over your ground properly or you'd have found that out for yourself."

"Should I? Why?" Alleyn asked and mentally touched wood.

"Because, my good Roderick, I used this shooting-stick and drove it so far into the ground that I was able to walk away and leave it, which I did repeatedly."

"Did you leave it there when you went home?"

"Certainly. As a landmark for the boy when he came to collect my things. I dumped them beside it."

"Lady Lacklander," Alleyn said, "I want to reconstruct the crucial bit of the landscape as it was after you left it. Will you lend us your shooting-stick and your sketching gear for an hour or so? We'll take the greatest care of them."

"I don't know what you're up to," she said, "and I suppose I may as well make up my mind that I won't find out. Here you are."

She heaved herself up and, sure enough, the disk and spike of her shooting-stick had been rammed down so hard into the path that both were embedded and the shooting-stick stood up of its own accord.

Alleyn desired above all things to release it with the most delicate care, perhaps dig it up, turf and all, and let the soil dry and fall away. But there was no chance of that; Lady Lacklander turned and with a single powerful wrench tore the shooting-stick from its bondage.

"There you are," she said indifferently and gave it to him.

"The sketching gear is up at the house. Come and get it?"

Alleyn thanked her and said that they would. He carried the shooting-stick by its middle and they all three went up to the house. George Lacklander was in the hall. His manner had changed overnight and he now spoke with the muted solemnity with which men of his type approach a sickroom or a church service. He made a further reference to his activities as a Justice of the Peace but otherwise was huffily reserved.

"Well, George," his mother said, and bestowed a peculiar smirk upon him, "I don't suppose they'll let me out on bail, but no doubt you'll be allowed to visit me."

"Really, Mama!"

"Roderick is demanding my sketching gear on what appears to me to be a sadly trumped-up excuse. He has not yet, however, administered what I understand to be the Usual Warning."

"Really, Mama!" George repeated with a miserable titter.

"Come along, Rory," Lady Lacklander continued and led Alleyn out of the hall into a cloakroom where umbrellas, an assortment of galoshes, boots and shoes, and a variety of rackets and clubs were assembled. "I keep them here to be handy," she said, "for garden peeps. I'm better at herbaceous borders than anything else, which just about places my prowess as a water-colourist, as, no doubt, your wife would tell you."

"She's not an aesthetic snob," Alleyn said mildly.

"She's a damn' good painter, however," Lady Lacklander continued. "There you are. Help yourself."

He lifted a canvas haversack to which were strapped an easel and an artist's umbrella. "Did you use the umbrella?" he asked.

"William, the boy, put it up. I didn't want it; the sun was gone from the valley. I left it, standing but shut, when I came home."

"We'll see if it showed above the hollow."

"Roderick," said Lady Lacklander, suddenly, "what exactly *were* the injuries?"

"Hasn't your grandson told you?"

"If he had I wouldn't ask you."

"They were cranial."

"You needn't be in a hurry to return the things. I'm not in the mood."

"It's very kind of you to lend them."

"Kettle will tell me," said Lady Lacklander, "all about it!"

"Of course she will," he agreed cheerfully, "much better than I can."

"What persuaded you to leave the Service for this unlovely trade?"

"It's a long time ago," Alleyn said, "but I seem to remember that it had something to do with a liking for facts."

"Which should never be confused with the truth."

"I still think they are the raw material of the truth. I mustn't keep you any longer. Thank you so much for helping us," Alleyn said and stood aside to let her pass.

He and Fox were aware of her great bulk, motionless on the steps, as they made their way back to the Home Coppice. Alleyn carried the shooting-stick by its middle and Fox the sketching gear. "And I don't mind betting," Alleyn said, "that from the rear we look as self-conscious as a brace of snowballs in hell."

When they were out of sight in the trees, they examined their booty.

Alleyn laid the shooting-stick on a bank and squatted beside it.

"The disk," he said, "screws on above the ferrule leaving a two-inch spike. Soft earth all over it and forced up under the collar of the disk, which obviously hasn't been disengaged for weeks! All to the good. If it's the weapon, it may have been washed in the Chyne and wiped, and it has, of course, been subsequently rammed down in soft earth, but it hasn't been taken apart. There's a good chance of a blood trace under the collar. We must let Curtis have this at once. Now let's have a look at her kit."

"Which we didn't really want, did we?"

"You never know. It's a radial easel with spiked legs, and it's a jointed gamp with a spiked foot. Lots of spikes available, but the shooting-stick fits the picture best. Now for the interior. Here we are," Alleyn said, unbuckling the straps and peering inside. "Large water-colour box. Several mounted boards of not-surface paper. Case of brushes. Pencils. Bunjy. Water-jar. Sponge. Paint-rag. Paint rag." he repeated softly and bent over the kit sniffing. He drew a length of stained cotton rag out of the kit. It was blotched with patches of watery colour with one dark brownish-reddish stain that was broken by a number of folds as if the rag had been twisted about some object.

Alleyn looked up at his colleague.

"Smell, Fox," he said.

Fox squatted behind him and sniffed stertorously.

"Fish," he said.

### iii

Before returning, they visited the second tee and looked down on the valley from the Nunspardon side. They commanded a view of the far end of the bridge and the reaches of the Chyne above it. As from the other side of the valley, the willow grove, the lower reaches and the Nunspardon end of the bridge were hidden by intervening trees through which they could see part of the hollow where Lady Lacklander had worked at her sketch.

"So you see," Alleyn pointed out, "it was from here that Mrs. Cartarette and that ass George Lacklander saw Mr. Phinn poaching under the bridge, and it was from down there in the hollow that Lady Lacklander glanced up and saw them." He turned and looked back at a clump of trees on the golf course. "And I don't mind betting," he added, "that all this chat about teaching her to play golf is the cover-story for a pompous slap-and-tickle."

"Do you reckon, Mr. Alleyn?"

"Well, I wouldn't be surprised. There's Oliphant at the bridge," Alleyn said, waving his hand. "We'll get him to take this stuff straight to Curtis, who'll be in Chyning by now. He's starting his P.M. by eleven. Dr. Lacklander's arranged for him to use the hospital mortuary. I want a report as soon as we can get it, on the rag and the shooting-stick."

"Will the young doctor attend the autopsy, do you think?"

"I wouldn't be surprised. I think our next move had better be a routine check-up on Commander Syce."

"That's the chap Miss Kettle mentioned, with lumbago, who lives in the middle house," Fox observed. "I wonder would he have seen anything."

"Depends on the position of his bed."

"It's a nasty thing, lumbago," Fox mused.

They handed over Lady Lacklander's property to Sergeant Oliphant with an explanatory note for Dr. Curtis and instructions to search the valley for the whole or part of the missing trout. They then climbed the river path to Uplands.

They passed through the Hammer Farm spinney and entered that of Commander Syce. Here they encountered a small notice nailed to a tree. It was freshly painted and bore in neatly executed letters the legend: "Beware of Archery."

"Look at that!" Fox said. "And we've forgotten our green tights."

"It may be a warning to Nurse Kettle," Alleyn said.

"I don't get you, sir?"

"Not to flirt with the Commander when she beats up his lumbago."

"Very far-fetched," Fox said stiffly.

As they emerged from Commander Syce's spinney into his garden, they heard a twang followed by a peculiar whining sound and the "tuck" of a penetrating blow.

"What the hell's that!" Fox ejaculated. "It sounded like the flight of an arrow."

"Which is not surprising," Alleyn rejoined, "as that is what it was."

He nodded at a tree not far from where they stood and there, astonishing and incongruous, was embedded an arrow prettily flighted in red and implanted in the centre of a neatly and freshly carved heart. It still quivered very slightly. "We can't say we weren't warned," Alleyn pointed out.

"Very careless!" Fox said crossly.

Alleyn pulled out the arrow and looked closely at it. "Deadly if they hit the right spot. I hope you've noticed the heart. It would appear that Commander Syce has recovered from his lumbago and fallen into love's sickness. Come on."

They emerged from the spinney to discover Commander Syce himself some fifty yards away, bow in hand, quiver at thigh, scarlet-faced and irresolute.

"Look here!" he shouted. "Damn' sorry and all that, but, great grief, how was I to know, and, damn it all, what about the notice!"

"Yes, yes," Alleyn rejoined. "We're here at our own risk."

He and Fox approached Syce, who, unlike Lady Lacklander, evidently found the interval between the first hail and, as it were, boarding distance extremely embarrassing. As they plodded up the hill, he looked anywhere but at them and when, finally, Alleyn introduced himself and Fox, he shied away from them like an unbroken colt.

"We are," Alleyn explained, "police officers."

"Good Lord!"

"I suppose you've heard of last night's tragedy?"

"What tragedy?"

"Colonel Cartarette."

"Cartarette?"

"He has been murdered."

"Great grief!"

"We're calling on his neighbours in case..."

"What time?"

"About nine o'clock, we think."

"How d'you know it's murder?"

"By the nature of the injuries, which are particularly savage ones, to the head."

"Who found him?"

"The District Nurse. Nurse Kettle."

Commander Syce turned scarlet. "Why didn't she get me!" he said.

"Would you expect her to?"

"No."

"Well then..."

"I say, come in, won't you? No good chattering out here,

what!" shouted Commander Syce.

They followed him into his desolate drawing-room and noted the improvised bed, now tidily made-up, and a table set out with an orderly array of drawing materials and water-colours. A large picture-map in the early stages of composition was pinned to a drawing board. Alleyn saw that its subject was Swevenings and that a number of lively figures had already been sketched in.

"Thet's very pleasant," Alleyn said, looking at it.

Commander Syce made a complicated and terrified noise and interposed himself between the picture-map and their gaze. He muttered something about doing it for a friend.

"Isn't she lucky?" Alleyn remarked lightly. Commander Syce turned, if anything, deeper scarlet, and Inspector Fox looked depressed.

Alleyn said he was sure Commander Syce would understand that as a matter of routine the police were calling upon Cartarette's neighbours. "Simply," he said, "to try and get a background. When one is casting about in a case like this..."

"Haven't you got the fellah?"

"No. But we hope that by talking to those of the Colonel's neighbours who were anywhere near..."

"I wasn't. Nowhere near."

Alleyn said with a scarcely perceptible modulation of tone, "Then you know where he was found?"

"'Course I do. You say nine o'clock. Miss... ah...the...ah...the lady who you tell me found him left here at five to nine and I saw her go down into the valley. If she found him at nine, he must have been in the perishing valley, mustn't he? I watched her go down."

"From where?"

"From up here. The window. She told me she was going down the valley."

"You were on your feet, then? Not completely prostrate with lumbago?"

Commander Syce began to look wretchedly uncomfortable. "I struggled up, don't you know," he said.

"And this morning you've quite recovered?"

"It comes and goes."

"Very tricky," said Alleyn. He still had the arrow in his hand and now held it up. "Do you often loose these things off into your spinney?" he asked.

Commander Syce muttered something about a change from target shooting.

"I've often thought I'd like to have a shot at archery," Alleyn lied amiably. "One of the more blameless sports. Tell me, what weight of bow do you use?"

"A sixty-pound pull."

"Really! What's the longest . . . is clout the word? . . . that can be shot with a sixty-pounder?"

"Two hundred and forty yards."

"Is that twelve score? 'A' would have clapped i' the clout at twelve score'?"

"That's right," Commander Syce agreed and shot what might have been an appreciative glance at Alleyn.

"Quite a length. However, I mustn't keep you gossiping about archery. What I really want to ask you is this. I understand that you've known Colonel Cartarette a great many years?"

"Off and on. Neighbours. Damn' nice fellah."

"Exactly. And I believe that when Cartarette was in the Far East, you ran up against him . . . at Hong Kong, was it?" Alleyn improvised hopefully.

"Singapore."

"Oh, yes. The reason why I'm asking you is this. From the character of the crime and the apparently complete absence of motive, here, we are wondering if it can possibly be a back-kick from his work out in the East."

"Wouldn't know."

"Look here, can you tell us anything at all about his life in the East? I mean, anything that might start us off. When actually did you see him out there?"

"Last time would be four years ago. I was still on the active list. My ship was based on Singapore and he looked me up when we were in port. I was axed six months later."

"Did you see much of them out there?"

"Them?"

"The Cartarettes."

Commander Syce glared at Alleyn. "He wasn't married," he said, "then."

"So you didn't meet the second Mrs. Cartarette until you came back here, I suppose?"

Commander Syce thrust his hands into his pockets and walked over to the window. "I had met her, yes," he mumbled. "Out there."

"Before they married?"

"Yes."

"Did you bring them together?" Alleyn asked lightly and he saw the muscles in the back of Syce's neck stiffen under the reddened skin.

"I introduced them, as it happens," Syce said loudly without turning his head.

"That's always rather amusing. Or I find it so, being," Alleyn said looking fixedly at Fox, "an incorrigible matchmaker."

"Good God, nothing like that!" Syce shouted. "Last thing I intended. Good God, no!"

He spoke with extraordinary vehemence and seemed to be moved equally by astonishment, shame and indignation. Alleyn wondered why on earth he himself didn't get the snub he had certainly invited and decided it was because Syce was too embarrassed to administer one. He tried to get something more about Syce's encounters with Cartarette in Singapore but was unsuccessful. He noticed the unsteady hands, moist skin and patchy colour, and the bewildered, unhappy look in the very blue eyes. "Alcoholic, poor devil," he thought.

"It's no good asking me anything," Syce abruptly announced. "Nobody tells me anything. I don't go anywhere. I'm no good to anybody."

"We're only looking for a background, and I hoped you might be able to provide a piece of it. Miss Kettle was saying last night how close the Swevenings people are to each other; it all sounded quite feudal. Even Sir Harold Lacklander had young Phinn as his secretary. What did you say?"

"Nothing. Young perisher. Doesn't matter."

". . . and as soon as your ship comes in, Cartarette naturally looks you up. You bring about his first meeting with Miss . . . I don't know Mrs. Cartarette's maiden name."

Commander Syce mumbled unhappily.

"Perhaps you can give it to me," Alleyn said apologetically. "We have to get these details for the files. Save me bothering her."

He gazed mildly at Syce, who threw one agonized glance at him, swallowed with difficulty, and said in a strangulated voice, "De Vere."

There was a marked silence. Fox cleared his throat.

"Ah, yes," Alleyn said.

*iv*

"Would you have thought," Fox asked as he and Alleyn made their way through Mr. Phinn's coppice to Jacob's Cottage, "that the present Mrs. Cartarette was born into the purple, Mr. Alleyn?"

"I wouldn't have said so, Br'er Fox. No."

"De Vere, though?"

"My foot."

"Perhaps," Fox speculated, reverting to the language in which he so ardently desired to become proficient, "perhaps she's . . . er . . . *declassee*."

"I think, on the contrary, she's on her way up."

"Ah. The baronet, now," Fox went on; "he's sweet on her, as anyone could see. Would you think it was a strong enough attraction to incite either of them to violence?"

"I should think he was going through the silly season most men of his type experience. I must say I can't see him raising an amatory passion to the power of homicide in any woman. You never know, of course; I should think she must find life in Swevenings pretty dim. What did you collect from Syce's general behaviour, Fox?"

"Well, now, he *did* get me wondering what exactly are his feelings about this lady? I mean, they seem to be old acquaintances, don't they? Miss Kettle said he made a picture of Mrs. Cartarette before she was married. And then he didn't seem to have fancied the marriage much, did he? Practically smoked when it was mentioned, he got so hot. My idea is there was something between him and her and the magnolia bush wherever East meets West."

"You dirty old man," Alleyn said absently. "We'll have to find out, you know."

*"Crime passionnel?"*

"Again you never know. We'll ring the Yard and ask them to look him up in the Navy List. They can find out when he was in Singapore and get a confidential report."

"Say," Fox ejaculated, "that he was sweet on her. Say they were engaged when he introduced her to the Colonel. Say he went off in his ship and then was retired from the navy and came home and found Kitty de Vere changed into the second Mrs. Cartarette. So he takes to the bottle and gets," said Mr. Fox, "an *idée fixe.*"

"So will you, if you go on speculating with such insatiable virtuosity. And what about his lumbago? Personally, I think he's having a dim fling with Nurse Kettle."

Fox looked put out.

"Very unsuitable," he said.

"Here is Mr. Phinn's spinney and here, I think, is our girlfriend of last night."

Mrs. Thomasina Twitchett was, in fact, taking a stroll. When she saw them, she wafted her tail, blinked and sat down.

"Good morning, my dear," said Alleyn.

He sat on his heels and extended his hand. Mrs. Twitchett did not advance upon it, but she broke into an extremely loud purring.

"You know," Alleyn continued severely, "if you could do a little better than purrs and mews, I rather fancy you could give us exactly the information we need. You were in the bottom meadow last night, my dear, and I'll be bound you were all eyes and ears."

Mrs. Twitchett half closed her eyes, sniffed at his extended forefinger and began to lick it.

"Thinks you're a kitten," Fox said sardonically.

Alleyn in his turn sniffed at his finger and then lowered his face almost to the level of the cat's. She saluted him with a brief dab of her nose.

"What a girl," Fox said.

"She no longer smells of raw fish. Milk and a little cooked rabbit, I fancy. Do you remember where we met her last night?"

"Soon after we began to climb the hill on this side, wasn't it?"

"Yes. We'll have a look over the terrain when we get the chance. Come on."

They climbed up through Mr. Phinn's spinney and finally emerged on the lawn before Jacob's Cottage. "Though if that's a cottage," Fox observed, "Buck House is a bungalow."

"Case of inverted snobbism, I daresay. It's a nice front, nevertheless. Might have been the dower house to Nunspardon at one time. Rum go, couple of unattached males living side-by-side in houses that are much too big for them."

"I wonder how Mr. Phinn and the Commander hit it off."

"I wouldn't mind having a bet that they don't. Look, here he comes."

"Cripes!" Mr. Fox ejaculated. "What a menagerie!"

Mr. Phinn had, in fact, come out of his house accompanied by an escort of cats and Mrs. Twichett's three fat kittens.

"No more!" he was saying in his curious alto voice. "All gone! Go and catch micey, you lazy lot of furs."

He set down the empty dish he had been carrying. Some object fell from his breast pocket and he replaced it in a hurry. Some of his cats pretended alarm and flounced off, the others merely stared at him. The three kittens, seeing their mother, galloped unsteadily towards her with stiff tails and a great deal of conversation. Mr. Phinn saw Alleyn and Fox. Staring at them, he clapped his hands like a mechanical toy that had not quite run down.

The tassel of his smoking cap had swung over his nose, but his sudden pallor undid its comic effect. The handle of the concealed object protruded from his breast pocket. He began to walk towards them, and his feline escort, with the exception of the Twitchetts, scattered before him.

"Good morning," Mr. Phinn fluted thickly. He swept aside his tassel with a not quite steady hand and pulled up a dingy handkerchief, thus concealing the protruding handle. "To what beneficent constabular breeze do I owe this enchanting surprise? Detectives, emerging from a grove of trees!" he exclaimed and clasped his hands. "Like fauns in pursuit of some elusive hamadryad! Armed, I perceive," he added with a malevolent glance at Commander Syce's arrow, which Alleyn had retained by the simple expedient of absent-mindedly walking away with it.

"Good morning, Mr. Phinn," Alleyn said. "I have been renewing my acquaintance with your charming cat."

"Isn't she sweet?" Mr. Phinn moistened his lips with the tip of his tongue. "Such a devoted mama, you can't think!"

Alleyn sat on his heels beside Mrs. Twitchett, who gently kicked away one of her too-greedy kittens. "Her fur's in wonderful condition for a nursing mother," he said, stroking it. "Do you give her anything special to eat?"

Mr. Phinn began to talk with the sickening extravagance of the feline-fanatic. "A balanced diet," he explained in a high-pitched voice, "of her own choosing. Fissy on Mondays and Fridays. Steaky on Tuesdays. Livvy on Wednesdays. Cooked bun on Thursdays and Sundays. Embellished," he added with a merciless smile, "by our own clever claws, with micey and birdie."

"Fish only twice a week," Alleyn mused, and Fox, suddenly feeling that something was expected of him, said, "Fancy!"

"She is looking forward to to-morrow," Mr. Phinn said, "with the devoted acquiescence of good Catholic, although, of course, theistically, she professes the mysteries of Old Nile."

"You don't occasionally catch her dinner for her in the Chyne?"

"When I am successful," Mr. Phinn said, "we share."

"Did you," Alleyn asked, fatuously addressing himself to the cat, "did you have fresh fissy for your supper last night, my angel?" Mrs. Twitchett turned contemptuously to her kittens.

"No!" said Mr. Phinn in his natural voice.

"You made no other catch then, besides the fabulous Old 'Un?"

"No!"

"May we talk?"

Mr. Phinn, silent for once, led the way through a side door and down a passage into a sizable library.

Alleyn's eye for other people's houses unobtrusively explored the room. The Colonel's study had been pleasant, civilized and not lacking in feminine graces. Commander Syce's drawing-room was at once clean, orderly, desolate and entirely masculine. Mr. Phinn's library was disorderly, dirty, neglected and ambiguous. It exhibited confused traces of Georgian grace, Victorian pomposity and Edwardian muddle. Cushions that had once been fashionably elaborate were now stained and tarnished. There were yards of dead canvas that had once been acceptable to Burlington House, including the portrait of a fragile-looking lady with a contradictory jaw that was vaguely familiar. There were rows and rows of "gift" books about cats, cheek-by-jowl with Edwardian novels which, if opened, would be found to contain illustrations of young women in dust coats and motoring veils making haughty little *moues* at gladiators in Norfolk jackets. But there were also one or two admirable chairs, an unmistakable Lyly and a lovely, though filthy, rug. And among the decrepit novels were books of distinction and authority. It was on Mr. Phinn's shelves that Alleyn noticed an unexpected link with the Colonel. For here among a collection of books on angling he saw again *The Scaly Breed* by Maurice Cartarette. But what interested Alleyn perhaps more than all these items was a state of chaos that was to be observed on and near a very nice serpentine-fronted bureau. The choked drawers were half out, one indeed was on the floor, the top was covered with miscellaneous objects which, to a police-trained eye, had clearly been dragged out in handfuls, while the carpet nearby was littered with a further assortment. A burglar, taken by surprise, could not have left clearer evidence behind him.

"How can I serve you?" asked Mr. Phinn. "A little refreshment, by the way? A glass of sherry? Does Tio Pepe recommend himself to your notice?"

"Not quite so early in the morning, thank you, and I'm afraid this is a duty call."

"Indeed? How I wish I could be of some help. I have spent a perfectly wretched night—such of it as remained to me—fretting and speculating, you know. A murderer in the Vale! Really, if it wasn't so dreadful, there would be a kind of grotesque humour in the thought. We are so very respectable in Swevenings. Not a ripple, one would have thought, on the surface of the Chyne!"

He flinched and made the sort of grimace that is induced by a sudden twinge of toothache.

"Would one not? What," Alleyn asked, "about the Battle of the Old 'Un?"

Mr. Phinn was ready for him. He fluttered his fingers. "*Nil nisi,*" he said, with rather breathless airiness, "and all the rest of it, but really the Colonel was most exasperating as an angler. A monument of integrity in every other respect, I daresay, but as a fly-fisherman I am sorry to say there were some hideous lapses. It is an ethical paradox that so noble a sport should occasionally be wedded to such lamentable malpractices."

"Such," Alleyn suggested, "as casting under a bridge into your neighbour's preserves?"

"I will defend my action before the Judgment Seat, and the ghost of the sublime Walton himself will thunder in my defence. It was entirely permissible."

"Did you and the Colonel," Alleyn said, "speak of anything else but this...ah...this ethical paradox?"

Mr. Phinn glared at him, opened his mouth, thought perhaps of Lady Lacklander and shut it again. Alleyn for his part remembered, with exasperation, the law on extra-judicial admissions. Lady Lacklander had told him there had been a further discussion between the two men but had refused to say what it was about. If Mr. Phinn should ever come to trial for the murder of Maurice Cartarette, or even if he should merely be called to give evidence against someone else, the use by Alleyn of the first of Lady Lacklander's admissions and the concealment of the second would be held by a court of law to be improper. He decided to take a risk.

"We have been given to understand," he said, "that there was, in fact, a further discussion."

There was a long silence.

"Well, Mr. Phinn?"

"Well. I am waiting."

"For what?"

"I believe it is known as the Usual Warning," Mr. Phinn said.

"The police are only obliged to give the Usual Warning when they have decided to make an arrest."

"And you have not yet arrived at this decision?"

"Not yet."

"You, of course, have your information from the Lady Gargantua, the Mammoth Chatelaine, the Great, repeat Great, Lady of Nunspardon," said Mr. Phinn, and then surprisingly turned pink. His gaze, oddly fixed, was directed past Alleyn's elbow to some object behind him. It did not waver. "Not," Mr. Phinn added, "that, in certain respects, her worth does not correspond by a rough computation with her avoirdupois. Did she divulge the nature of my further conversation with the Colonel?"

"No."

"Then neither," said Mr. Phinn, "shall I. At least, not yet. Not unless I am obliged to do so."

The direction of his gaze had not shifted.

"Very well," Alleyn said and turned away with an air of finality.

He had been standing with his back to a desk. Presiding over an incredibly heaped-up litter were two photographs in tarnished silver frames. One was of the lady of the portrait. The other was of a young man bearing a strong resemblance to her as was inscribed in a flowing hand: "Ludovic."

It was at this photograph that Mr. Phinn had been staring.

# CHAPTER VIII

## Jacob's Cottage

Alleyn decided to press home what might or might not be an advantage and so did so with distaste. He had been in the police service for over twenty years. Under slow pressure his outward habit had toughened, but, like an ice cube that under warmth will yield its surface but retain its inward form, so his personality had kept its pattern intact. When an investigation led him, as this did, to take action that was distasteful to him, he imposed a discipline upon himself and went forward. It was a kind of abstinence, however, that prompted him to do so.

He said, looking at the photograph, "This is your son, sir, isn't it?"

Mr. Phinn, in a voice that was quite unlike his usual emphatic alto, said, "My son, Ludovic."

"I didn't meet him, but I was in the Special Branch in 1937. I heard about his tragedy, of course."

"He was a good boy," Mr. Phinn said. "I think I may have spoiled him. I fear I may have done so."

"One can't tell about these things."

"No. One can't tell."

"I don't ask you to forgive me for speaking of him. In a case of homicide I'm afraid no holds are barred. We have discovered that Sir Harold Lacklander died with the name 'Vic' on his lips and full of concern about the publication of his own memoirs which he had entrusted to Colonel Cartarette. We know that your son was Sir Harold's secretary during a crucial period of his administration in Zlomce and that Sir Harold could hardly avoid mention of the tragedy of your son's death if he was to write anything like a definitive record of his own career."

"You need go no further," said Mr. Phinn with a wave of his hand. "I see very clearly what is in your mind." He looked at Fox, whose notebook was in his palm. "Pray write openly, Inspector. Mr. Alleyn, you wonder, do you not, if I quarrelled with Colonel Cartarette because he proposed to make public, through Lacklander's memoirs, the ruin of my boy. Nothing could be further from the truth."

"I wonder," Alleyn said, "if the discussion, that Lady Lacklander overheard but doesn't care to reveal, was about some such matter."

Mr. Phinn suddenly beat his pudgy hands together, once. "If Lady L. does not care to tell you," he announced, "then neither for the time being do I."

"I wonder, too," Alleyn continued, "if it wouldn't be easy to misjudge completely your own motives and those of Lady Lacklander."

"Ah," Mr. Phinn said, with extraordinary complacency, "you are on dangerous ground indeed, my dear Alleyn. Peel away the layers of motive from the ethical onion and your eyes may well begin to water. It is no occupation, believe me, for a Chief Detective-Inspector."

A faint smile played conceitedly about the corners of his mouth. Alleyn might have supposed him to have completely recovered his equanimity if it had not been for the slightest possible tic in the lower lid of his right eye and a movement of the fingers of one hand across the back of the other.

"I wonder," Alleyn said, "if you'd mind showing us your fishing gear . . . the whole equipment as you took it down yesterday to the Chyne?"

"And why not?" Mr. Phinn rejoined. "But I demand," he added loudly, "to know if you suspect me of this crime. Do you? Do you?"

"Come now," Alleyn said, "you must know very well that you can't in the same breath refuse to answer our questions and demand an answer to your own. If we may, we would like to see your fishing gear."

Mr. Phinn stared at him. "It's not here," he said. "I'll get it."

"Fox will help you."

Mr. Phinn looked as if he didn't much relish this offer but appeared to think better of refusing it. He and Fox went out together. Alleyn moved over to the book-lined wall on his left and took down Maurice Cartarette's work on *The Scaly Breed*. It was inscribed on the title page: "January 1930. For Viccy on his eighteenth birthday with good wishes for many happy castings," and was signed by the author. The Colonel, Alleyn reflected, had evidently been on better terms with young Phinn than with his father.

He riffled through the pages. The book had been published in 1929 and appeared to be a series of short and pleasantly written essays on the behaviour and eccentricities of fresh-water fish. It contained an odd mixture of folkishness, natural history, mild flights of fancy and, apparently, a certain amount of scientific fact. It was illustrated, rather charmingly, with marginal drawings. Alleyn turned back to the title page and found that they were by Geoffrey Syce: another instance, he thought, of the way the people of Swevenings stick together, and he wondered if, twenty-six years ago, the Colonel in his regiment and the Commander in his ship had written to each other about the scaly breed and about how they should fashion their book. His eye fell on a page-heading, "No Two Alike," and with astonishment he saw what at first he took to be a familiar enough kind of diagram: that of two magnified fingerprints, showing the essential dissimilarities. At first glance they might have been lifted from a manual on criminal investigation. When, however, he looked more closely, he found, written underneath: "Microphotographs. Fig. 1. Scale of Brown Trout. 6 years. 2 1/2 lbs. Chyne River. Showing 4 years' poor growth followed by 2 years' vigorous growth. Fig. 2 Scale of Trout. 4 years. 1 lb. Chyne River. Note differences in circuli, winter bands and spawning marks." With sharpened interest he began to read the accompanying letter-press:

> It is not perhaps generally known [the Colonel had written] that the scales of no two trout are alike: I mean microscopically alike in the sense that no two sets of finger-prints correspond. It is amusing to reflect that in the watery world a rogue-trout may leave incriminating evidence behind him in the form of what might be called scales of justice.

For the margin Commander Syce had made a facetious picture of a roach with meerschaum and deerstalker hat examining through a lens the scales of a very tough-looking trout.

Alleyn had time to re-read the page. He turned back to the frontispiece—a drawing of the Colonel himself. Alleyn found in the face a duel suggestion of soldier and diplomat superimposed, he fancied, on something that was pure countryman. "A nice chap, he looks. I wonder if it would have amused him to know that he himself has put into my hands the prize piece of information received."

He replaced the book and turned to the desk with its indescribable litter of pamphlets, brochures, unopened and opened letters, newspapers and magazines. Having inspected the surface, he began, gingerly, to disturb the top layer and in a moment or two had disclosed a letter addressed to "Octavius Phinn, Esq." in the beautiful and unmistakable handwriting of Colonel Cartarette.

Alleyn had just had time enough to discover that it contained about thirty pages of typescript marked on the outside: "7," when he heard Fox's voice on the stairs. He turned away and placed himself in front of the portrait.

Mr. Phinn and Fox reappeared with the fishing gear.

"I have," Alleyn said, "been enjoying this very charming portrait."

"My wife."

"Am I imagining—perhaps I am—a likeness to Dr. Mark Lacklander?"

"There was," Mr. Phinn said shortly, "a distant connection. Here are my toys."

He was evidently one of those anglers who cannot resist the call of the illustrated catalogue and the lure of the gadget. His creel, his gaff, his net, his case of flies and his superb rod were supplemented by every conceivable toy, all of them, Alleyn expected, extremely expensive. His canvas bag was slotted and pocketted to receive these mysteries, and Alleyn drew them out one after another to discover that they were all freshly cleaned and in wonderful order.

"With what fly," he asked Mr. Phinn, "did you hook the Old 'Un? It must have been a Homeric struggle, surely?"

"Grant me the bridge," Mr. Phinn shouted excitedly, "grant me that, and I'll tell you."

"Very well," Alleyn conceded with a grin, "we'll take the bridge in our stride. I concede it. Let's have the story."

Mr. Phinn went strongly into action. It appeared that, at the mention of his prowess, the emotions that had so lately seemed to grip him were completely forgotton. Fear, if he had known fear, paternal anguish, if he had in fact experienced it, and anger, if it was indeed anger that had occasionally moved him, were all abandoned for the absolute passion of the angler. He led them out of doors, exhibited his retrospective prowess in casting, led them in again and re-enacted in the strangest pantomime his battle with the Old 'Un: how he was played, with breath-taking reverses, up through the waters under the bridge and into Mr. Phinn's indisputable preserves; how he was nearly lost, and what cunning he displayed, and how Mr. Phinn countered with even greater cunning of his own. Finally there was the great capitulation, the landing and the *coup de grace*, this last being administered, as Mr. Phinn made clear in spirited pantomime, with a sort of angler's cosh: a short, heavily leaded rod.

Alleyn took this instrument in his hand and balanced it. "What do you call the thing?" he asked.

"A priest," Mr. Phinn said. "It is called a priest. I don't know why."

"Perhaps because of its valedictory function." He laid it on the desk and placed Commander Syce's arrow beside it. Mr. Phinn stared but said nothing.

"I really must return his arrow to Commander Syce," Alleyn said absently. "I found it in the spinney, embedded in a tree trunk."

He might have touched off a high-explosive. The colour flooded angrily into Mr. Phinn's face and he began to shout of the infamies of Commander Syce and his archery. The death of Thomasina Twitchett's mother at the hands of Commander Syce was furiously recalled. Syce, Mr. Phinn said, was a monster, an alcoholic sadist, possessed of a blood-lust. It was with malice aforethought that he had transfixed the dowager Twitchett. The plea of accident was ridiculous: the thing was an obsession. Syce would drink himself into a sagittal fury and fire arrows off madly into the landscape. Only last night, Mr. Phinn continued, when he himself was returning from the Chyne after what he now called his little *mesentente* with Colonel Cartarette, the Commander's bow was twanging away on the archery lawn and Mr. Phinn had actually heard the "tuck" of an arrow in a tree trunk dangerously near to himself. The time was a quarter past eight. He remembered hearing his clock chime at the same time.

"I think you must be mistaken," Alleyn put in mildly. "Nurse Kettle tells us that last evening Commander Syce was completely incapacitated by an acute attack of lumbago."

Mr. Phinn shouted out a rude and derisive word. "A farrago of nonsense!" he continued. "Either she is his accomplice or his paramour or possibly," he amended more charitably, "his dupe. I swear he was devilishly active last night. I swear it. I trembled lest my Thomasina, who had accompanied me to the Chyne, should share the fate of her mama. She did not join me on my return but had preferred to linger in the evening air. Indeed, the reason for my perhaps slightly dramatic entry into Hammer in the early hours of this morning was my hope of retrieving my errant Fur. The dreadful news with which you met me quite put her out of my head," Mr. Phinn concluded and did not look as if he expected to be believed.

"I see," Alleyn said and did not look as if he believed him. "Quite a chapter of accidents. Do you mind if we take possession of your fishing gear for a short time? Part of a routine check, you know."

Mr. Phinn was at a loss for words. "But how quite extraordinary!" he at last exclaimed. "My fishing gear? Well, I suppose one must not refuse."

"We shan't keep it any longer than is necessary," Alleyn assured him.

Fox put the kit in order and slung it over his massive shoulder.

"And also, I'm afraid," Alleyn said apologetically, "the shoes and suit that you wore on your fishing expedition."

"My shoes? My suit! But why, why! I don't like this. I don't like it at all."

"It may be some comfort to you to know that I shall make the same awkward demands of at least four other persons."

Mr. Phinn seemed to brighten a little. "Blood?" he asked.

"Not necessarily," Alleyn said coolly. "This and that, you know, and the other thing. May we have them?"

"A fat lot of use," Mr. Phinn muttered, "if I said no. And in any case you are perfectly welcome to every garment I possess. Homicidally speaking, they are as pure as the driven snow."

When he saw them, Alleyn reflected that although, homicidally speaking, this might be true, from any other point of view it was grossly inaccurate: Mr. Phinn's angling garments were exceedingly grubby and smelt strongly of fish.

Alleyn saw with satisfaction a slimy deposit on the right leg of a pair of old-fashioned knickerbockers. The shoes were filthy and the stockings in holes. With a gesture of defiance, their owner flung on top in them a dilapidated tweed hat with the usual collection of flies in the band.

"Make what you like of them," he said grandly, "and see that you let me have them back in the order in which you receive them."

Alleyn gave him grave assurance to this effect and wrapped up the garments. Fox wrote out a receipt for the unlovely bundle.

"We won't keep you any longer," Alleyn said, "unless by any chance you would care to give us a true account of your ramblings in the watches of the night."

Mr. Phinn gaped at him and in doing so resembled for the moment the Old 'Un himself.

"Because," Alleyn went on, "you haven't done so yet, you know. I mean, your story of seeing lighted windows and calling to tell the Colonel of your catch was completely blown-up by Lady Lacklander. And your latest version...that you were on the hunt for your mother-cat...really won't do at all. Feline nursing mothers, and you tell us this is a particularly devoted one, do not desert their kittens for six hours on end. Moreover, we came upon Mrs. Twitchett last night on her way home about half past twelve. And why, if the Twitchett story was the true one, did you not produce it in the first instance?" Alleyn waited for some seconds. "You see," he said, "you have no answer to any of these questions."

"I shall not make any further statements. I prefer to remain silent."

"Shall I tell you what I think may have happened last night? I think that when you made your first remark as you stood in the French window at Hammer, you said something that was near the truth. I think that either then, or perhaps earlier in the evening, you had sallied out in search of your great trout. I think you regretted having flung it down on the bridge during your quarrel with Colonel Cartarette. You knew he wouldn't touch it, because he had told you so and had gone off, leaving it there. Did you not go down into the valley of the Chyne to retrieve the trout, and did you not find it gone from the bridge when you got there?"

The colour mounted in Mr. Phinns' face in uneven patches. He lowered his chin and looked quickly at Alleyn from under his meagre brows. But he said nothing.

"If this is so," Alleyn went on, "and I am encouraged by your silence to hope that it may be, I can't help wondering what you did next. Did you come straight back to Hammer and seeing the lighted windows make up your mind to accuse the Colonel of having pinched your fish after all? But no. If that had been so, your behaviour would have been different. You would not, before you were aware of his death, have trembled and gone white to the lips. Nor would you have invented your cock-and-bull story of wanting to tell the Colonel all about your catch: a story that was at once disproved when Lady Lacklander told us about your row with the Colonel over that very catch and by the fact that for a long time you have not been on visiting terms with your neighbour."

Mr. Phinn had turned aside, and Alleyn walked round him until they were again face-to-face.

"How," he said, "is one to explain your behaviour of last night? Shall I tell you what I think? I think that when you arrived at Hammer Farm at five past one this morning, you knew already that Colonel Cartarette was dead."

Still Mr. Phinn said nothing.

"Now if this is true," Alleyn said, "and again you don't deny it, you have misinformed us about your movements. You let us understand that you returned to the bottom meadow just before you came to Hammer Farm at about one o'clock. But your coat was as dry as a chip. So it must have been much earlier in the evening before the rain that you returned to the bridge in the hope of retrieving the fish and found it gone. And knowing that the Colonel was fishing his own waters not far away, would you not seek him out? Now, if you did behave as I suggested, you did so at a time when nobody saw you. That must have been after Lady Lacklander, Mrs. Cartarette and Dr. Lacklander had all gone home. Mrs. Cartarette reached Hammer Farm at about five past eight, and Dr. Lacklander went home at a quarter past eight. Neither of them saw the trout. On my work hypothesis, then, you revisited the valley after a quarter past eight and, one would suppose, before a quarter to nine when Nurse Kettle did so. And there, Mr. Phinn, in the willow grove you found Colonel Cartarette's dead body with your mammoth trout beside it. And didn't Nurse Kettle very nearly catch you in the willow grove?"

Mr. Phinn ejaculated, "Has she said—" and caught his voice back.

"No," Alleyn said. "Not specifically. It is I who suggest that you hid and watched her and crept away when she had gone. I suggest, moreover, that when you bolted for cover, your reading spectacles were snatched from your hat by an envious sliver and that in your panic and your terror of being seen, you dared not look for them. Possibly you did not realize they had gone until you got home. And that's why, after the rain, you stole out again—to try and find your glasses in case they were lost in a place where they might incriminate you. Then you saw the lights of Hammer Farm and dared go no further. You couldn't endure the suspense of not knowing if the Colonel had been found. You drew nearer and Sergeant Oliphant's torchlight shone in your eyes."

Alleyn turned to the window and looked down at Mr. Phinn's spinney, at the upper reaches of the Chyne and at a glimpse, between trees, of the near end of the bridge.

"That," he said, "is how I think you moved the landscape yesterday evening and last night." Alleyn drew a pair of spectacles from the breast pocket of his coat and dangled them before Mr. Phinn. "I'm afraid I can't let you have them back just yet. But"—he extended his long finger toward Mr. Phinn's breast pocket—"isn't that a magnifying glass you have managed to unearth?"

Mr. Phinn was silent.

"Well," Alleyn said, "there's our view of your activities. It's a picture based on your own behaviour and one or two known facts. If it is accurate, believe me, you will be wise to say so."

Mr. Phinn said in an unrecognizable voice, "And if I don't choose to speak?"

"You will be within your rights, and we shall draw our own conclusions."

"You still don't give me the famous Usual Warning one hears so much about?"

"No."

"I suppose," Mr. Phinn said, "I am a timid man, but I know, in respect of this crime, that I am an innocent one."

"Well, then," Alleyn said and tried to lend the colour of freshness to an assurance he had so often given, "your innocence should cancel your timidity. You have nothing to fear."

It seemed to Alleyn as he watched Mr. Phinn that he was looking on at the superficial signs of a profound disturbance. It was as if Mr. Phinn's personality had been disrupted from below like a thermal pool and in a minute or two would begin to boil.

Some kind of climax was in fact achieved, and he began to talk very rapidly in his high voice.

"You are a very clever man. You reason from character to fact and back again. There! I have admitted everything. It's all quite true. I tiffed with Cartarette. I flung my noble Fin on the bridge. I came home but did not enter my house. I walked distractedly about my garden. I repented of my gesture and returned. The Fin had gone. I sought out my rival and because of the howl of his dog—a disagreeable canine—I found him—" here Mr. Phinn shut his eyes very tight—"no, really, it was too disagreeable! Even though his hat was over his face, one knew at a glance. And the dog never even looked at one. Howl! Howl! I didn't go near them, but I saw my fish! My trout! My Superfin! And then, you know, I heard *her*. Kettle. Stump, stump, stump past the willow grove. I ran, I doubled, I flung myself on my face in the undergrowth and waited until she had gone. And then I came home," said Mr. Phinn, "and as you have surmised, I discovered the loss of my reading glasses, which I frequently keep in my hatband. I was afraid. And there you are."

"Yes," Alleyn said, "there we are. How do you feel about making a signed statement to this effect?"

"Another statement. O, tedious task! But I am resigned."

"Good. We'll leave you to write it with the aid of your reading glasses. Will you begin with the actual catching of the Old 'Un?"

Mr. Phinn nodded.

"And you are still disinclined to tell us the full substance of your discussion with Colonel Cartarette?"

Mr. Phinn nodded.

He had his back to the windows and Alleyn faced them. Sergeant Oliphant had come out of the spinney and stood at the foot of the garden. Alleyn moved up to the windows. The sergeant, when he saw him, put his thumb up and turned back into the trees.

Fox picked up the parcel of clothes.

Alleyn said, "We'll call later for the statement. Or perhaps you would bring it to the police-station in Chyning this evening?"

"Very well." Mr. Phinn swallowed and his Adam's apple bobbed in his throat. "After all," he said, "I would hardly desert my Glorious Fin. Would I?"

"You did so before. Why shouldn't you do so again?"

"I am completely innocent."

"Grand. We mustn't bother you any longer. Good-bye, then, until, shall we say, five o'clock in Chyning."

They went out by a side door and down the garden to the spinney. The path wound downhill amongst trees to a stile that gave onto the river path. Here Sergeant Oliphant waited for them. Alleyn's homicide bag, which had been entrusted to the sergeant, rested on the stile. At the sound of their voices he turned, and they saw that across his palms there lay a sheet of newspaper.

On the newspaper were the dilapidated remains of a trout.

"I got 'er," said Sergeant Oliphant.

*ii*

"She was a short piece above the bridge on this side," explained the sergeant, who had the habit of referring to inanimate but recalcitrant objects in the feminine gender. "Laying in some long grass to which I'd say she'd been dragged. Cat's work, sir, as you can see by the teeth-marks."

"As we supposed," Alleyn agreed. "Mrs. Tomasina Twitchett's work."

"A nice fish; she's been, say, two pound, but nothing to the Old 'Un," said the sergeant.

Alleyn laid the paper and its contents on a step of the stile and hung fondly over it. Mrs. Twitchett, if indeed it was she, had made short work of most of the Colonel's trout, if indeed this was his trout. The body was picked almost clean and some of the smaller bones had been chewed. The head appeared to have been ejected after a determined onslaught and the tail was semi-detached. But from the ribs there still depended some pieces of flesh and rags of skin that originally covered part of the flank and belly of the fish, and it was over an unlovely fragment of skin that Alleyn pored. He laid it out flat, using two pairs of pocket tweezers for the purpose, with a long finger pointed to something that might have been part of an indented scar. It was about a quarter of an inch wide and had a curved margin. It was pierced in one place as if by a short spike.

"Now blow me down flat," Alleyn exulted, "if this isn't the answer to the good little investigating officer's prayer. See here, Fox, isn't this a piece of the sort of scar we would expect to find? And look here."

Very gingerly he turned the trout over and discovered, clinging to the other flank, a further rag of skin with the apex of a sharp triangular gap in it.

"Sink me if I don't have a look," Alleyn muttered.

Under Oliphant's enchanted gaze, he opened his case, took

from it a flat enamel dish, which he laid on the bottom step of the stile, and a small glass jar with a screw-on lid. Using his tweezers, he spread out the piece of skin with the triangular gap on the plate. From the glass jar he took the piece of skin that had been found on the sharp stone under the Old 'Un. Muttering and whistling under his breath, and with a delicate dexterity, he laid the second fragment bside the first, opened it out and pushed and fiddled the one into the other as if they were pieces of a jigsaw puzzle. They fitted exactly.

"And that," Alleyn said, "is why Mrs. Twitchett met us last night smelling of fresh fish when she should have been stinking of liver. O, Fate! O, Nemesis! O, Something or Another!" he apostrophized. "Thy hand is here!" And in answer to Oliphant's glassy stare he added, "You've done damned handily, Sergeant, to pick this up so quickly. Now, listen, and I'll explain."

The explanation was detailed and exhaustive. Alleyn ended it with an account of the passage he had read in Colonel Cartarette's book. "We'll send out a signal to some piscatorial pundit," he said, "and get a check. But if the Colonel was right, and he seems to have been a conscientious, knowledgeable chap, our two trout cannot exhibit identical scales. The Colonel's killer, and only his killer can have, handled both fish. We do a round-up of garments, my hearties, and hope for returns."

Sergeant Oliphant cleared his throat and with an air of modest achievement stooped behind a briar bush. "There's one other matter, sir," he said. "I found this at the bottom of the hill in a bit of underbrush."

He straightened up. In his hand was an arrow. "It appears," he said, "to have blood on it."

"Does it, indeed?" Alleyn said and took it. "All right, Oliphant. Damn' good show. We're getting on very prettily. And if," he summarized for the benefit of the gratified and anxious Oliphant, "if it all tallies up as I believe it must, then the pattern will indeed begin to emerge, won't it, Fox?"

"I hope so, Mr. Alleyn," Fox rejoined cheerfully.

"So off you go, Oliphant," Alleyn said. "Drive Mr. Fox to

the station, where he will ring the Yard and the Natural History Museum. Deliver your treasure-trove to Dr. Curtis. I hope to have the rest of the exhibits before this evening. Come on, chaps, this case begins to ripen."

He led them back to the valley, saw Oliphant and Fox on their way with an accumulation of gear and objects of interest, and himself climbed up the hill to Nunspardon.

Here, to his surprise, he ran into a sort of party. Shaded from the noontide sun on the terrace before the great house were assembled the three Lacklanders, Kitty Cartarette and Rose. It was now half past twelve, and a cocktail tray gave an appearance of conviviality to a singularly wretched-looking assembly. Lady Lacklander seemed to have retired behind her formidable facade leaving in her wake an expression of bland inscrutability. George stood in a teapot attitude: one hand in his jacket pocket, the other on the back of a chair; one neatly knickered leg straight, one bent. Mark scowled devotedly upon Rose, who was pale, had obviously wept a great deal and seemed in addition to her grief to be desperately worried. Kitty, in a tweed suit, high heels and embroidered gloves, was talking to George. She looked exhausted and faintly sulky, as if tragedy had taken her by surprise and let her down. She lent an incongruous note to a conversation piece that seemed only to lack the attendant figures of grooms with hounds in leashes. Her voice was a high-pitched one. Before she noticed Alleyn, she had completed a sentence and he had heard it. "That's right," she had said, "Brierley and Bentwood," and then she saw him and made an abrupt movement that drew all their eyes upon him.

He wondered how many more times he would have to approach these people through their gardens and from an uncomfortable distance. In a way, he was beginning to enjoy it. He felt certain that this time, if George Lacklander could have managed it, the waiting group would have been scattered by a vigorous gesture, George himself would have retired to some manly den and Alleyn, in the ripeness of time, would have been admitted by a footman.

As it was, all of them except Lady Lacklander made

involuntary movements which were immediately checked. Kitty half rose as if to beat a retreat, looked disconsolately at George and sank back in her chair.

"They've been having a council of war," thought Alleyn.

After a moment's further hesitation Mark, with an air of coming to a decision, put his chin up, said loudly, "It's Mr. Alleyn," and came to meet him. As they approached each other, Alleyn saw Rose's face, watchful and anxious, beyond Mark's advancing figure, and his momentary relish for the scene evaporated.

"Good morning," Alleyn said. "I'm sorry to reappear so soon and to make a further nuisance of myself. I won't keep you long."

"That's all right," Mark said pleasantly. "Who do you want to see?"

"Why, in point of fact, all of you, if I may. I'm lucky to find you in a group like this."

Mark had fallen into step with him and together they approached the group.

"Well, Rory," Lady Lacklander shouted as soon as he was within range, "you don't give us much peace, do you? What do you want this time? The clothes off our backs?"

"Yes," Alleyn said, "I'm afraid I do. More or less."

"And what may that mean? More or less?"

"The clothes off your yesterday-evening backs, if you please."

"Is this what my sporadic reading has led me to understand as 'a matter of routine'?"

"In a way," Alleyn said coolly, "yes. Yes, it is. Routine."

"And who," Kitty Cartarette asked in a careworn voice of nobody in particular, "said that a policeman's lot is not a happy one?"

This remark was followed by a curious little gap. It was if her audience had awarded Kitty a point for attempting, under the circumstances, her small joke but at the same time were unable to accept her air of uncertain intimacy, which apparently even George found embarrassing. He laughed uncomfortably. Lady Lacklander raised her eyebrows, and Mark scowled at his boots.

"Do you mean," Lady Lacklander said, "the clothes that we were all wearing when Maurice Cartarette was murdered?"

"I do, yes."

"Well," she said, "you're welcome to mine. What *was* I wearing yesterday, George?"

"Really, Mama, I'm afraid I don't..."

"Nor do I. Mark?"

Mark grinned at her. "A green tent, I fancy, Gar darling, a solar topee and a pair of grandfather's boots."

"You're perfectly right. My green Harris, it was. I'll tell my maid, Roderick, and you shall have them."

"Thank you." Alleyn looked at George. "Your clothes and boots, please?"

"Ah, spiked shoes and stockings and plus fours," George said loudly. "Very old-fogeyish. Ha-ha."

"I think they're jolly good," Kitty said wearily. "On the right man." George's hand went to his moustache, but he didn't look at Kitty. He seemed to be exquisitely uncomfortable. "I," Kitty added, "wore a check shirt and a twin set. Madly county, you know," she added, desperately attempting another joke, "on account we played golf." She sounded near to tears.

"And your shoes?" Alleyn asked.

Kitty stuck out her feet. Her legs, Alleyn noted, were good. Her feet, which were tiny, were shod in lizard-skin shoes with immensely high heels. "Not so county," Kitty said, with a ghost of a grin, "but the best I had."

George, apparently in an agony of embarrassment, glanced at the shoes, at his mother and at the distant prospect of the Home Spinney.

Alleyn said, "If I may, I'll borrow the clothes, gloves and stockings. We'll pick them up at Hammer Farm on our way back to Chyning."

Kitty accepted this. She was looking at Alleyn with the eye, however wan, of a woman who spots a genuine Dior in a bargain basement.

"I'll hurry back," she said, "and get them ready for you."

"There's no immediate hurry."

Mark said, "I was wearing whites. I put brogues on for going home and carried my tennis shoes."

"And your racket?"

"Yes."

"And, after Bottom Bridge, Lady Lacklander's sketching gear and shooting-stick?"

"That's right."

"By the way," Alleyn asked him, "had you gone straight to your tennis party from Nunspardon?"

"I looked in on a patient in the village."

"And on the gardener's child, didn't you?" Kitty said. "They told me you'd lanced its gumboil."

"Yes. An abscess, poor kid," Mark said cheerfully.

"So you had your professional bag, too?" Alley suggested.

"It's not very big."

"Still, quite a load."

"It was rather."

"But Lady Lacklander had left it all tidily packed up, hadn't she?"

"Well," Mark said with a smile at his grandmother, "more or less."

"Nonsense," Lady Lacklander said; "there was no more or less about it. I'm a tidy woman and I left everything tidy."

Mark opened his mouth and shut it again.

"Your paint-rag, for instance?" Alleyn said, and Mark glanced sharply at him.

"I overlooked the rag, certainly," said Lady Lacklander rather grandly, "when I packed up. But I folded it neatly and tucked it under the strap of my haversack. Why have you put on that look, Mark?" she added crossly.

"Well, darling, when I got there, the rag, far from being neatly folded and stowed, was six yards away on a briar bush. I rescued it and put it into your haversack."

They all looked at Alleyn as if they expected him to make some comment. He was silent, however, and after a considerable pause Lady Lacklander said, "Well, it couldn't be of less significance, after all. Go indoors and ask them to get the clothes together. Fisher knows what I wore."

"Ask about mine, old boy, will you?" said George, and Alleyn wondered how many households there were left in England where orders of this sort were still given.

Lady Lacklander turned to Rose. "And what about you, child?"

But Rose stared out with unseeing eyes that had filled again with tears. She dabbed at them with her handkerchief and frowned to herself.

"Rose?" Lady Lacklander said quietly.

Still frowning, Rose turned and looked at her. "I'm sorry," she said.

"They want to know what clothes you wore, my dear."

"Tennis things, I imagine," Alleyn said.

Rose said, "Oh, yes. Of course. Tennis things."

Kitty said, "It's the day for the cleaner. I saw your tennis things in the box, didn't I, Rose?"

"I—? Yes," Rose said. "I'm sorry. Yes, I did put them in."

"Shall we go and rescue them?" Mark asked.

Rose hesitated. He looked at her for a moment and then said in a level voice, "O.K. I'll come back," and went into the house. Rose turned away and stood at some distance from the group.

"It's toughest for Rose," Kitty said, unexpectedly compassionate, and then with a return to her own self-protective mannerisms she sipped her sherry. "I wish you joy of my skirt, Mr. Alleyn," she added loudly. "You won't find it very delicious."

"No?" Alleyn said, "Why not?"

"It absolutely reeks of fish."

*iii*

Alleyn observed the undistinguished little face and wondered if his own was equally blank. He then, under the guise of bewilderment, looked at the others. He found that Lady Lacklander seemed about as agitated as a Buddha and

**173**

that George was in the process of becoming startled. Rose was still turned away.

"Are you a fisherman too, then, Mrs. Cartarette?" Alleyn asked.

"God forbid!" she said with feeling. "No. I tried to take a fish away from a cat last evening." The others gaped at her.

"My dear Kitty," Lady Lacklander said, "I suggest that you consider what you say."

"Why?" Kitty countered, suddenly common and arrogant. "Why? It's the truth. What are you driving at?" she added nervously. "What's the matter with saying I've got fish on my skirt? Here," she demanded of Alleyn, "what are they getting at?"

"My good girl—" Lady Lacklander began, but Alleyn cut in. "I'm sorry, Lady Lacklander, but Mrs. Cartarette's perfectly right. There's nothing the matter, I assure you, with speaking the truth." Lady Lacklander shut her mouth with a snap. "Where did you meet your cat and fish, Mrs. Cartarette?"

"This side of the bridge," Kitty muttered resentfully.

"Did you, now?" Alleyn said with relish.

"It looked a perfectly good trout to me, and I thought the cat had no business with it. I suppose," Kitty went on, "it was one of old Occy Phinn's swarm; the cat, I mean. Anyhow, I tried to get the trout away from it. It hung on like a fury. And then when I did jerk the trout away, it turned out to be half eaten on the other side, sort of. So I let the cat have it back," Kitty said limply.

Alleyn said, "Did you notice any particular mark or scar on the trout?"

"Well, hardly. It was half eaten."

"Yes, but on the part that was left?"

"I don't think so. Here! What sort of mark?" Kitty demanded, beginning to look alarmed.

"It doesn't matter. Really."

"It was quite a nice trout. I wondered if Maurice had caught it, and then I thought old Occy Phinn must have hooked it and given it to the cat. He's crazy enough on his cats to give them anything, isn't he, George?"

"Good God, yes!" George ejaculated automatically, without looking at Kitty.

"It's a possible explanation," Alleyn said as if it didn't much matter either way.

Mark came back from the house. "The clothes," he said to Alleyn, "will be packed up and put in your car, which has arrived, by the way. I rang up Hammer and asked them to keep back the things for the cleaner."

"Thank you so much," Alleyn said. He turned to Lady Lacklander. "I know you'll understand that in a case like this we have to fuss about and try to get as complete a picture as possible of the days, sometimes even the weeks and months, before the event. It generally turns out that ninety-nine per cent of the information is quite useless, and then everybody thinks how needlessly inquisitive and impertinent the police are. Sometimes, however, there is an apparently irrelevant detail that leads, perhaps by accident, to the truth."

Lady Lacklander stared at him like a basilisk. She had a habit of blinking slowly, her rather white eyelids dropping conspicuously like shutters: a slightly reptilian habit that was disconcerting. She blinked twice in this manner at Alleyn and said, "What are you getting at, my dear Roderick? I hope you won't finesse too elaborately. Pray tell us what you want."

"Certainly. I want to know if, when I arrived, you were discussing Sir Harold Lacklander's memoirs."

He knew by their very stillness that he had scored. It struck him, not for the first time, that people who have been given a sudden fright tend to look alike: a sort of homogeneous glassiness overtakes them.

Lady Lacklander first recovered from whatever shock they had all received.

"In point of fact we were," she said. "You must have extremely sharp ears."

"I caught the name of my own publishers," Alleyn said at once. "Brierley and Bentwood. An admirable firm. I

**175**

wondered if they are to do the memoirs."

"I'm glad you approve of them," she said dryly. "I believe they are."

"Colonel Cartarette was entrusted with the publication, wasn't he?"

There was a fractional pause before Mark and Rose together said, "Yes."

"I should think," Alleyn said pleasantly, "that that would have been a delightful job."

George in a strangulated voice, said something about "responsibility" and suddenly offered Alleyn a drink.

"My good George," his mother said impatiently, "Roderick is on duty and will have none of your sherry. Don't be an ass."

George blushed angrily and glanced, possibly for encouragement, at Kitty.

"Nevertheless," Lady Lacklander said with a sort of grudging bonhomie, "you may as well sit down, Rory. One feels uncomfortable when you loom. There *is*, after all, a chair."

"Thank you," Alleyn said, taking it. "I don't want to loom any more than I can help, you know, but you can't expect me to be all smiles and prattle when you, as a group, close your ranks with such a deafening clank whenever I approach you."

"Nonsense," she rejoined briskly, but a dull colour actually appeared under her weathered skin, and for a moment there was a fleeting likeness to her son. Alleyn saw that Rose Cartarette was looking at him with a sort of anguished appeal and that Mark had taken her hand.

"Well," Alleyn said cheerfully, "if it's all nonsense, I can forget all about it and press on with the no doubt irrelevant details. About the autobiography, for instance. I'm glad Mr. Phinn is not with us at the moment because I want to ask you if Sir Harold gives a full account of young Phinn's tragedy. He could scarcely, one imagines, avoid doing so, could he?"

Alleyn looked from one blankly staring face to another. "Or could he?" he added.

Lady Lacklander said, "I haven't read my husband's memoirs. Nor, I think, has anyone else, except Maurice."

"Do you mean, Lady Lacklander, that you haven't read them in their entirety, or that you haven't read or heard a single word of them?"

"We would discuss them. Sometimes I could refresh his memory."

"Did you discuss the affair of young Ludovic Phinn?"

"Never!" she said very loudly and firmly, and George made a certain noise in his throat.

Alleyn turned to Kitty and Rose.

"Perhaps," he suggested, "Colonel Cartarette may have said something about the memoirs?"

"Not to me," Kitty said and added, "Too pukka sahib."

There was an embarrassed stirring among the others.

"Well," Alleyn said, "I'm sorry to labour the point, but I should like to know, if you please, whether Sir Harold Lacklander or Colonel Cartarette ever said anything to any of you about the Ludovic Phinn affair in connection with the memoirs."

"Damned if I see what you're getting at!" George began, to the dismay, Alleyn felt sure, of everybody who heard him. "Damned if I see how you make out my father's memoirs can have anything to do with Maurice Cartarette's murder. Sorry, Kitty. I beg pardon, Rose. But I mean to say!"

Alleyn said, "It's eighteen years since young Ludovic Danberry-Phinn committed suicide, and a war has intervened. Many people will have forgotten his story. One among those who have remembered it . . . his father . . . must dread above all things any revival." He leant forward on his chair, and as if he had given some kind of order or exercised some mesmeric influence on his audience, each member of it imitated this movement. George Lacklander was still empurpled, the others had turned very pale, but one expression was common to them all: they looked, all of them, extremely surprised. In Kitty and George and perhaps in Lady Lacklander, Alleyn thought he sensed a kind of relief. He raised his hand. "Unless, of course," he said, "it has come about that in reviving the tragedy through the memoirs, young Phinn's name will be cleared."

It was as if out of a cloth that had apparently been wrung dry an unexpected trickle was induced. George, who seemed to be the most vulnerable of the group, shouted, "You've no right to assume..." and got no further. Almost simultaneously Mark and Rose, with the occasional unanimity of lovers, said, "This won't do..." and were checked by an imperative gesture from Lady Lacklander.

"Roderick," Lady Lacklander demanded, "have you been talking to Octavius Phinn?"

"Yes," Alleyn said. "I have come straight here from Jacob's Cottage."

"Wait a bit, Mama," George blurted out. "Wait a bit! Octavius can't have said anything. Otherwise, don't you see, Alleyn wouldn't try to find out from us."

In the now really deathly silence that followed this speech, Lady Lacklander turned and blinked at her son.

"You ninny, George," she said, "you unfathomable fool."

And Alleyn thought he now knew the truth about Mr. Phinn, Colonel Cartarette and Sir Harold Lacklander's memoirs.

# CHAPTER IX

## Chyning

The next observation was made by Mark Lacklander.
"I hope you'll let me speak, Grandmama," he said. "And
Father," he added, obviously as a polite afterthought.
"Although, I must confess, most of the virtue has already gone
from what I have to say."

"Then, why, my dear boy, say it?"

"Well, Gar, it's really, you know, a matter of principle.
Rose and I are agreed on it. We've kept quiet under your
orders, but we both have felt, haven't we, Rose, that by far the
best thing is to be completely frank with Mr. Alleyn. Any
other course, as you've seen for yourself, just won't do."

"I have not changed my mind, Mark. Wait, a little."

"O, yes," Kitty said eagerly. "I do think so, honestly. Wait.
I'm sure," she added, "it's what he would have said. Maurie, I
mean." Her face quivered unexpectedly and she fumbled for
her handkerchief.

Rose made one of those involuntary movements that are so much more graphic than words, and Alleyn, whom for the moment they all completely disregarded, wondered how the Colonel had enjoyed being called Maurie.

George, with a rebellious glance at his mother, said, "Exactly what I mean. Wait."

"By all means, wait," Alleyn interjected, and stood up. They all jumped slightly. "I expect," he suggested to Lady Lacklander, "you would like, before taking any further steps, to consult with Mr. Phinn. As a matter of fact, I think it highly probable that he will suggest it himself." Alleyn looked very straight at Lady Lacklander. "I suggest," he said, "that you consider just exactly what is at stake in this matter. When a capital crime is committed, you know, all sorts of long-buried secrets are apt to be discovered. It's one of these things about homicide." She made no kind of response to this, and, after a moment, he went on, "Perhaps when you have all come to a decision, you will be kind enough to let me know. They'll always take a message at the Boy and Donkey. And now, if I may, I'll get on with my job."

He bowed to Lady Lacklander and was about to move off when Mark said, "I'll see you to your car, sir. Coming, Rose?"

Rose seemed to hesitate, but she went off with him, entirely, Alleyn sensed, against the wishes of the remaining three.

Mark and Rose conducted him round the east wing of the great house to the open platform in front of it. Here Fox waited in the police car. A sports model with a doctor's sticker and a more domestic car, which Alleyn took to be the Cartarette's, waited side by side. The young footman, William, emerged with a suitcase. Alleyn watched him deliver this to Fox and return to the house.

"There goes our dirty washing," Mark said, and then looked uncomfortable.

Alleyn said, "But you carried a tennis racket, didn't you, and Sir George, I suppose, a golf bag? May we have them too?"

Mark said, "Yes, I see. Yes. All right, I'll get them."

He ran up the steps and disappeared. Alleyn turned to Rose. She stared at the doorway through which Mark had gone, and it was if some kind of threat had overtaken her.

"I'm so frightened," she said. "I don't know why, but I'm so frightened."

"Of what?" Alleyn asked gently.

"I don't know. One of those things, I suppose. I've never felt it before. It's as if my father was the only person that I ever really knew. And now he's gone; someone's murdered him, and I feel as if I didn't properly understand anyone at all."

Mark came back with a bag of clubs and a tennis racket in a press.

"This is it," he said.

"You didn't have it in one of those waterproof-cover things?"

"What? Oh, yes, actually, I did."

"May I have that too, please?"

Mark made a second trip to get it and was away rather longer. "I wasn't sure which was the one," he said, "but I think this is right."

Alleyn put it with the bag and racket in the car.

Mark had caught Rose's hand in his. She hung back a little. "Mr. Alleyn," Mark said, "Rose and I are in the hell of a spot over this. Aren't we, darling? We're engaged, by the way."

"You amaze me," Alleyn said.

"Well, we are. And, of course, wherever it's humanly possible, I'm going to see that Rose is not harried and fussed. She's had a very severe shock and ..."

"No, don't," Rose said. "Please, Mark, don't."

Mark gazed at her, seemed to lose the thread of his subject, and then collected himself.

"It's just this," he said. "I feel strongly that as far as you and our two families are concerned, everything ought to be perfectly straightforward. We're under promise not to mention this and that, and so we can't, but we are both very worried about the way things are going, I mean, in respect of Octavius Phinn. You see, sir, we happen to know that poor old Occy Phinn had every possible reason *not* to commit this crime. Every possible reason. And if," Mark said, "you've guessed, as I rather think you may have, what I'm driving at, I can't help it."

"And you agree with all this, Miss Cartarette?" Alleyn asked.

Rose held herself a little aloof now. Tear-stained and obviously exhausted, she seemed to pull herself together and shape her answer with care and difficulty.

"Mr. Alleyn, my father would have been appalled if he could have known that because he and Octavius had a row over the trout, poor Occy might be thought to—to have a motive. They'd had rows over trout for years. It was a kind of joke—nothing. And—whatever else they had to say to each other, and as you know, there *was* something else, it would have made Octavius much more friendly. I promise you. You see, I know my father had gone to see Octavius."

Alleyn said quickly. "You mean he went to his house? Yesterday afternoon?"

"Yes. I was with him before he went and he said he was going there."

"Did he say why? I think you spoke of some publishing business."

"Yes. He—he had something he wanted to show Occy."

"What was that, can you tell us?"

"I can't tell you," Rose said looking wretchedly unhappy. "I *do* know, actually, but it's private. But I'm sure he went to Occy's because I saw him take the envelope out of the desk and put it in his pocket—" she put her hand to her eyes—"but," she said, "where is it, then?"

Alleyn said, "Where exactly was the envelope? In which drawer of his desk?"

"I think the bottom one on the left. He kept it locked, usually."

"I see. Thank you. And, of course, Mr. Phinn was not at home?"

"No. I suppose, finding him not at home, Daddy followed him down to the stream. Of course, I mustn't tell you what his errand was, but if ever," Rose said in a trembling voice, "if ever there was an errand of—well, of mercy—Daddy's was one, yesterday afternoon."

Rose had an unworldly face with a sort of Pre-Raphaelitish beauty: very unmodish in its sorrow and very touching.

Alleyn said gently, "I know. Don't worry. I can promise we won't blunder."

"How kind you are," she said. Mark muttered indistinguishably.

As Alleyn turned away towards the police car, her voice halted him: "It must be somebody mad," she said. "Nobody who wasn't mad could possibly do it. Not possibly. There's somebody demented that did it for no reason at all." She extended her hand towards him a little way, the palm turned up in a gesture of uncertainty and appeal. "Don't you think so?" she said.

Alleyn said, "I think you are very shocked and bewildered, as well you might be. Did you sleep last night?"

"Not much. I am sorry, Mark, but I didn't take the thing you gave me. I felt I mustn't. I had to wake for him. The house felt as if he was looking for me."

"I think it might be a good idea," Alleyn said to Mark, "if you drove Miss Cartarette to Hammer Farm, where perhaps she will be kind enough to hunt up her own and Mrs. Cartarette's garments of yesterday. Everything, please, shoes, stockings and all. And treat them, please, like eggshell china."

Mark said, "As important as that?"

"The safety of several innocent persons may depend upon them."

"I'll take care," Mark said.

"Good. We'll follow you and collect them."

"Fair enough," Mark said. He smiled at Rose. "And when that's done," he said, "I'm going to bring you back to Nunspardon and put my professional foot down about nembutal. Kitty'll drive herself home. Come on."

Alleyn saw Rose make a small gesture of protest. "I think perhaps I'll stay at Hammer, Mark."

"No, you won't, darling."

"I can't leave Kitty like that."

"She'll understand. Anyway, we'll be back here before she leaves. Come on."

Rose turned as if to appeal to Alleyn and then seemed to give up. Mark took her by the elbow and led her away.

Alleyn watched them get into the sports car and shoot off down a long drive. He shook his head slightly and let himself into the front seat beside Fox.

"Follow them, Br'er Fox," he said. "But sedately. There's no hurry. We're going to Hammer Farm."

On the way he outlined the general shape of his visit to Nunspardon.

"It's clear enough, wouldn't you agree," he ended, "what has happened about the memoirs. Take the facts as we know them. The leakage of information at Zlomce was of such importance that Sir Harold Lacklander couldn't, in what is evidently an exhaustive autobiography, ignore it. At the time of the catastrophe we learnt in the Special Branch from Lacklander himself that after confessing his treachery, young Phinn, as a result of his wigging, committed suicide. We know Lacklander died with young Phinn's name on his lips, at the same time showing the greatest anxiety about the memoirs. We know that Cartarette was entrusted with the publication. We know Cartarette took an envelope from the drawer that was subsequently broken open and went to see old Phinn on what Miss Cartarette describes as an errand of mercy. When he didn't find him at home, he followed him into the valley. Finally, we know that after they fell out over the poaching, they had a further discussion about which, although she admits she heard it, Lady Lacklander will tell us nothing. Now, my dear Br'er Fox, why should the Lacklanders or Mr. Phinn or the Cartarettes be so uncommonly touchy about all this? I don't know what you think, but I can find only one answer."

Fox turned the car sedately into the Hammer Farm drive and nodded his head.

"Seems pretty obvious when you put it like that, Mr. Alleyn, I must say. But is there sufficient motive for murder in it?"

"Who the hell's going to say what's a sufficient motive for murder? And anyway, it may be one of a bunch of motives. Probably is. Stick to *ubi, quibus, auxilius, quomodo* and *quando*, Foxkin; let *cur* look after itself, and blow me down if *quis* won't walk in when you're least expecting it."

"So you always tell us, sir," said Fox.

"All right, all right; I grow to a dotage and repeat myself. There's the lovelorn C. P.'s car. We wait here while they hunt up the garments of the two ladies. Mrs. Cartarette's will be brand-new extra-loud tweeds smelling of Schiaparelli and, presumably, of fish."

"Must be a bit lonely," Fox mused.

"Who?"

"Mrs. Cartarette. An outsider, you might say, dumped down in a little place where they've known each other's pedigrees since the time they were *all* using bows and arrows. Bit lonely. More she tries to fit in, I daresay, the less they seem to take to her. More polite they get, the more uncomfortable they make her feel."

"Yes," Alleyn said, "true enough. You've shoved your great fat finger into the middle of one of those uncomfortable minor tragedies that the Lacklanders of this world prefer to cut dead. And I'll tell you something else, Fox. Of the whole crowd of them, *not* excluding your girl-friend, there isn't one that wouldn't feel a *kind* of relief if she turned out to have murdered her husband."

Fox looked startled. "One, surely?" he ejaculated.

"No," Alleyn insisted with a sort of violence that was very rare with him. "Not one. Not one. For all of them she's the intruder, the disturber, the outsider. The very effort some of them have tried to make on her behalf has added to their secret resentment. I bet you. How did you get on in Chyning?"

"I saw Dr. Curtis. He's fixed up very comfortably in the hospital mortuary and was well on with the P.M. Nothing new cropped up about the injuries. He says he thinks it's true enough about the fish scales and will watch out for them and do the microscope job with all the exhibits. The Yard's going to look up the late Sir Harold's will and check Commander Syce's activities in Singapore. They say it won't take long if the Navy List gives them a line on anybody in the Service who was there at the time and has a shore job now. If they strike it lucky, they may call us back in a couple of hours. I said the Boy and Donkey and the Chyning station to be sure of catching us."

"Good," Alleyn said without much show of interest. "Hullo, listen who's coming! Here we go."

He was out of the car before Fox could reply and with an abrupt change of speed began to stroll down the drive. His pipe was in his hands and he busied himself with filling it. The object of this unexpected pantomime now pedalled into Mr. Fox's ken: the village postman.

Alleyn, stuffing his pipe, waited until the postman was abreast with him.

"Good morning," said Alleyn.

"Morning, sir," said the postman, braking his bicycle.

"I'll take them shall I?" Alleyn suggested.

The postman steadied himself with one foot on the ground. "Well, ta," he said and with a vague suggestion of condolence added, "Save the disturbance, like, won't it, sir? Only one, anyway." He fetched a long envelope from his bag and held it out. "For the deceased," he said in a special voice. "Terrible sad, if I may pass the remark."

"Indeed, yes," Alleyn said, taking, with a sense of rising excitement, the long, and to him familiar, envelope.

"Terrible thing to happen in the Vale," the postman continued. "What I mean, the crime, and the Colonel that highly respected and never a word that wasn't kindness itself. Everybody's that upset and that sorry for the ladies. Poor Miss Rose, now! Well, it's terrible."

The postman, genuinely distressed and at the same time consumed with a countryman's inquisitiveness, looked sideways at Alleyn. "You'd be a relative, I daresay, sir."

"How very kind of you," Alleyn said, blandly ignoring this assumption. "I'll tell them you sent your sympathy, shall I?"

"Ta," said the postman. "And whoever done it; what I mean, I'm sure I hope they get 'em. I hear it's reckoned to be a job for the Yard and altogether beyond the scope of Bert Oliphant, which won't surprise us in the Vale, although the man's active enough when it comes to after hours at the Boy and Donkey. Well, I'll be getting along."

When he had gone, Alleyn returned to Fox.

"Look what I've got," he said.

Fox contemplated the long envelope and, when Alleyn showed him the reverse side, read the printed legend on the flap: "From Brierley and Bentwood, St. Peter's Place, London, W.1."

"Publishers?" said Fox.

"Yes. We've got to know what this is, Fox. The flap's very sketchily gummed down. A little tweak and—how easy it would be. Justifiable enough, too, I suppose. However, we'll go the other way round. Here comes Miss Cartarette."

She came out, followed by Mark carrying a suitcase, a tennis racket in a press and a very new golf bag and clubs.

"Here you are, sir," Mark said. "We had to fish the clothes out of the dry cleaner's box, but they're all present and correct. Rose said you might want her racket, which is absurd, but this is it."

"Thank you," Alleyn said, and Fox relieved Mark of his load and put it in the police car. Alleyn showed Rose the envelope.

He said. "This has come for your father. I'm afraid we may have to ask for all his recent correspondence and certainly for anything that comes now. They will, of course, be returned and, unless used in evidence, will be treated as strictly confidential. I'm so sorry, but that's how it is. If you wish, you may refuse to let me have this one without an official order."

He was holding it out with the typed superscription uppermost. Rose looked at it without interest.

Mark said, "Look, darling, I think perhaps you shouldn't—"

"Please take it," she said to Alleyn. "It's a pamphlet, I should think."

Alleyn thanked her and watched her go off with Mark in his car.

"Shame to take the money," said Fox.

Alleyn said, "I hope, if he knows, the Colonel doesn't think too badly of me."

He opened the envelope, drew out the enclosure and unfolded it.

> Colonel M. C. V. Cartarette, M.V.O., D.S.C.
>    Hammer Farm
>    Swevenings

Dear Sir:

The late Sir Harold Lacklander, three weeks before he died, called upon me for a discussion about his memoirs, which my firm is to publish. A difficulty had arisen in respect of Chapter 7, and Sir Harold informed me that he proposed to take your advice in this matter. He added that if he should not live to see the publication of his memoirs, he wished you, if you would accept the responsibility, to edit the work in toto. He asked me, in the event of his death, to communicate directly with you and with nobody else and stressed the point that your decision in every respect must be considered final.

We have had no further instructions or communications of any kind from Sir Harold Lacklander, and I now write, in accordance with his wishes, to ask if you have, in fact, accepted the responsibility of editing the memoirs, if you have received the manuscript, and if you have arrived at a decision in the delicate and important matter of Chapter 7.

I shall be most grateful for an early reply. Perhaps you would give me the pleasure of lunching with me when next you are in London. If you would be kind enough to let me know the appropriate date, I shall keep it free.

> I am, my dear sir,
> Yours truly,
> TIMOTHY BENTWOOD

"And I'll give you two guesses, Br'er Fox," Alleyn said as he refolded the letter and returned it to its envelope, "what constitutes the delicate and important matter of Chapter 7."

*ii*

When Mark had turned in at the Nunspardon Lodge gates, Rose asked him to stop somewhere on the drive.

"It's no use going on," she said. "There's something I've got to say. Please stop."

"Of course." Mark pulled into an open space alongside the drive. He stopped his engine and turned to look at her. "Now," he said, "tell me."

"Mark, he doesn't think it was a tramp."

"Alleyn?"

"Yes. He thinks it was—one of us. I know he does."

Rose made a little faint circling movement of her hand.

"Someone that knew him. A neighbour. Or one of his own family."

"You can't tell. Honestly. Alleyn's got to do his stuff. He's got to clear the decks."

"He doesn't think it was a tramp," Rose repeated. Her voice, exhausted and drained of its colour, rose a little. "He thinks it was one of us."

Mark said after a long pause, "Well, suppose—and I don't for a moment admit—suppose at this stage he does wonder about all of us. After all—"

"Yes," Rose said, "after all, he has cause, hasn't he?"

"What do you mean?"

"You see what's happening to us? You're pretending to misunderstand. It's clear enough he's found out about Chapter 7."

She saw the colour drain out of his face and cried out, "O! What am I doing to us both!"

"Nothing as yet," Mark said. "Let's get this straight. You

think Alleyn suspects that one of us—me or my father or, I suppose, my grandmother—may have killed your father because he was going to publish the amended version of my grandfather's memoirs. That it?"

"Yes."

"I see. Well, you may be right. Alleyn may have some such idea. What I want to know now is this: You yourself, Rose—do you—can it be possible that you too—? No," he said, "not now. I won't ask you now when you're so badly shocked. We'll wait."

"We can't wait. I can't go on like this. I can't come back to Nunspardon and pretend the only thing that matters is for me to take a nembutal and go to sleep."

"Rose, look at me. No, please. Look at me."

He took her face between his hands and turned it towards him.

"My God," he said, "you're afraid of me."

She did not try to free herself. Her tears ran down between his fingers. "No," she cried, "no, it's not true. I can't be afraid of you; I love you."

"Are you sure? Are you sure that somewhere in the back of your mind you're not remembering that your father stood between us and that I was jealous of your love for him? And that his death has made you an heiress? Because it has, hasn't it? And that the publication of the memoirs would have set my family against our marriage and brought disrepute upon my name? Are you sure you don't suspect me, Rose?"

"Not you. I promise. Not you."

"Then—who? Gar? My father? Darling, can you see how fantastic it sounds when one says it aloud?"

"I know it sounds fantastic," Rose said in despair. "It's fantastic that anyone should want to hurt my father, but all the same, somebody has killed him. I've got to learn to get used to that. Last night somebody killed my father."

She pulled his hands away from her face. "You must admit," she said, "that takes a bit of getting used to."

Mark said, "What am I to do about this!"

"Nothing; you can't do anything; that's what's so awful,

isn't it? You want me to turn to you and find my comfort in you, don't you, Mark? and I want it, too. I long for it. And then, you see, I can't. I can't, because there's no knowing who killed my father."

There was a long silence. At last she heard Mark's voice. "I didn't want to say this, Rose, but now I'm afraid I've got to. There are, after all, other people. If my grandmother and my father and I fall under suspicion—Oh, yes, and Occy Phinn—isn't there somebody else who can't be entirely disregarded?"

Rose said, "You mean Kitty, don't you?"

"I do. Yes—equally with us."

"Don't!" Rose cried out. "Don't! I won't listen."

"You've got to. We can't stop now. Do you suppose I enjoy reminding myself—or you—that my father—"

"No! No, Mark! Please!" Rose said and burst into tears.

Sometimes there exists in people who are attached to each other a kind of ratio between the degree of attraction and the potential for irritation. Strangely, it is often the happiness of one that arouses an equal degree of irascibility in the other. The tear-blotted face, the obstinate misery, the knowledge that the distress is genuine and the feeling of incompetence it induces, all combine to exasperate and inflame.

Rose thought she recognized signs of this exasperation in Mark. His look darkened and he had moved away from her. "I can't help it, Mark," she stammered.

She heard his expostulations and reiterated arguments. She thought she could hear, too, a note of suppressed irritation in his voice. He kept saying that the whole thing had better be threshed out between them. "Let's face it," he said on a rising note. "Kitty's *there*, isn't she? And what about Geoffrey Syce or Nurse Kettle? We needn't concentrate exclusively on the Lacklanders, need we?" Rose turned away. Leaning her arm on the ledge of the open window and her face on her arm, she broke down completely.

"Ah, hell!" Mark shouted. He pushed open the door, got out and began to walk angrily to and fro.

It was upon this situation that Kitty appeared, driving

herself home from Nunspardon. When she saw Mark's car, she pulled up. Rose made a desperate effort to collect herself. After a moment's hesitation, Kitty got out of her car and came over to Rose. Mark shoved his hands into his pockets and moved away.

"I don't want to butt in," Kitty said, "but can I do anything? I mean, just say—I'll get out if I'm no use."

Rose looked up at her and for the first time saw in her stepmother's face the signs of havoc that Kitty had been at pains to repair. For the first time it occurred to Rose that there are more ways than one of meeting sorrow, and for the first time she felt a sense of fellowship for Kitty.

"How kind of you," she said. "I'm glad you stopped."

"That's all right. I was sort of wondering," Kitty went on, with an unwonted air of hesitation; "I daresay you'd rather sort of move out. Say if you would. I'm not talking about what you said about the future but of now. I mean, I daresay Mark's suggested you stay up at Nunspardon. Do, if you'd like to. I mean, I'll be O.K."

It had never occurred to Rose that Kitty might be lonely if she herself went to Nunspardon. A stream of confused recollections and ideas flooded her thoughts. She reminded herself again that Kitty would now be quite desperately hard-up and that she had a responsibility towards her. She wondered if her stepmother's flirtations with Mark's father had not been induced by a sense of exclusion. She looked into the careworn, over-painted face and thought, "After all, we both belonged to him."

Kitty said awkwardly, "Well, anyway, I'll push off."

Suddenly Rose wanted to say, "I'll come with you, Kitty. Let's go home." She fumbled with the handle of the door, but before she could speak or make a move, she was aware of Mark. He had come back to the car and had moved round to her side and was speaking to Kitty.

"That's what I've been telling her," he said. "In fact, as her doctor, those are my orders. She's coming to Nunspardon. I'm glad you support me."

Kitty gave him the look she bestowed quite automatically

on any presentable male. "Well, anyway, she's in good hands," she said. She gave them a little wave of her own hand and returned to her car.

With a feeling of desolation and remorse Rose watched her drive away.

### iii

On the way to Chyning, Alleyn propounded his theory on Chapter 7.

"Bear in mind," he said, "the character of Colonel Cartarette as it emerges from the welter of talk. With the exception of Danberry-Phinn, they are all agreed, aren't they, that Cartarette was a nice chap with uncommonly high standards and a rather tender conscience. All right. For the last time let us remind ourselves that, just before he died, old Lacklander was very much bothered by something to do with Cartarette and the memoirs and that he died with the name Vic on his lips. All right. Whenever the memoirs and/or young Viccy Phinn are mentioned, everybody behaves as if they're concealing the fact that they are about to have kittens. Fair enough. Phinn and Lady Lacklander both agree that there was further discussion, after the row, between Phinn and the Colonel. Lady Lacklander flatly refuses to divulge the subject-matter, and Phinn says if she won't, neither will he. The Colonel left his house with the intention of calling upon Phinn, with whom he had been on bad terms for a long time. Now put all those bits together, remembering the circumstances of young Phinn's death, George Lacklander's virtual admission that the memoirs exonerated young Phinn, Rose Cartarette's statement that her father's visit to old Phinn was an errand of mercy, and the contents of the publisher's letter. Put 'em together and what do you get?"

"Chapter 7 was the bit that exonerated young Phinn. Colonel Cartarette was given the responsibility of including it in this book. He couldn't decide one way or the other and took it to Mr. Phinn," Fox speculated, "to see which way he felt about it. Mr. Phinn was out fishing and the Colonel followed him up. After their dust-up the Colonel—now what does the Colonel do?"

"In effect," Alleyn said, "the Colonel says, 'All right, you unconscionable old poacher. All right. Look what I'd come to do for you?' And he tells him about Chapter 7. And since we didn't find Chapter 7 on the Colonel, we conclude that he gave it there and then to Mr. Phinn. This inference is strongly supported by the fact that I saw an envelope with a wad of typescript inside, addressed in the Colonel's hand to Mr. Phinn, on Mr. Phinn's desk. So what, my old Foxkin, are we to conclude?"

"About Chapter 7?"

"About Chapter 7."

"You tell me," said Fox with a stately smile.

Alleyn told him.

"Well, sir," Fox said, "it's possible. It's as good a motive as any for the Lacklanders to do away with the Colonel."

"Except that if we're right in our unblushing conjectures, Fox, Lady Lacklander overheard the Colonel give Chapter 7 to Mr. Phinn; in which case if any of the Lacklanders were after blood, Mr. Phinn's would be the more logical blood to tap."

"Lady Lacklander may not have heard much of what they said."

"In which case, why is she so cagey about it all now, and what did she and the Colonel talk about afterwards?"

"Ah, blast!" said Fox in disgust. "Well, then, it may be that the memoirs and Chapter 7 and Who—Stole—the—Secret—Document—in—Zlomce haven't got anything to do with the case."

"My feeling is that they do belong but are not of the first importance."

"Well, Mr. Alleyn, holding the view you do hold, it's the only explanation that fits."

"Quite so. And I tell you what, Fox, motive, as usual, is a secondary consideration. And here is Chyning and a petrol pump and here (hold on to your hat, Fox; down, down, little flutterer) is the Jolly Kettle filling up a newly painted car which I'll swear she calls by a pet name. If you can control yourself, we'll put in for some petrol. Good morning, Miss Kettle."

"The top of the morning to you, Chief," said Nurse Kettle turning a beaming face upon them. She slapped the back of her car as if it were a rump. "Having her elevenses," she said. "First time we've met for a fortnight on account she's been having her face lifted. And how *are* you?"

"Bearing up," Alleyn said, getting out of the car. "Inspector Fox is turning rather short-tempered."

Fox ignored him. "Very nice little car, Miss Kettle," he said.

"Araminta? She's a good steady girl on the whole," said Nurse Kettle, remorselessly jolly. "I'm just taking her out to see a case of lumbago."

"Commander Syce?" Alleyn ventured.

"That's right."

"He is completely recovered."

"You don't say," Nurse Kettle rejoined, looking rather disconcerted. "And him tied up in knots last evening. Fancy!"

"He was a cot case, I understand, when you left him round about eight o'clock last night."

"*Very* sorry for ourselves we were, yes."

"And yet," Alleyn said. "Mr. Phinn declares that at a quarter past eight Commander Syce was loosing off arrows from his sixty-pound bow."

Nurse Kettle was scarlet to the roots of her mouse-coloured hair. Alleyn heard his colleague struggling with some subterranean expression of sympathy.

"Well, fancy!" Nurse Kettle was saying in a high voice. "There's 'bago for you! Now you see it, now you don't." And she illustrated this aphorism with sharp snaps of her finger and thumb.

Fox said in an unnatural voice, "Are you sure, Miss Kettle, that the Commander wasn't having you on?" Excuse the suggestion."

Nurse Kettle threw him a glance that might perhaps be best described as uneasily roguish.

"And why not?" she asked. "Maybe he was. But not for the

**195**

reason you mere men suppose."

She got into her car with alacrity and sounded her horn. "Home, John, and don't spare the horses," she cried waggishly and drove away in what was evidently an agony of self-consciousness.

"Unless you can develop a deep-seated and obstinate malady, Br'er Fox," Alleyn said, "you haven't got a hope."

"A thoroughly nice woman," Fox said and added ambiguously, "What a pity!"

They got their petrol and drove on to the police station. Here Sergeant Oliphant awaited them with two messages from Scotland Yard.

"Nice work," Alleyn said. "Damn' quick."

He read aloud the first message. "Information re trout scales checked with Natural History Museum, Royal Piscatorial Society, Institute for Preservation of British Trout Streams, and D.R.S.K.K. Solomon expert and leading authority. All confirm that microscopically your two trout cannot exhibit precisely the same characteristics in scales. Cartarette regarded an authority."

"Fine!" said Inspector Fox. "Fair enough!"

Alleyn took up the second slip of paper. "Report," he read, "on the late Sir Harold Lacklander's will." He read to himself for a minute, then looked up. "Couldn't be simpler," he said. "With the exception of the usual group of legacies to dependents the whole lot goes to to the widow and to the son, upon whom most of it's entailed."

"What Miss Kettle told us."

"Exactly. Now for the third. Here we are. Report on Commander Geoffrey Syce, R.N., retired. Singapore, March 1, 195- to April 9, 195-. Serving in H. M. S. ——, based on Singapore. Shore duty. Activities, apart from duties: At first, noticeably quiet tastes and habits. Accepted usual invitations but spent considerable time alone, sketching. Later, cohabited with a so-called Miss Kitty de Vere, whom he is believed to have met at a taxi-dance. Can follow up history of de Vere if required. Have ascertained that Syce rented apartment occupied by de Vere, who subsequently met and married

Colonel Maurice Cartarette, to whom she is believed to have been introduced by Syce. Sources—"

The followed a number of names, obtained from the Navy List, and a note to say that H. M. S.——being now in port, it had been possible to obtain information through the appropriate sources at the "urgent and important" level.

Alleyn dropped the chit on Oliphant's desk.

"Poor Cartarette," he said with a change of voice, "and, if you like, Poor Syce."

"Or, from the other point of view," Fox said, "poor Kitty."

*iv*

Before they returned to Swevenings, Alleyn and Fox visited Dr. Curtis in the Chyning Hospital mortuary. It was a very small mortuary attached to a sort of pocket-hospital, and there was a ghastly cosiness in the close proximity of the mall to the now irrevocably and dreadfully necrotic Colonel. Curtis, who liked to be thorough in his work, was making an extremely exhaustive autopsy and had not yet completed it. He was able to confirm that there had been an initial blow, followed, it seemed, rather than preceded by, a puncture, but that neither the blow nor the puncture quite accounted for some of the multiple injuries, which were the result, he thought, of pressure. *Contrecoup*, he said, was present in a very marked degree. He would not entirely dismiss Commander Syce's arrows nor Lady Lacklander's umbrella spike, but he thought her shooting-stick the most likely of the sharp instruments produced. The examination of the shooting-stick for blood traces might bring them nearer to a settlement of this point. The paint-rag, undoubtedly, was stained with blood, which had not yet been classified. It smelt quite strongly of fish. Alleyn handed over the rest of his treasure-trove.

"As soon as you can," he said, "do, like a good chap, get on to the fishy side of the business. Find me scales of both trout on one person's article, and only on one person's, and the rest will follow as the night the day."

"You treat me," Curtis said without malice, "like a tympanist in a jazz band perpetually dodging from one instrument to another. I'll finish my P.M., blast you, and Willy Roskill can muck about with your damned scales." Sir William Roskill was an eminent Home Office analyst.

"I'll ring him up now," Alleyn said.

"It's all right; I've rung him. He's on his way. As soon as we know anything, we'll ring the station. What's biting you about this case, Rory?" Dr. Curtis asked. "You're always slinging off at the 'expeditions' officer and raising your cry of *festina lente*. Why the fuss and hurry? The man was only killed last night."

"It's a pig of a case," Alleyn said, "and on second thoughts I'll keep the other arrow—the bloody one. If it is blood. What the hell can I carry it in? I don't want him to—" He looked at the collection of objects they had brought with them. "That'll do," he said. He slung George Lacklander's golf bag over his shoulder, wrapped up the tip of Syce's arrow and dropped it in.

"A pig of a case," he repeated; "I hate its guts."

"Why this more than another?"

But Alleyn did not answer. He was looking at the personal effects of the persons under consideration. They were laid out in neat groups along a shelf opposite the dissecting table, almost as if they were component parts of the autopsy. First came the two fish: the Old 'Un, 4 pounds of cold, defeated splendour, and beside it on a plate the bones and rags of the Colonel's catch. Then the belongings of the men who had caught them: the Colonel's and Mr. Phinn's clothes, boots, fishing gear and hat. Kitty's loud new tweed skirt and twin set. Sir George's plus fours, stockings and shoes. Mark's and Rose's tennis clothes. Lady Lacklander's tent-like garments, her sketching kit and a pair of ancient but beautifully made brogues. Alleyn stopped, stretched out a hand and lifted one of these brogues.

"Size about four," he said. "They were hand-made by the best bootmaker in London in the days when Lady Lacklander still played golf. Here's her name sewn in. They've been cleaned, but the soles are still dampish and—" He turned the shoe over and was looking at the heel. It carried miniature spikes. Alleyn looked at Fox, who, without a word, brought from the end of the shelf a kitchen plate on which were laid out, as if for some starvation-diet, the remains of the Colonel's fish. The flap of skin with its fragment of an impression was carefully spread out. They waited in silence.

"It'll fit all right," Alleyn said. "Do your stuff, of course, but it's going to fit. And the better it fits, the less I'm going to like it."

And with this illogical observation he went out of the mortuary.

"What *is* biting him?" Dr. Curtis asked Fox.

"Ask yourself, Doctor," Fox said. "It's one of the kind that he's never got, as you might say, used to."

"Like that, is it?" Dr. Curtis, for the moment unmindful of his own terrible explicit job, muttered, "I often wonder why on earth he entered the Service."

"I've never like to enquire," Fox said in his plain way, "but I'm sure I'm very glad he did. Well, I'll leave you with your corpse."

". . . seeing you," Dr. Curtis said absently, and Fox rejoined his principal. They returned to the police station, where Alleyn had a word with Sergeant Oliphant. "We'll leave you here, Oliphant," Alleyn said. "Sir William Roskill will probably go straight to the hospital, but as soon as there's anything to report, he or Dr. Curtis will ring you up. Here's a list of people I'm going to see. If I'm not at one of these places, I'll be at another. See about applying for a warrant; we may be making an arrest before nightfall."

"'T, 't, 't," Sergeant Oliphant clicked. "Reely? In what name, sir? Same as you thought?"

Alleyn pointed his forefinger at a name on the list he had given the sergeant, who stared at it for some seconds, his face perfectly wooden.

"It's not positive," Alleyn said, "but you'd better warn your tame J.P. about the warrant in case we need it in a hurry. We'll get along with the job now. Put a call through to Brierley and Bentwood, will you. Oliphant? Here's the number. Ask for Mr. Timothy Bentwood and give my name."

He listened while Sergeant Oliphant put the call through and noticed abstractedly that he did this in a quiet and business-like manner.

Alleyn said, "If Bentwood will play, this should mean the clearing-up of Chapter 7."

Fox raised a massive finger and they both listened to Oliphant.

"O, yerse?" Oliphant was saying. "Yerse? Will you hold the line, sir, while I enquire?"

"What is it?" Alleyn demanded sharply.

Oliphant placed the palm of his vast hand over the mouthpiece. "Mr. Bentwood, sir," he said, "is in hopital. Would you wish to speak to his secretary?"

"Damnation, blast and bloody hell!" Alleyn said. "No, I wouldn't. Thank you, Oliphant. Come on, Fox. That little game's gone cold. We'd better get moving. Oliphant, if we can spare the time, we'll get something to eat at the Boy and Donkey, but on the way, we'll make at least one call." His finger again hovered over the list. The sergeant followed its indication.

"At Uplands?" he said. "Commander Syce?"

"Yes," Alleyn said. "Have everything laid on, and if you get a signal from me, come at once with suitable assistance. It'll mean an arrest. Come on, Fox."

He was very quiet on the way back over Watt's Hill.

As they turned the summit and approached Jacob's Cottage, they saw Mr. Phinn leaning over his gate with a kitten on his shoulder.

Alleyn said, "It might as well be now as later. Let's stop." Fox pulled up by the gate and Alleyn got out. He walked over to the gate and Mr. Phinn blinked at him.

"Dear me, Chief Inspector," he said, taking the kitten from his neck and caressing it, "how very recurrent you are. Quite decimalite, to coin an adjective."

"It's our job, you know," Alleyn said mildly. "You'll find we do tend to crop up."

Mr. Phinn blinked and gave a singular little laugh. "Am I to conclude, then, that I am the subject of your interest? Or are you on your way to fresh fields of surmise and conjecture? Nunspardon, for instance. Do you perhaps envisage my Lady Brobdignagia, the Dowager Tun, the Mammoth Matriarch, stealing a tip-toe through the daisies? Or George aflame with his newly acquired dignities, thundering through the willow grove in plus fours? Or have the injuries a clinical character? Do we suspect the young Aesculapius with scalpel or probe? You are thinking I am a person of execrable taste, but the truth is there *are* other candidates for infamy. Perhaps we should look nearer at hand. At our elderly and intemperate merryman of the shaft and quiver. Or at the interesting and mysterious widow with the dubious antecedents? Really, how very footling, if you will forgive me, it all sounds, doesn't it? What can I do for you?"

Alleyn looked at the pallid face and restless eyes. "Mr. Phinn," he said, "will you let me have your copy of Chapter 7?"

The kitten screamed, opening its mouth and showing its tongue. Mr. Phinn relaxed his fingers, kissed it and put it down.

"Forgive me, my atom," he said. "Run to Mother." He opened the gate. "Shall we go in?" he suggested, and they followed him into a garden dotted about with rustic furniture of an offensive design.

"Of course," Alleyn said, "you can refuse. I shall then have to use some other form of approach."

"If you imagine," Mr. Phinn said, wetting his lips, "that as far as I am concerned this Chapter 7, which I am to suppose you have seen on my desk but not read, is in any way incriminating, you are entirely mistaken. It constitutes, for me, what may perhaps be described as a contra-motive."

"So I had supposed," Alleyn said. "But don't you think you had better let me see it?"

There was a long silence. "Without the consent of Lady Lacklander," Mr. Phinn said, "never. Not for all the sleuths in Christendom."

"Well," Alleyn said, "that's all very correct, I daresay.

Would you suggest, for the sake of argument, that Chapter 7 constitutes a sort of confession on the part of the author? Does Sir Harold Lacklander, for instance, perhaps admit that he was virtually responsible for the leakage of information that tragic time in Zlomce?"

Mr. Phinn said breathlessly, "Pray, what inspires this gush of unbridled empiricism?"

"It's not altogether that," Alleyn rejoined with perfect good-humour. "As I think I told you this morning, I have some knowledge of the Zlomce affair. You tell us that the new version of Chapter 7 constitutes for you a contra-motive. If this is so, if, for instance, it provides exoneration, can you do anything but welcome its publication?"

Mr. Phinn said nothing.

"I think I must tell you," Alleyn went on, "that I shall ask the prospective publishers for the full story of Chapter 7."

"They have not been informed—"

"On the contrary, unknown to Colonel Cartarette, they were informed by the author."

"Indeed?" said Mr. Phinn, trembling slightly. "If they profess any vestige of professional rectitude, they will refuse to divulge the content."

"As you do?"

"As I do. I shall refuse any information in this affair, no matter what pressure is put upon me, Inspector Alleyn."

Mr. Phinn had already turned aside when his garden gate creaked and Alleyn said quietly, "Good morning once again, Lady Lacklander."

Mr. Phinn spun round with an inarticulate ejaculation.

She stood blinking in the sun, huge, without expression and very slightly tremulous.

"Roderick," said Lady Lacklander, "I have come to confess."

# CHAPTER **X**

## Return to Swevenings

Lady Lacklander advanced slowly towards them.

"If that contraption of yours will support my weight, Octavius," she said, "I'll take it."

They stood aside for her. Mr. Phinn suddenly began to gabble. "No, no, no! Not another word! I forbid it."

She let herself down on a rustic seat.

"For God's sake," Mr. Phinn implored her frantically, "hold your tongue, Lady L."

"Nonsense, Occy," she rejoined, panting slightly. "Hold yours, my good fool." She stared at him for a moment and then gave a sort of laugh.

"Good Lord, you think I did it myself, do you?"

"No, no, no. What a thing to say!"

She shifted her great torso and addressed herself to Alleyn. "I'm here, Roderick, virtually on behalf of my husband. The confession I have to offer is his.".

"At last," Alleyn said. "Chapter 7."

"Precisely. I've no idea how much you think you already know or how much you may have been told."

"By me," Mr. Phinn cried out, "nothing!"

"Humph!" she said. "Uncommon generous of you, Octavius."

Mr. Phinn began to protest, threw up his hands and was silent.

"There are, however, other sources," she went on. "I understand his wife has been kept posted." She stared at Alleyn, who thought, "George has told Kitty Cartarette about Chapter 7 and Lady Lacklander has found out. She thinks Kitty has told me." He said nothing.

"You may suppose, therefore," Lady Lacklander continued, "that I am merely making a virtue of necessity."

Alleyn bowed.

"It is not altogether that. To begin with, we are, as a family, under a certain obligation to you, Octavius."

"Stop!" Mr. Phinn shouted. "Before you go on much further, before you *utter*—"

"Mr. Phinn," Alleyn cut in, breaking about three vital items of the police code in one sentence, "if you don't stop chattering, I shall take drastic steps to make you. Shut up, Mr. Phinn."

"Yes, Occy," Lady Lacklander said, "I couldn't agree more. Either shut up or take yourself off, my dear fellow." She lifted a tiny, fat hand, holding it aloft as if it was one of Mr. Phinn's kittens. "Do me the favour," she said, "of believing I have thought things over very carefully, and be quiet."

While Mr. Phinn still hesitated, eyeing Alleyn and fingering his lips, Lady Lacklander made a brief comprehensive gesture with her short arms and said, "Roderick, my husband was a traitor."

### ii

They made a strange group, sitting there on uncomfortable rustic benches. Fox took unobtrusive notes, Mr. Phinn held his head in his hands, Lady Lacklander, immobile behind the great facade of her fat, talked and talked. Cats came and went, gracefully indifferent to the human situation.

"That," Lady Lacklander said, "is what you will find in Chapter 7." She broke off and, after a moment, said, "This is not going to be easy and I've no wish to make a fool of myself. Will you forgive me for a moment?"

"Of course," Alleyn said, and they waited while Lady Lacklander, staring before her, beat her puffball palms on her knees and got her mouth under control. "That's better," she said at last. "I can manage now." And she went on steadily. "At the time of the Zlomce incident my husband was in secret negotiation with a group of Prussian fascists. The top group: the men about Hitler. They looked upon him, it appears, as their trump card: a British diplomat whose name—" her voice creaked and steadied—"was above reproach in his own country. He was absolutely and traitorously committed to the Nazi programme." Alleyn saw that her eyes were bitter with tears. "They never found that out at your M.I.5., Roderick, did they?"

"No."

"And yet this morning I thought that perhaps you knew."

"I wondered. That was all."

"So she didn't say anything."

"She?"

"Maurice's wife, Kitty."

"No."

"You never know," she muttered, "with that sort of people what they may do."

"Nor," he said, "with other sorts either, it seems."

A dark unlovely flush flooded her face.

"The extraordinary thing," Mr. Phinn said suddenly, "*is*

*why. Why* did Lacklander do it?"

"The Herrenvolk heresy?" Alleyn suggested. "An aristo-cratic Anglo-German alliance as the only alternative to war and communism and the only hope for the survival of his own class? It was a popular heresy at that time. He wasn't alone. No doubt he was promised great things."

"You don't spare him," Lady Lacklander said under her breath.

"How can I? In the new Chapter 7, I imagine, he doesn't spare himself."

"He repented bitterly. His remorse was frightful."

"Yes," Mr. Phinn said "That is clear enough."

"Ah, yes!" she cried out. "Ah, yes, Occy, yes. And most of all for the terrible injury he did your boy—most of all for that."

"The injury?" Alleyn repeated, cutting short an attempt on Mr. Phinn's part to intervene. "I'm sorry, Mr. Phinn. We must have it."

Lady Lacklander said, "Why do you try to stop me, Occy? You've read it. You must want to shout it from the roof-tops."

Alleyn said, "Does Sir Harold exonerate Ludovic Phinn?"

"Of everything but carelessness."

"I see."

Lady Lacklander put her little fat hands over her face. It was a gesture so out of key with the general tenor of her behaviour that it was as shocking in its way as a bout of hysteria.

Alleyn said, "I think I understand. In the business of the railway concessions in Zlomce, was Sir Harold, while apparently acting in accordance with his instructions from the British Government, about to allow the German interest to get control?"

He saw that he was right and went on, "And at the most delicate stage of these negotiations, at the very moment where he desired above all things that no breath of suspicion should be aroused, his private secretary goes out on a Central European bender and lets a German agent get hold of the contents of the vital cable which Sir Harold had left him to decode. Sir Harold is informed by his own government of the leakage. He is obliged to put up a terrific show of ambassadorial rage. He has no alternative but to send for young Phinn. He accuses him of such things and threatens him with such disastrous exposures, such disgrace and ruin, that the boy goes out and puts an end to it all. Was it like that?"

He looked from one to the other.

"It was like that," Lady Lacklander said. She raised her voice as if she repeated some intolerable lesson. "My husband writes that he drove Viccy Phinn to his death as surely as if he had killed him with his own hands. He was instructed to do so by his Nazi masters. It was then that he began to understand what he had done and to what frightful lengths his German associates could drive him. I knew, at that time, he was wretchedly unhappy, but put it down to the shock of Viccy's death and—as I, of course, thought—treachery. But the treachery, Occy, was ours, and your Viccy was only a foolish and tragically careless boy." She looked at Mr. Phinn and frowned. "Yesterday," she said, "after your row with Maurice over the trout, he came to me and told me he'd left a copy of the amended Chapter 7 at your house. Why haven't you produced it, Occy? Why just now did you try to stop me? Was it because—"

"Dear me, no," Mr. Phinn said very quietly, "not from any high-flown scruples, I assure you. It was, if you will believe me, in deference to my boy's wishes. Before he killed himself, Viccy wrote to his mother and to me. He begged us to believe him innocent. He also begged us most solemnly, whatever the future might hold, never to take any action that might injure Sir Harold Lacklander. You may not have noticed, my dear Lady L., that my foolish boy hero-worshipped your husband. We decided to respect his wishes."

Mr. Phinn stood up. He looked both old and shabby. "I am not concerned," he said, "with the Lacklander conscience, the Lacklander motive, or the Lacklander remorse. I no longer desire the Lacklanders to suffer for my dear boy's death. I do not, I think, believe any more in human expiation. Now if I may, I shall ask you to excuse me. And if you want to know what I did with Chapter 7, I burnt it to ashes, my dear Chief Inspector, half an hour ago."

He raised his dreadful smoking cap, bowed to Lady Lacklander and walked into his house, followed by his cats.

Lady Lacklander stood up. She began to move towards the gate, seemed to recollect herself and paused. "I am going to Nunspardon," she said. Alleyn opened the gate. She went out without looking at him, got into her great car and was driven away.

Fox said, "Painful business. I suppose the young fellow suspected what was up at the last interview. Unpleasant."

"Very."

"Still, as Mr. Phinn says, this Chapter 7 really puts him in the clear as far as killing Colonel Cartarette is concerned."

"Well no," Alleyn said.

"No?"

"Not exactly. The Colonel left Chapter 7 at Jacob's Cottage. Phinn, on his own statement, didn't re-enter the house after his row with the Colonel. He returned to the willow grove, found the body and lost his spectacles He read Chapter 7 for the first time this morning, I fancy, by the aid of a magnifying glass."

### iii

"Of course," Fox said, as they turned into Commander Syce's drive, "it will have been a copy. The Colonel'd never hand over the original."

"No. My guess is he locked the original in the bottom drawer of the left-hand side of his desk."

"Ah! Now!" Fox said with relish. "That might well be."

"In which case one of his own family or one of the Lacklanders or any other interested person has pinched it, and it's probably gone up in smoke like its sister-ship. On the other hand, the bottom drawer may have been empty and the original typescript in Cartarette's bank. It doesn't very much matter, Fox. The publisher was evidently given a pretty sound idea of the alternative version by its author. He could always be called. We may not have to bring the actual text in evidence. I hope we won't."

"What d'you reckon is the dowager's real motive in coming so remarkably clean all of a sudden?"

Alleyn said crossly, "I've had my bellyfull of motives. Take your choice, Br'er Fox."

"Of course," Fox said, "she's a very sharp old lady. She must have guessed we'd find out anyway."

Alleyn muttered obscurely. "The mixture as before. And here we go with a particularly odious little interview. Look out for squalls, Br'er Fox. Gosh! See who's here!"

It was Nurse Kettle. She had emerged from the front door, escorted by Commander Syce, who carred a napkin in his hand. She was about to enter her car, and this process was accelerated by Commander Syce, who quite obviously drew her attention to the approaching police car and then, limping to her own, opened the door and waited with some evidence of trepidation for her to get in. She did so without glancing at him and started her engine.

"She's told him," Alleyn said crossly, "that we've rumbled the 'bago."

"Acting, no doubt," Fox rejoined stiffly, "from the kindest of motives."

"No doubt." Alleyn lifted his hat as Nurse Kettle, having engaged her bottom gear with some precipitance, shot past them like a leaping eland. She was extremely red in the face.

Syce waited for them.

Fox pulled up and they both got out. Alleyn slung the golf bag over his shoulder as he addressed himself to Syce.

"May we speak to you indoors somewhere?" Alleyn asked.

Without a word Syce led the way into his living-room, where a grim little meal, half consumed, was laid out on a small table in close proximity to a very dark whisky-and-water.

The improvised bed was still in commission. A dressing-gown was folded neatly across the foot.

"Sit down?" Syce jerked out, but, as he evidently was not going to do so himself, neither Alleyn nor Fox followed his suggestion.

"What's up now?" he demanded.

Alleyn said, "I've come to ask you a number of questions, all of which you will find grossly impertinent. They concern the last occasion when you were in Singapore. The time we discussed this morning, you remember, when you told us you introduced the present Mrs. Cartarette to her husband?"

Syce didn't answer. He thrust his hands into the pockets of his coat and stared out of the window.

"I'm afraid," Alleyn said, "I shall have to press this a little further. In a word, I must ask you if you were not, in fact, on terms of the greatest intimacy with Miss de Vere, as she was then."

"Bloody impertinence."

"Well, yes. But so, when one comes to think of it, is murder."

"What the hell are you driving at?"

"Ah!" Alleyn exclaimed with one of his very rare gestures. "How footling all this is! You know damn' well what I'm driving at. Why should we stumble about like a couple of maladroit fencers? See here. I've information from the best possible sources that before she was married, you were living with Mrs. Cartarette in Singapore. You yourself have told me you introduced her to Cartarette. You came back here and found them man and wife: the last thing, so you told me, that you had intended. All right. Cartarette was murdered last night in the bottom meadow, and there's a hole in his head that might have been made by an arrow. You gave out that you were laid by with lumbago, but you were heard twanging away at your sixty-pound bow when you were supposed to be incapacitated on your bed. Now, send for your solicitor if you like and refuse to talk till he comes, but for the love of Mike don't pretend you don't know what I'm driving at."

"Great grief!" Syce exclaimed with exactly the same inflection he had used of cats. "I *liked* Cartarette."

"You may have liked Cartarette, but did you love his wife?"

"'Love,'" Syce repeated turning purple. "What a word!"

"Well, my dear man—put it this way. Did she love you?"

"Look here, are you trying to make out that she egged me on or—or—I egged her on or any perishing rot of that sort! Thompson," Commander Syce shouted angrily, "and Bywaters, by God!"

"What put them into your head, I wonder? The coincidence that he was a seafaring man and she, poor woman, an unfaithful wife?"

"A few more cracks like that and I bloody well will send for a solicitor."

"You *are* being difficult," Alleyn said without rancour. "Will you let me have the clothes you were wearing last evening?"

"What the hell for?"

"For one thing, to see if Cartarette's blood is on them."

"How absolutely piffling."

"Well, may I have them?"

"I'm wearing them, blast it."

"Would you mind wearing something else?"

Commander Syce fixed his intensely blue and slightly bloodshot eyes on a distant point in the landscape and said, "I'll shift."

"Thank you. I see you've been using this as a bedsitting-room during, no doubt, your attack of lumbago. Perhaps for the time being you could shift into your dressing-gown and slippers."

Syce followed this suggestion. Little gales of whisky were wafted from him, and his hands were unsteady, but he achieved his change with the economy of movement practised by sailors. He folded up the garments as they were discarded, pass a line of cord round them, made an appropriate knot and gave the bundle to Fox, who wrote out a receipt for it.

Syce tied his dressing-gown cord with a savage jerk.

"No return," Alleyn remarked, "of the ailment?"

Syce did not reply.

Alleyn said, "Why not tell me about it? You must know damn' well that I can't cut all this background stuff dead. Why the devil did you pretend to have lumbago last evening? Was it for the love of a lady?"

It would be innaccurate to say that Commander Syce blushed, since his face, throughout the interview, had been suffused. But at this juncture it certainly darkened to an alarming degree.

"Well, *was* it?" Alleyn insisted on a note of exasperation. Fox clapped the bundle of clothes down on a table.

"I know what it's like," Commander Syce began incomprehensibly. He moved his head in the direction of Hammer Farm. "Lonely as hell. Poor little Kit. Suppose she wanted security. Natural. Ever seen that play? I believe they put it on again a year or two ago. I don't go in for poodle-faking, but it was damn' true. In the end she pitched herself out of a top window, poor thing. Frozen out. County."

"Can you mean *The Second Mrs. Tanqueray?*"

"I daresay. And they'd better change their course or she'll do the same thing. Lonely. I know what it's like."

His gaze travelled to a corner cupboard. "You have to do something," he said and then eyed the tumbler on his luncheon table. "No good offering you a drink," he mumbled.

"None in the world, worse luck."

"Well," Syce said. He added something that sounded like "luck" and suddenly drained the tumbler.

"As a matter of fact," he said, "I'm thinking of giving it up myself. Alcohol."

"It's a 'good familiar creature,'" Alleyn quoted, "'if it is well used.'"

"That's all right as far as it goes, but what sort of a perisher," Syce surprisingly observed, "took the bearings? A nasty little man and a beastly liar into the bargain."

"True enough. But we're not, after all, discussing Iago and alcohol but you and lumbago. Why—"

"All right, I heard you before. I'm just th͟ink͟ ng what to say."

He went to the corner cupboard and returned with a half-empty bottle of whisky. "I've got to think," he said. "It's damn' ticklish, I'd have you know." He helped himself to a treble whisky.

"In that case, wouldn't you do better without that snorter you've just poured out?"

"Think so?"

Fox, with his masterly command of the totally unexpected, said, "*She* would."

"Who?" shouted Commander Syce looking terrified. He drank half his whisky.

"Miss Kettle."

"She would what?"

"Think you'd be better without it, sir."

"She knows what to do," he muttered, "if she wants to stop me. Or rather she doesn't. I wouldn't tell *her*," Commander Syce added in a deeper voice than Alleyn could have imagined him to produce, "I wouldn't mention it to her on any account whatsoever, never."

"I'm afraid you really are very tight."

"It's the last time so early; in future I'm going to wait till the sun's over the yard-arm. It happens to be a promise."

"To Miss Kettle?"

"Who else?" Syce said grandly. "Why not?"

"An admirable idea. Was it," Alleyn asked, "on Miss Kettle's account, by any chance, that you pretended to have lumbago last evening?"

"Who else's?" admitted Syce, who appeared to have got into one unchangeable gear. "Why not?"

"Does she know?"

Fox muttered something indistinguishable and Syce said, "She guessed." He added wretchedly, "We parted brass rags."

"You had a row about it?" Alleyn ventured.

"Not about that. About *that*." He indicated the tumbler. "So I promised. After to-day. Yard-arm."

"Good luck to it."

With the swiftest possible movement Alleyn whisked the arrow from the golf bag and held it under Syce's nose. "Do you know anything about that?" he asked.

"That's mine. You took it away."

"No. This is another of your arrows. This was found in Bottom Meadow at the foot of Watt's Hill. If you examine it, you'll see there's a difference."

Alleyn whipped the cover off the tip of the arrow. "Look," he said.

Syce stared owlishly at the point.

"Bloody," he observed.

"Looks like it. What blood? Whose blood?"

Syce thrust his fingers distractedly through his thin hair. "Cat's blood," he said.

### iv

This was the selfsame arrow, Commander Syce urged, with which some weeks ago he had inadvertently slain the mother of Thomasina Twitchett. He himself had found the body and in his distress had withdrawn the arrow and cast it from him into the adjacent bushes. He had taken the body to Mr. Phinn, who had refused to accept his explanation and apologies, and they had parted, as Commander Syce again put it, brass rags.

Alleyn asked him if he did not consider it at all dangerous to fire off arrows at random into his neighbours' spinneys and over them. The reply was confused and shamefaced. More by surmise and conjecture than by any positive means, Alleyn understood Syce to suggest a close relationship between the degree of his potations and the incontinence of his archery. At this juncture he became morose, and they could get no more out of him.

"It appears," Alleyn said as they drove away, "that when he's completely plastered, he gets a sort of cupid fixation and looses off his shafts blindly into the landscape with a classic disregard for their billets. It's a terrifying thought, but I suppose his immediate neighbours have learnt to look after themselves."

"I'm afraid," Fox said heavily, "she's bitten off more than she can chew. I'm afraid so.".

"My dear old Fox, there's no end to the punishment some women will take."

"Of course," Fox said dismally, "in a manner of speaking, she's trained for it. There is that."

"I rather think, you know, that she's one of the sort that has got to have somebody to cosset."

"I daresay. Whereas, barring the odd bilious turn, I'm never out of sorts. What do we do now, Mr. Alleyn?" Fox continued, dismissing the more intimate theme with an air of finality.

"We can't do anything really conclusive until we get a lead from Curtis. But we interview George Lacklander all the same, Br'er Fox, and, I hope, lay the ghost of young Ludovic Phinn. It's half past one. We may as well let them have their luncheon. Let's see what they can do for us at the Boy and Donkey."

They ate their cold meat, potato and beetroot with the concentration of men whose meals do not occur as a matter of course but are consumed precariously when chances present themselves. Before they had finished, Dr. Curtis rang up to give an interim report. He now plumped unreservedly for a blow on the temple with a blunt instrument while Colonel Cartarette squatted over his catch. Subsequent injuries had been inflicted with a pointed instrument after he lay on his side, unconscious or possibly already lifeless. The second injury had all but obliterated the first. He was unable with any certainty to name the first instrument, but the second was undoubtedly the shooting-stick. Sir William Roskill had found traces of recently shed blood under the collar of the disk. He was now checking for the blood group.

"I see," Alleyn said. "And the shooting-stick was used—?"

"My dear chap, in the normal way, one must suppose."

"Yes, one must, mustn't one? Deliberately pushed home and sat on. Horrid-awful behavior."

"Brutal," Dr. Curtis said dispassionately.

"All the brutality in the world. Has Willy tackled the fish scales?"

"Give him time. But yes, he's begun. No report yet."

"We're going to Nunspardon. Telephone me if there's anything, Curtis, will you? You or Willy?"

"O.K."

Alleyn turned away from the telephone to discover Sergeant Bailey waiting for him with the air of morose detachment that meant he had something of interest to impart. He had, in fact, come from a further detailed overhaul of Colonel Cartarette's study. The bottom drawer on the left of the desk carried an identifiable finger-print of Sir George Lacklander's.

"I checked it with his grog glass," Bailey said, looking at his boots. "The drawer seems to have been wiped over, but a dab on the underside must have been missed or something. It's his all right."

"Very useful," Alleyn said.

Fox wore that expression of bland inscrutability that always seemed to grow upon him as a case approached its close. He would listen attentively to witnesses, suspects, colleagues or his chief and would presently glance up and move the focus of his gaze to some distant object of complete unimportance. This mannerism had the same effect as a change of conversation. It was as if Mr. Fox had become rather pleasurably abstracted. To his associates it was a sign of a peculiar wiliness.

"Remove your attention from the far horizon, Br'er Fox," Alleyn said, "and bring it to bear on the immediate future. We're going to Nunspardon."

They were taken there by the Yard driver, who was now released from his duties in Bottom Meadow.

As they drove past the long wall that marked the Nunspardon marches, Fox began to speculate. "Do you suppose that they throw it open to the public? They must, mustn't they? Otherwise, how do they manage these days?"

"They manage by a freak. Within the last two generations the Lacklanders have won first prizes in world lotteries. I remember because I was still in the Foreign Service when George Lacklander rang the bell in the Calcutta Sweep. In addition to that, they're fantastically lucky race-horse owners and possess one of the most spectacular collections of private jewels in England, which I suppose they could use as a sort of lucky dip if they felt the draught. Really, they're one of the few remaining country families who are wealthy through sheer luck."

"Is that so?" Fox observed mildly. "And Miss Kettle tells me they've stood high in the county for something like a thousand years. Never a scandal, she says, but then I daresay she's partial."

"I daresay. A thousand years," Alleyn said dryly, "is a tidy reach even for the allegedly blameless Lacklanders."

"Well, to Miss Kettle's knowledge there's never been the slightest hint of anything past or present."

"When, for the love of wonder, did you enjoy this cosy chat with Nurse Kettle?"

"Last evening, Mr. Alleyn. When you were in the study, you know, Miss Kettle, who was saying at the time that the Colonel was quite one of the old sort, a real gentleman and so on, mentioned that she and her ladyship had chatted on the subject only that afternoon!" Fox stopped, scraped his chin and became abstracted.

"What's up? What subject?"

"Well, er—class obligation and that style of thing. It didn't seem to amount to anything last night, because at that stage no connection had been established with the family."

"Come on."

"Miss Kettle mentioned in passing that her ladyship had talked about the—er—the—er—as you might say—the—er— principle of 'noblesse oblige' and had let it be known she was very worried."

"About what?"

"No particular cause was named."

"And you're wondering now if she was worried about the prospect of an imminent debunking through Chapter 7 of the blameless Lacklanders?"

"Well, it makes you think," Fox said.

"So it does," Alleyn agreed as they turned into the long drive to Nunspardon.

"She's being a great lady."

"Are you reminding me of her character, her social position or what Mr. Phinn calls her avoirdupois?"

"She must be all of seventeen stone," Fox mused, "and I wouldn't mind betting the son'll be the same at her age. Very heavy-built."

"And damn' heavy-going into the bargain."

"Mrs. Cartarette doesn't seem to think so."

"My dear man, as you have already guessed, he's the only human being in the district, apart from her husband, who's sent out any signals of any kind at all, and he's sent plenty."

"You don't reckon she's in love with him, though?"

"You never know—never. I daresay he has his ponderous attractions."

"Ah, well," Fox said and with an air of freshening himself up stared at a point some distance ahead. It was impossible to guess whether he ruminated upon the tender passion, the character of George Lacklander or the problematical gratitude of Kitty Cartarette. "You never know," he sighed, "he may even be turning it over in his mind how long he ought to wait before it'll be all right to propose to her."

"I hardly think so, and I must say I hope she's not building on it."

"You've made up your mind, of course," Fox said after a pause.

"Well, I have, Fox. I can only see one answer that will fit all the evidence, but unless we get the go-ahead sign from the experts in Chyning, we haven't a case. There we are again."

They had rounded the final bend in the drive and had come out before the now familiar facade of Nunspardon.

The butler admitted them and contrived to suggest with next to no expenditure of behaviour that Alleyn was a friend of the family and Fox completely invisible. Sir George, he said, was still at luncheon. If Alleyn would step this way, he would inform Sir George. Alleyn, followed by the unmoved Fox, was shown into George Lacklander's study: the last of the studies they were to visit. It still bore, Alleyn recognized, the imprint of Sir Harold Lacklander's personality, and he looked with interest at a framed caricature of his erstwhile chief made a quarter of a century ago when Alleyn was a promising young man in the Foreign Service. The drawing revived his memories of Sir Harold Lacklander; of his professional charm, his conformation to type, his sudden flashes of wit and his extreme sensitiveness to criticism. There was a large photograph of George on the desk, and it was strange to see in it, as Alleyn fancied he could, these elements adulterated and transformed by the addition of something that was either stupidity or indifference. Stupidity? Was George, after all, such an ass? It depended, as usual, on "what one meant" by an ass.

At this point in Alleyn's meditations, George himself, looking huffily postprandial, walked in. His expression was truculent.

"I *should* have thought, I *must* say, Allen," he said, "that one's luncheon hour at least might be left to one."

"I'm sorry," Alleyn said, "I thought you'd finished. Do you smoke between the courses, perhaps?"

Lacklander angrily pitched his cigarette into the fireplace. "I wasn't hungry," he said.

"In that case I am relieved that I didn't, after all, interrupt you."

"What are you driving at? I'm damned if I like your tone, Alleyn. What do you want?"

"I want," Alleyn said, "the truth. I want the truth about what you did yesterday evening. I want the truth about what you did when you went to Hammer Farm last night. I want the truth, and I think I have it, about Chapter 7 of your father's memoirs. A man has been murdered. I am a policeman and I want facts."

"None of these matters has anything to do with Cartarette's

death," Lacklander said and wet his lips.

"You won't persuade me of that by refusing to discuss them."

"Have I said that I refuse to discuss them?"

"All right," Alleyn sighed. "Without more ado, then, did you expect to find a copy of Chapter 7 when you broke open the drawer in Colonel Cartarette's desk last night?"

"You're deliberately insulting me, by God!"

"Do you deny that you broke open the drawer?"

Lacklander made a small gaping movement with his lips and an ineffectual gesture with his hands. Then, with some appearance of boldness he said, "Naturally, I don't do anything of the sort. I did it by—at the desire of his family. The keys seemed to be lost and there were certain things that had to be done—people to be told and all that. She didn't even know the name of his solicitors. And there were people to ring up. They thought his address book might be there."

"In the locked drawer? The address book?"

"Yes."

"Was it there?"

He boggled for a moment and then said, "No."

"And you did this job before we arrived?"

"Yes."

"At Mrs. Cartarette's request?"

"Yes."

"And Miss Cartarette? Was she in the search party?"

"No."

"Was there, in fact, anything in the drawer?"

"No," George said hardily. "There wasn't." His face had begun to look coarse and blank.

"I put it to you that you did not break open the drawer at Mrs. Cartarette's request. It was you, I suggest, who insisted upon doing it because you were in a muck-sweat wanting to find out where the amended Chapter 7 of your father's memoirs might be. I put it to you that your relationship with Mrs. Cartarette is such that you were in a position to dictate this manoeuvre."

"No. You have no right, damn you—"

"I suggest that you are very well aware of the fact that your father wrote an amended version of Chapter 7 which was, in effect, a confession. In this version he stated firstly that he himself was responsible for young Ludovic Phinn's suicide and secondly that he himself had traitorously conspired against his own government with certain elements in the German Government. This chapter, if it were published, would throw such opprobrium upon your father's name that in order to stop its being made public, I suggest, you were prepared to go to the lengths to which you have, in fact, gone. You are an immensely vain man with a confused, indeed a fanatical sense of your family prestige. Have you anything to say to all this?"

A tremor has begun to develop in George Lacklander's hands. He glanced down at them and with an air of covering up a social blunder, thrust them into his pockets. Most unexpectedly he began to laugh, an awkward, rocketing sound made on the intake of breath, harsh as a hacksaw.

"It's ridiculous," he gasped, hunching his shoulders and bending at the waist in a spasm that parodied an ecstacy of amusement. "No, honestly, it's too much!"

"Why," Alleyn asked sedately, "are you laughing?"

Lacklander shook his head and screwed up his eyes. "I'm so sorry," he gasped. "Frightful of me, I know, but really!" Alleyn saw that through his almost sealed eyelids he was peeping out, wary and agitated. "You don't mean to say you think that I—?" He waved his uncompleted sentence with a flap of his pink freckled hand.

"That you murdered Colonel Cartarette, were you going to say?"

"Such a notion! I mean, how? When? With what?"

Alleyn, watching his antics, found them insupportable.

"I know I shouldn't laugh," Lacklander gabbled, "but it's so fantastic. How? When? With What?" And through Alleyn's mind dodged a disjointed jingle. *"Quomodo? Quando? Quibus auxiliis?"*

"He was killed," Alleyn said, "by a blow and a stab. The injuries were inflicted at about five past eight last evening.

The murderer stood in the old punt. As for 'with what'—"

He forced himself to look at George Lacklander, whose face, like a bad mask, was still crumpled in a false declaration of mirth.

"The puncture," Alleyn said, "was made by your mother's shooting-stick and the initial blow—" he saw the pink hands flex and stretch, flex and stretch—"by a golf-club. Probably a driver."

At that moment the desk telephone rang. It was Dr. Curtis for Alleyn.

He was still talking when the door opened and Lady Lacklander came in followed by Mark. They lined themselves up by George and all three watched Alleyn.

Curtis said, "Can I talk?"

"Ah yes," Alleyn said airily. "That's all right. I'm afraid I can't do anything to help you, but you can go ahead quietly on your own."

"I suppose," Dr Curtis's voice said very softly, "you're in a nest of Lacklanders?"

"Yes, indeed."

"All right. I've rung up to tell you about the scales. Willy can't find both types on any of the clothes or gear."

"No?"

"No. Only on the rag: the paint-rag."

"Both types on that?"

"Yes. And on the punt seat."

"Yes?"

"Yes. Shall I go on?"

"Do."

Dr. Curtis went on. Alleyn and the Lacklanders watched each other.

# CHAPTER **XI**

## Between Hammer and Nunspardon

Nurse Kettle had finished her afternoon jobs in Swevenings, but before she returned to Chyning, she thought she should visit the child with the abscess in the gardener's cottage at Hammer Farm. She felt some delicacy about this duty because of the calamity that had befallen the Cartarettes. Still, she could slip quietly round the house and down to the cottage without bothering anybody, and perhaps the gardener's wife would have a scrap or two of mournful gossip for her about when the funeral was to take place and what the police were doing and how the ladies were bearing up and whether general opinion favoured an early marriage between Miss Rose and Dr. Mark. She also wondered privately what, if anything, was being said about Mrs. Cartarette and Sir George Lacklander, though her loyalty to The Family, she told herself, would oblige her to give a good slap down to any nonsense that was talked in *that* direction.

Perhaps her recent interview with Commander Syce had a little upset her. It had been such a bitter and unexpected disappointment to find him at high noon so distinctly the worse for wear. Perhaps it was disappointment that had made her say such astonishingly snappish things to him; or, more likely, she thought, anxiety. Because, she reflected as she drove up Watt's Hill, she *was* dreadfully anxious about him. Of course, she knew very well that he had pretended to be prostrate with lumbago because he wanted her to go on visiting him, and this duplicity, she had to admit, gave her a cosy feeling under her diaphragm. But Chief Detective-Inspector Alleyn would have a very different point of view about the deception; perhaps a terrifying point of view. Well, there, she thought, turning in at the Hammer Farm drive, it was no good at her age getting the flutters. In her simple snobbishness she comforted herself with the thought that "Handsome Alleyn," as the evening papers called him, was the Right Sort, by which Nurse Kettle meant the Lacklander as opposed to the Kettle or Fox or Oliphant sort or, she was obliged to add to herself, the Kitty Cartarette sort. As this thought occurred to her, she compressed her generous lips. The memory had arisen of Commander Syce trying half-heartedly to conceal a rather exotic water-colour of Kitty Cartarette. It was a memory that, however much Nurse Kettle might try to shove it out of sight, recurred with unpleasant frequency.

By this time she was out of the car and stumping round the house by a path that ran down to the gardener's cottage. She carried her bag and looked straight before her, and she quite jumped when she heard her name called: "Hullo, there! Nurse Kettle!"

It was Kitty Cartarette sitting out on the terrace with a tea-table in front of her. "Come and have some," she called.

Nurse Kettle was dying for a good cup of tea, and what was more, she had a bone to pick with Kitty Cartarette. She accepted and presently was seated before the table.

"You pour out," Kitty said. "Help yourself."

She looked exhausted and had made the mistake of overpainting her face. Nurse Kettle asked her briefly if she had had any sleep.

"Oh, yes," she said, "doped myself up to the eyebrows last night, but you don't feel so good after it, do you?"

"You certainly do *not*. You want to be careful about that sort of thing, you know, dear."

"Ah, what the hell!" Kitty said impatiently and lit a cigarette at the stub of her old one. Her hands shook. She burnt her finger and swore distractedly.

"Now, then," Nurse Kettle said making an unwilling concession to the prompting of her professional conscience. "Steady." And thinking it might help Kitty to talk, she asked, "What have you been doing with yourself all day, I wonder?"

"Doing? God, I don't know. This morning for my sins I had to go over to the Lacklanders'."

Nurse Kettle found this statement deeply offensive in two ways. Kitty had commonly referred to the Lacklanders as if they were shopkeepers. She had also suggested that they were bores.

"To Nunspardon?" Nurse Kettle said with refinement. "What a lovely old home it is! A show place if ever there was one," and she sipped her tea.

"The *place* is all right," Kitty muttered under her breath. This scarcely veiled slight upon the Lacklanders angered Nurse Kettle still further. She began to wish that she had not accepted tea from Kitty. She replaced her cucumber sandwich on her plate and her cup and saucer on the table.

"Perhaps," she said, "you prefer Uplands."

Kitty stared at her. "*Uplands?*" she repeated, and after a moment's hesitation she asked without any great display of interest, "Here! what are you getting at?"

"I thought," Nurse Kettle said with mounting colour, "you might find the company at Uplands more to your taste than the company at Nunspardon."

"Geoff Syce?" Kitty gave a short laugh. "God, that old bit of wreckage! Have a heart!"

Nurse Kettle's face was scarlet. "If the Commander isn't

the man he used to be," she said, "I wonder whose fault it is."

"His own, I should think," Kitty said indifferently.

"Personally, I've found it's more often a case of *cherchez*," Nurse Kettle said carefully, "*la femme.*"

"What?"

"When a nice man takes to solitary drinking, it's generally because some woman's let him down."

Kitty looked at her guest with the momentarily deflected interest of a bitter preoccupation. "Are you suggesting I'm the woman in this case?" she asked.

"I'm not suggesting anything. But you knew him out in the East, I believe?" Nurse Kettle added with a spurious air of making polite conversation.

"Oh, yes," Kitty agreed contemptuously. "I knew him all right. Did he tell you? Here, what *has* he told you?" she demanded, and unexpectedly there was a note of something like desperation in her voice.

"Nothing, I'm sure, that you could take exception to; the Commander, whatever you like to say, *is* a gentleman."

"How can you be such a fool," Kitty said drearily.

"Well, really!"

"Don't talk to me about gentlemen. I've had them, thank you. If you ask me, it's a case of the higher you go the fewer. "Look," Kitty said with savagery, "at George Lacklander."

"Tell me this," Nurse Kettle cried out; "did he love you?"

"Lacklander?"

"No." She swallowed and with dignity corrected Kitty, "I was referring to the Commander."

"You talk like a kid. Love!"

"*Honestly!*"

"Look!" Kitty said. "You don't know anything. Face it; you don't know a single damn' thing. You haven't got a clue."

"Well, I must say! You can't train for nursing, I'll have you know—"

"O, well, all right. O.K. From that point of view. But from my point of view, honestly, you have no idea."

"I don't know what we're talking about," Nurse Kettle said in a worried voice.

"I bet you don't."

"The Commander—" She stopped short and Kitty stared at her incredulously.

"Do I see," Kitty asked, "what I think I see! You don't tell me you and Geoff Syce—God, that's funny!"

Words, phrases, whole speeches suddenly began to pour out of Nurse Kettle. She had been hurt in the most sensitive part of her emotional anatomy, and her reflex action was surprising. She scarcely knew herself what she said. Every word she uttered was spoken in defence of something that she would have been unable to define. It is possible that Nurse Kettle, made vulnerable by her feeling for Commander Syce—a feeling that in her cooler moments she would have classed as "unsuitable"—found in Kitty Cartarette's contempt an implicit threat to what Lady Lacklander had called her belief in degree. In Kitty, over-painted, knowledgeable, fantastically "not-quite," Nurse Kettle felt the sting of implied criticism. It was as if, by her very existence, Kitty Cartarette challenged the hierarchy that was Nurse Kettle's symbol of perfection.

"—so you've no business," she heard herself saying, "you've no business to be where you are and behave the way you're behaving. I don't care what's happened. I don't care how *he* felt about you in Singapore or wherever it was. That was *his* business. I don't care."

Kitty had listened to this tirade without making any sign that she thought it exceptional. Indeed, she scarcely seemed to give it her whole attention but snuffed it with an air of brooding discontent. When at last Nurse Kettle ran out of words and breath, Kitty turned and stared abstractedly at her.

"I don't know why you're making such a fuss," she said. "Is he game to marry you?"

Nurse Kettle felt dreadful. "I wish I hadn't said anything," she muttered. "I'm going."

"I suppose he might like the idea of being dry-nursed. *You've* nothing to moan about. Suppose I was friends with him in Singapore? What of it? Go right ahead. Mix in with the bloody county and I hope you enjoy yourself."

"Don't talk about them like that," Nurse Kettle shouted. "Don't do it! You know nothing about them. You're ignorant. I always say they're the salt of the earth."

"Do you!" With methodical care Kitty moved the tea-tray aside as if it prevented her in some way from getting at Nurse Kettle. "Listen," she continued, holding the edges of the table and leaning forward, "listen to me. I asked you to come and sit here because I've got to talk and I thought you might be partly human. I didn't know you were a yes-girl to this gang of fossils. God! You make me sick! What have they got, except money and snob-value, that you haven't got?"

"Lots," Nurse Kettle declaimed stoutly.

"Like hell they have! No, listen. Listen! O.K., I lived with your boy-friend in Singapore. He was bloody dull, but I was in a bit of a jam and it suited us both. O.K., he introduced me to Maurice. O.K., he did it like they do: 'Look what I've found,' and sailed away in his great big boat and got the shock of his life when he came home and found me next door as Mrs. Cartarette. So what does he do? He couldn't care less what happened to *me*, of course, but could he be just ordinary-friendly and give me a leg up with these survivals from the ice-age? Not he! He shies off as if I was a nasty smell and takes to the bottle. Not that he wasn't pretty expert at that before."

Nurse Kettle made as if to rise, but Kitty stopped her with a sharp gesture. "Stay where you are," she said. "I'm talking. So here I was. Married to a—I don't know what—the sort they call a nice chap. Too damn' nice for me. I'd never have pulled it off with him in Singapore if it hadn't been he was lonely and missing Rose. He couldn't bear not to have Rose somewhere about. He was a real baby, though, about other women: more like a mother's darling than an experienced man. You had to laugh sometimes. He wasn't my cup of tea, but I was down to it, and anyway, his sort owed me something."

"O, dear!" Nurse Kettle lamented under her breath. "O, dear, dear, dear!" Kitty glanced at her and went on.

"So how did it go? We married and came here and he started writing some god-awful book and Rose and he sat in each other's pockets and the county called. Yes, they called, all right, talking one language to each other and another one to me. Old Occy Phinn, as mad as a meat-axe and doesn't even keep himself clean. The Fat Woman at Nunspardon, who took one look at me and then turned polite for the first time in history. Rose, trying so hard to be nice it's a wonder she didn't rupture something. The parson and his wife, and half a dozen women dressed in tweed sacks and felt buckets with faces like the backsides of a mule. My God, what have they *got*? They aren't fun, they aren't gay, they don't *do* anything and they look like the wreck of the schooner *Hesperus*. Talk about the living death! And me! Dumped like a sack and meant to be grateful!"

"You don't understand," Nurse Kettle began and then gave it up. Kitty had doubled her left hand into a fist and was screwing it into the palm of the right, a strangely masculine gesture at odds with her enamelled nails.

"Don't!" Nurse Kettle said sharply. "Don't do that."

"Not one of them, not a damn' one was what you might call friendly."

"Well, dear me, I must say! What about Sir George!" Nurse Kettle cried, exasperated and rattled into indiscretion.

"George! George wanted what they all want, and now things have got awkward, he doesn't want that. George! George, the umpteenth baronet, is in a mucksweat. George can't think," Kitty said in savage mimicry, "what people might not be saying. He told me so himself! If you knew what I know about George—" Her face, abruptly, was as blank as a shuttered house. "Everything," she said, "has gone wrong. I just don't have the luck."

All sorts of notions, scarcely comprehensible to herself, writhed about in the mid-region of Nurse Kettle's thoughts. She was reminded of seaweed in the depths of a marine pool. Monstrous revelations threatened to emerge and were suppressed by a sort of creaming-over of the surface of her mind. She wanted to go away from Kitty Cartarette before any more damage was done to her innocent idolatries and yet found herself unable to make the appropriate gestures of departure. She was held in thrall by a convention. Kitty had been talking dismally for some time, and Nurse Kettle had not listened. She now caught a desultory phrase.

"Their fault!" Kitty was saying. "You can say what you like, but whatever has happened is their fault."

"No, no, no!" Miss Kettle cried out, beating her short scrubbed hands together. "How can you think that! You terrify me. What are you suggesting?"

## ii

"What are you suggesting?" George Lacklander demanded as Alleyn at last put down the receiver. "Who have you been speaking to? What did you mean by what you said to me just now—about—" he looked around at his mother and son—"an instrument," he said.

Lady Lacklander said, "George, I don't know what you and Roderick have been talking about, but I think it's odds on that you'd better hold your tongue."

"I'm sending for my solicitor."

She grasped the edge of the desk and let herself down into a chair. The folds of flesh under her chin began to tremble. She pointed at Alleyn.

"Well, Rory?" she demanded, "what is all this? What are you suggesting?"

Alleyn hesitated for a moment and then said, "At the moment, I suggest that I see your son alone."

"No."

Mark, looking rather desperate, said, "Gar, don't you think it might be better?"

"No." She jabbed her fat finger at Alleyn. "What have you said and what were you going to say to George?"

"I told him that Colonel Cartarette was knocked out by a golf-club. I'll now add for the information of you all, since you choose to stay here, that he was finally killed by a stab through the temple made by your shooting-stick, Lady Lacklander. Your paint-rag was used to wipe the scales of two trout from the murderer's hands. The first blow was made from the punt. The murderer, in order to avoid being seen from Watt's Hill, got into the punt and slid down the stream using the long mooring rope as you probably did when you yourself sketched from the punt. The punt, borne by the current, came to rest in the little bay by the willow grove, and the murderer stood in it idly swinging a club at the daisies growing on the edge of the bank. This enemy of the Colonel's was so well known to him that he paid little attention, said something, perhaps, about the trout he had caught and went on cutting grass to wrap it in. Perhaps the last thing he saw was the shadow of the club moving swiftly across the ground. Then he was struck on the temple. We think there was a return visit with your shooting-stick, Lady Lacklander, and that the murderer quite deliberately used the shooting-stick on Colonel Cartarette as you used it this morning on your garden path. Placed it over the bruised temple and sat on it. What did you say? Nothing? It's a grotesque and horrible thought, isn't it? We think that on getting up and releasing the shooting-stick, there was literally a slip. A stumble, you know. It would take quite a bit of pulling out. There was a backward lunge. A heel came down on the Colonel's trout. The fish would have slid away, no doubt, if it had not been lying on a sharp triangular stone. A flap of skin was torn away and the foot, instead of sliding off, sank in and left an impression. An impression of the spiked heel of a golf shoe."

George Lacklander said in an unrecognizable voice, "All this conjecture!"

"No," Alleyn said, "I assure you. Not conjecture." He looked at Lady Lacklander and Mark. "Shall I go on?"

Lady Lacklander, using strange uncoordinated gestures, fiddled with the brooches that, as usual, were stuck about her bosom. "Yes," she said, "go on."

Mark, who throughout Alleyn's discourse had kept his gaze fixed on his father, said, "Go on. By all means. Why not?"

"Right," Alleyn said. "Now the murderer was faced with evidence of identity. One imagines the trout glistening with a clear spiked heel-mark showing on its hide. It wouldn't do to throw it into the stream or the willow grove and run away. There lay the Colonel with his hands smelling of fish and pieces of cut grass all round him. For all his murderer knew, there might have been a witness to the catch. This, of course, wouldn't matter as long as the murderer's identity was unsuspected. But there is a panic sequel to most crimes of violence, and it is under its pressure that the fatal touch of over-cleverness usually appears. I believe that while the killer stood there, fighting down terror, the memory of the Old 'Un lying on Bottom Bridge, arose. Hadn't Danberry-Phinn and the Colonel quarrelled loudly, repeatedly and vociferously— quarrelled that very afternoon—over the Old 'Un? Why not replace the Colonel's catch with the fruits of Mr. Phinn's poaching tactics and drag, not a red-herring, but a whacking great trout across the trail? Would that not draw attention towards the known enemy and away the secret one? So there was a final trip in the punt. The Colonel's trout was removed and the Old 'Un substituted. It was at this juncture that Fate, in the person of Mrs. Thomasina Twitchett, appeared to come to the murderer's aid."

"For God's sake," George Lacklander shouted, "stop talking—" He half formed an extremely raw epithet, broke off and muttered something indistinguishable.

"Who are you talking about, Rory?" Lady Lacklander demanded. "Mrs. *who?*"

"Mr. Phinn's cat. You will remember, Mrs. Cartarette told us that in Bottom Meadow she came upon a cat with a half-eaten trout. We have found the remains. There is a triangular gash corresponding with the triangular flap of skin torn off by the sharp stone, and as if justice or nemesis or somebody had assuaged the cat's appetite at the crucial moment, there is also a shred of skin bearing the unmistakable mark of part of a heel and the scar of a spike."

"But can all this—" Mark began. "I mean, when you talk of correspondence—"

"Our case," Alleyn said, "will, I assure you, rest upon scientific evidence of an unusually precise character. At the moment, I'm giving you the sequence of events. The Colonel's trout was bestowed upon the cat. Lady Lacklander's paint-rag was used to clean the spike of the shooting-stick and the murderer's hands. You may remember, Dr. Lacklander, that your grandmother said she had put all her painting gear tidily away, but you, on the contrary, said you found the rag caught up in a briar bush."

"You suggest then," Mark said evenly, "that the murder was done some time between ten to eight, when my grandmother went home, and a quarter past eight, when I went home." He thought for a moment and then said, "I suppose that's quite possible. The murderer might have heard or caught sight of me, thrown down the rag in a panic and taken to the nearest cover only to emerge after I'd picked up the sketching gear and gone on my way."

Lady Lacklander said after a long pause, "I find that a horrible suggestion. Horrible."

"I daresay," Alleyn agreed dryly. "It was an abominable business, after all."

"You spoke of scientific evidence," Mark said.

Alleyn explained about the essential dissimilarities in individual fish scales. "It's all in Colonel Cartarette's book," he said and looked at George Lacklander. "You had forgotten that perhaps."

"Matter of fact, I—ah—I don't know that I ever read poor old Maurice's little book."

"It seems to me to be both charming," Alleyn said, "and instructive. In respect of the scales it is perfectly accurate. A trout's scales, the Colonel tells us, are his diary in which his whole life-history is recorded for those who can read them. Only if two fish have identical histories will their scales correspond. Our two sets of scales, luckily, are widely dissimilar. There is Group A, the scales of a nine- or ten-year old fish who has lived all his life in one environment. And there is group B, belonging to a smaller fish who, after a slow growth of four years, changed his environment, adopted possibly a sea-going habit, made a sudden sput of growth and was very likely a newcomer to the Chyne. You will see where this leads us, of course?"

"I'm damned if I do," George Lacklander said.

"Oh, but yes, surely. The people who, on their own and other evidence, are know to have handled one fish or the other are Mr. Phinn, Mrs. Cartarette and the Colonel himself. Mr. Phinn caught the Old 'Un; Mrs. Cartarette tells us she tried to take a fish away from Thomasina Twitchett. The Colonel handled his own catch and refused to touch the Old 'Un. Lady Lacklander's paint-rag with the traces of both types of fish scales tells us that somebody, we believe the murderer, handled both fish. The further discovery of minute blood-stains tells us that the spike of the shooting-stick was twisted in the rag after being partially cleaned in the earth. If, therefore, with the help of the microscope we could find scales from both fish on the garments of any of you, that one would be Colonel Cartarette's murderer. That," Alleyn said, "was our belief."

"Was?" Mark said quickly, and Fox, who had been staring at a facetious Victorian hunting print, refocussed his gaze on his senior officer.

"Yes," Alleyn said. "The telephone conversation I have just had was with one of the Home Office men who are looking after the pathological side. It is from him that I got all this expert's stuff about scales. He tells me that on none of the garments submitted are the scales of both types."

The normal purplish colour flooded back into George Lacklander's face. "I said from the beginning," he shouted, "it was some tramp. Though why the devil you had to—to—" he seemed to hunt for a moderate word—"to put us through the hoops like this—" His voice faded. Alleyn had lifted his hand. "Well?" Lacklander cried out. "What is it? What the hell is it? I beg your pardon, Mama."

Lady Lacklander said automatically, "Don't be an ass, George."

"I'll tell you," Alleyn said, "exactly what the pathologist has found. He has found traces of scales where we expected to find them: on the Colonel's hands and the edge of one cuff, on Mr. Phinn's coat and knickerbockers and, as she warned us, on Mrs. Cartarette's skirt. The first of these traces belongs to group B and the other two a group A. Yes?" Alleyn said, looking at Mark, who had begun to speak and then stopped short.

"Nothing," Mark said. "I—no, go on."

"I've almost finished. I've said that we think the initial blow was made by a golf-club, probably a driver. I may as well tell you at once that so far none of the clubs has revealed any trace of blood. On the other hand, they have all been extremely well cleaned."

George said, "Naturally. My chap does mine."

"When it comes to shoes, however," Alleyn went on, "it's a different story. They too have been well cleaned. But in respect of the right foot of a pair of golfing shoes there is something quite definite. The pathologist is satisfied that the scar left on the Colonel's trout was undoubtedly made by the spiked heel of this shoe."

"It's a bloody lie!" George Lacklander bawled out. "Who are you accusing? Whose shoe?"

"It's a hand-made job. Size four. Made, I should think, as long as ten years ago. From a very old, entirely admirable and hideously expensive bootmaker in the Burlington Arcade. It's your shoe, Lady Lacklander."

Her face was too fat to be expressive. She seemed merely to stare at Alleyn in a meditative fashion, but she had gone very pale. At last she said without moving, "George, it's time to tell the truth."

"That," Alleyn said, "is the conclusion I hoped you would come to."

### iii

"What are you suggesting?" Nurse Kettle repeated and then, seeing the look in Kitty's face, she shouted, "No! Don't tell me!"

But Kitty had begun to tell her. "It's each for himself in their world," she said, "just the same as in anybody else's. If George

Lacklander dreams he can make a monkey out of me, he's
going to wake up in a place where he won't have any more
funny ideas. What about the old family name then! Look! Do
you know what he gets me to do? Break open Maurice's desk
because there's something Maurice was going to make public
about old Lacklander and George wants to get in first. And
when it isn't there, he asks me to find out if it was on the body.
No! And when I won't take that one on, what does he say?"

"I don't know. Don't tell me!"

"O, yes, I will. You listen to this and see how you like it.
After all the fun and games! Teaching me how to swing—"
She made a curious little retching sound in her throat and
looked at Nurse Kettle with a kind of astonishment. "You
know," she said, "golf. Well, so what does he do? He says, this
morning, when he comes to the car with me, he says he thinks
it will be better if we don't see much of each other." She
suddenly flung out a string of adjectives that Nurse Kettle
would have considered unprintable. "That's George Lacklander for you," Kitty Cartarette said.

"You're a wicked woman," Nurse Kettle said. "I forbid you
to talk like this. Sir George may have been silly and infatuated.
I daresay you've got what it takes, as they say, and he's a
widower and I always say there's a trying time for gentlemen
just as there is—but that's by the way. What I mean, if he's
been silly, it's you that's led him on," Nurse Kettle said, falling
back on the inexorable precepts of her kind. "You caught our
dear Colonel and not content with that, you set your cap at
poor Sir George. You don't mind who you upset or how
unhappy you make other people. I know your sort. You're no
good. You're no good at all. I shouldn't be surprised if you
weren't responsible for what's happened. Not a scrap
surprised."

"What the hell do you mean?" Kitty whispered. She curled
back in her chair and staring at Nurse Kettle, she said, "You
with your poor Sir George! Do you know what I think about
your poor Sir George? I think he murdered your poor dear
Colonel, Miss Kettle."

Nurse Kettle sprang to her feet. The wrought-iron chair rocked against the table. There was a clatter of china and a jug of milk overturned into Kitty Cartarette's lap.

"How dare you!" Nurse Kettle cried out. "Wicked! Wicked! *Wicked!*" She heard herself grow shrill and in the very heat of her passion she remembered an important item in her code: Never Raise the Voice. So although she would have found it less difficult to scream like a train, she did contrive to speak quietly. Strangely commonplace phrases emerged, and Kitty, slant-eyed, listened to them. "I would advise you," Nurse Kettle quavered, "to choose your words. People can get into serious trouble passing remarks like that." She achieved an appalling little laugh. "Murdered the Colonel!" she said, and her voice wobbled desperately. "The idea! If it wasn't so dreadful, it'd be funny. With what, may I ask? And how?"

Kitty, too, had risen, and milk dribbled from her ruined skirt to the terrace. She was beside herself with rage.

"How?" she stammered. "I'll tell you how and I'll tell you with what. With a golf-club and his mother's shooting-stick. That's what. Just like a golf ball it was. Bald and shining. Easy to hit. Or an egg. Easy—"

Kitty drew in her breath noisily. Her gaze was fixed, not on Nurse Kettle, but beyond Nurse Kettle's left shoulder. Her face was stretched and stamped with terror. It was as if she had laid back her ears. She was looking down the garden towards the spinney.

Nurse Kettle turned.

The afternoon was far advanced and the men who had come up through the spinney cast long shadows across the lawn, reaching almost to Kitty herself. For a moment she and Alleyn looked at each other and then he came forward. In his right hand he carried a pair of very small old-fashioned shoes: brogues with spikes in the heels.

"Mrs. Cartarette," Alleyn said, "I am going to ask you if when you played golf with Sir George Lacklander, he lent you his mother's shoes. Before you answer me, I must warn you—"

Nurse Kettle didn't hear the Usual Warning. She was

looking at Kitty Cartarette, in whose face she saw guilt itself. Before this dreadful symptom her own indignation faltered and was replaced, as it were professionally, by a composed, reluctant and utterly useless compassion.

# CHAPTER **XII**

## Epilogue

"George," Lady Lacklander said to her son, "we shall, if you please, get this thing straightened out. There must be no reservations before Mark or—" she waved her fat hand at a singularly still figure in a distant chair—"or Octavius. Everything will come out later on. We may as well know where we are now, among ourselves. There must be no more evasions."

George looked up and muttered, "Very well, Mama."

"I knew, of course," his mother went on, "that you were having one of your elephantine flirtations with this wretched, unhappy creature. I was afraid that you had been fool enough to tell her about your father's memoirs and all the fuss over Chapter 7. What I must know, now, is how far your affair with her may be said to have influenced her in what she did."

"My God!" George said. "I don't know."

"Did she hope to marry you, George? Did you say things like: 'If only you were free,' to her?"

"Yes," George said, "I did." He looked miserably at his mother and added, "You see, she wasn't. So it didn't seem to matter."

Lady Lacklander snorted but not with her usual brio. "And the memoirs? What did you say to her about them?"

"I just told her about that damned Chapter 7. I just said that if Maurice consulted her, I hoped she'd sort of weigh in on our side. And I—when that was no use—I—I said—that if he did publish, you know, it'd make things so awkward between the families that we—well—"

"All right. I see. Go on."

"She knew he had the copy of Chapter 7 when he went out. She told me that—afterwards—this morning. She said she couldn't ask the police about it, but she knew he'd taken it."

Lady Lacklander moved slightly. Mr. Phinn made a noise in his throat.

"Well, Occy?" she said.

Mr. Phinn, summoned by telephone and strangely acquiescent, said, "My dear Lady L., I can only repeat what I've already told you; had you all relied on my discretion, as I must acknowledge Cartarette did, there would have been no cause for anxiety on any of your parts over Chapter 7."

"You've behaved very handsomely, Occy."

"No, no," he said. "Believe me, no."

"Yes, you have. You put us to shame. Go on, George."

"I don't know that there's anything more. Except—"

"Answer me this, George. Did you suspect her?"

George put his great elderly hand across his eyes and said, "I don't know, Mama. Not at once. Not last night. But this morning. She came by herself, you know. Mark called for Rose. I came downstairs and found her in the hall. It seemed queer. As if she'd been doing something odd."

"From what Rory tells us, she'd been putting my shoes, that you lent her without my leave, in the downstairs cloakroom," Lady Lacklander said grimly.

"I am completely at a loss," Mr. Phinn said suddenly.

"Naturally you are, Occy." Lady Lacklander told him about the shoes. "She felt, of course, that she had to get rid of them. They're the ones I wear for sketching when I haven't got a bad toe, and my poor fool of a maid packed them up with the other things. Go on, George."

"Later on, after Alleyn had gone and you went indoors, I talked to her. She was sort of different," said poor George. "Well, damned hard. Sort of almost suggesting—well, I mean, it wasn't exactly the thing."

"I wish you would contrive to be more articulate. She suggested that it wouldn't be long before you'd pay your addresses?"

"Er—er—"

"And then?"

"I suppose I looked a bit taken aback. I don't know what I said. And then—it really was pretty frightful—she sort of began, not exactly hinting, but—well—"

"Hinting," Lady Lacklander said, "will do."

"—that if the police found Chapter 7, they'd begin to think that I—that we—that—"

"Yes, George. We understand. Motive."

"It really was frightful. I said I thought it would be better if we didn't sort of meet much. It was just that I suddenly felt I couldn't. Only that, I assure you, Mama. I assure you, Octavius."

"Yes, yes," they said. "All right, George."

"And then, when I said that, she suddenly looked—" George said this with an unexpected flash—"like a snake."

"And you, my poor boy," his mother added, "looked, no doubt, like the proverbial rabbit."

"I feel I've behaved like one, anyway," George rejoined with a unique touch of humour.

"You've behaved very badly, of course," his mother said without rancour. "You've completely muddled your values. Just like Poor Maurice himself, only he went still further. You led a completely unscrupulous trollop to suppose that if she was a widow, you'd marry her. You would certainly have bored her even more than poor Maurice, but Occy will forgive me if I suggest that your title and your money and Nunspardon offered sufficient compensation. You may, on second thoughts, even have attracted her, George," his mother added. "I mustn't, I suppose, underestimate your simple charms. "She contemplated her agonized son for a few minutes and then said, "It all comes to this, and I said as much to Kettle a few days ago: we can't afford to behave shabbily, George. We've got to stick to our own standards, such as they are, and we daren't muddle our values. Let's hope Mark and Rose between them will pick up the pieces." She turned to Mr. Phinn. "If any good has come out of this dreadful affair, Occy," she said, "it is this. You have crossed the Chyne after I don't know how many years and paid a visit to Nunspardon. God knows we have no right to expect it. We can't make amends, Occy. We can't pretend to try. And there it is. It's over, as they say nowadays, to you." She held out her hand and Mr. Phinn, after a moment's hesitation came forward to take it.

## ii

"You see, Oliphant," Alleyn said with his customary air of diffidence, "at the outset it tied up with what all of you told me the Colonel himself. He was an unusually punctilious man. 'Oddly formal,' the Chief Constable said, 'and devilishly polite, especially with people he didn't like or had fallen out with.' He had fallen out with the Lacklanders. One couldn't imagine him squatting on his haunches and going on with his job if Lacklander or his mother turned up in the punt. Or old Phinn, with whom he'd had a flaring row. Then, as you and Gripper pointed out, the first injury had been the sort of blow that is struck by a quarryman on a peg projecting from a cliff-face at knee level, or by an underhand service. Or, you might have added, by a golfer. It seemed likely, too, that the murderer knew the habit of the punt and the counter-current of the Chyne and the fact that where the punt came to rest in the willow-grove bay it was completely masked by trees. You will remember that we found one of Mrs. Cartarette's distinctive yellow hairpins in the punt in close association with a number of cigarette butts, some with lipstick and some not."

"Ah," Sergeant Oliphant said. "Dalliance, no doubt."

"No doubt. When I floated down the stream into the little bay and saw how the daisy heads had been cut off and where they lay, I began to see, also, a figure in the punt idly swinging a club: a figure so familiar to the Colonel that after an upward glance and a word of greeting, he went on cutting grass for his fish. Perhaps, urged by George Lacklander, she asked her husband to suppress the alternative version to Chapter 7 and perhaps he refused. Perhaps Lacklander, in his infatuation, had told her that if she was free, he'd marry her. Perhaps anger and frustration flooded suddenly up to her savage little brain and down her arms into her hands. There was that bald head, like an immense exaggeration of the golf balls she had swiped at under Lacklander's infatuated tuition. She had been slashing idly at the daisies, now she made a complete backswing, and in a moment her husband was curled up on the bank with the imprint of her club on his temple. From that time on she became a murderess fighting down her panic and frantically engaged in the obliteration of evidence. The print of the golf-club was completely wiped out by her nightmare performance with the shooting-stick, which she had noticed on her way downhill. She tramped on the Colonel's trout, and there was the print of her spiked heel on its hide. She grabbed up the trout and was frantic to get rid of it when she saw Mr. Phinn's cat. One can imagine her watching to see if Thomasina would eat the fish and her relief when she found that she would. She had seen the Old 'Un on the bridge. No doubt she had heard at least the fortissimo passages of Phinn's quarrel with the Colonel. Perhaps the Old 'Un would serve as false evidence. She fetched it and put it down by the body, but in handling the great trout, she let it brush against her skirt. Then she replaced the shooting-stick. Lady Lacklander's paint-rag was folded under the strap of her rucksack. Kitty Cartarette's hands were fishy. She used the rag to wipe them. Then, although she was about to thrust the shooting-stick back into the earth, she saw, probably round the collar of the spike, horrible traces of the use she had made of it. She twisted it madly about in the rag, which was, of course, already extensively stained with paint. No doubt she would have refolded the rag and replaced it, but she heard, may even have seen, Dr. Lacklander. She dropped the rag and bolted for cover. When she emerged, she found he had taken away all the painting gear." Alleyn paused and rubbed his nose. "I wonder," he said "if it entered her head that Lady Lacklander might be implicated. I wonder exactly when she remembered that she herself was wearing Lady Lacklander's shoes."

He looked from Fox to Oliphant and the attentive Gripper.

"When she got home," he said, "no doubt she at once bathed and changed. She put out her tweed skirt to go to the cleaners. Having attended very carefully to the heel, she then polished Lady Lacklander's shoes. I think that heel must have worried her more than anything else. She guessed that Lacklander hadn't told his mother he'd borrowed the shoes. As we saw this morning, she had no suitable shoes of her own, and her feet are much smaller than her stepdaughter's. She drove herself over to Nunspardon this morning and instead of ringing, walked in and put the shoes in the downstairs cloakroom. I suppose Lady Lacklander's maid believed her mistress to have worn them and accordingly packed them up with her clothes instead of the late Sir Harold's boots which she had actually worn."

Fox said, "When you asked for everybody's clothes, Mrs. Cartarette remembered, of course, that her skirt would smell of fish."

"Yes. She'd put it in the box for the dry cleaning. When she realized we might get hold of the skirt, she remembered the great trout brushing against it. With a mixture of bravado and cunning which is, I think, very characteristic, she boldly told me it would smell of fish and had the nerve and astuteness to use Thomasina as a sort of near-the-truth explanation. She only altered one fact. She said she tried to take a fish away from a cat, whereas she had given a fish to a cat. If she'd read her murdered husband's book, she'd have known that particular cat wouldn't jump, and the story was, in fact, a bit too fishy. The scales didn't match."

Oliphant said suddenly, "It's a terrible thing to happen in the Vale. Terrible the things that'll come out! How's Sir George going to look?"

"He's going to look remarkably foolish," Alleyn said with some heat, "which is no more than he deserves. He's behaved very badly, as his mother has no doubt pointed out to him. What's more, he's made things beastly and difficult for his son, who's a good chap, and for Rose Cartarette, who's a particularly nice child. I should say Sir George Lacklander has let his side down. Of course, he was no match at all for a woman of her hardihood; he'd have been safer with a puff-adder than with Kitty Cartarette, nee, Heaven help her, de Vere."

"What, sir, do you reckon—" Oliphant began, and catching sight of his superior's face, was silent.

Alleyn said harshly, "The case will rest on expert evidence of a sort never introduced before. If her counsel is clever and lucky, she'll get an acquittal. If he's not so clever and a bit unlucky, she'll get a lifer." He looked at Fox. "Shall we go?" he said.

He thanked Oliphant and Gripper for their work and went out to the car.

Oliphant said, "Has something upset the Chief, Mr. Fox?"

"Don't worry," Fox said. "It's the kind of case he doesn't fancy. Capital charge and a woman. Gets to thinking about what he calls first causes."

"First causes?" Oliphant repeated dimly.

"Society. Civilization. Or something," Fox said. "I mustn't keep him waiting. So long."

### iii

"Darling, darling Rose," Mark said. "We're in for a pretty ghastly time, I know. But we're in for it together, my dearest love, and I'll watch over you and be with you, and when it's all done with, we'll have each other and love each other more than ever before. Won't we? Won't we?"

"Yes," Rose said clinging to him. "We will, won't we?"

"So that something rather wonderful will come out of it all," Mark said. "I promise it will. You'll see."

"As long as we're together."

"That's right," Mark said. "Being together is everything."

And with one of those tricks that memory sometimes plays upon us, Colonel Cartarette's face, as Mark had last seen it in life, rose up clearly in his mind. It wore a singularly compassionate smile.

Together, they drove back to Nunspardon.

### iv

Nurse Kettle drove in bottom gear to the top of Watt's Hill and there paused. On an impulse, or perhaps inspired by some acknowledged bit of wishful thinking, she got out and looked down on the village of Swevenings. Dusk had begun to seep discreetly into the valley. Smoke rose in cosy plumes from one or two chimneys; roofs cuddled into their surrounding greenery. It was a circumspect landscape. Nurse Kettle revived her old fancy. "As pretty as a picture," she thought wistfully and was again reminded of an illustrated map. With a sigh, she turned back to her faintly trembling car. She was about to seat herself when she heard a kind of strangulated hail. She looked back and there, limping through the dusk, came Commander Syce. The nearer he got to Nurse Kettle, the redder in the face they both became. She lost her head slightly, clambered into her car, turned her engine off and turned it on again. "Pull yourself together, Kettle," she said and leaning out shouted in an unnatural voice. "The top of the evening to you."

Commander Syce came up with her. He stood by the open driving window, and even in her flurry, she noticed that he no longer smelt of stale spirits.

"Ha, ha," he said, laughing hollowly. Sensing perhaps that this was a strange beginning, he began again. "Look here!" he shouted. "Good Lord! Only just heard. Sickening for you. Are you all right? Not too upset and all that? What a thing!"

Nurse Kettle was greatly comforted. She had feared an entirely different reaction to Kitty Cartarette's arrest in Commander Syce.

"What about yourself?" she countered. "It must be a bit of a shock to *you*, after all."

He made a peculiar dismissive gesture with the white object he carried.

"Never mind me. Or rather," Commander Syce amended, dragging feverishly at his collar, "if you can bear it for a moment—"

She now saw that the object was a rolled paper. He thrust it at her. "There you are," he said. "It's nothing, whatever. Don't say a word."

She unrolled it, peering at it in the dusk. "Oh," she cried in an ecstasy, "how lovely! How lovely! It's my picture-map! Oh, *look!* There's Lady Lacklander, sketching in Bottom Meadow. And the doctor with a stork over his head—aren't you a *trick*—and there's me, only you've been much too kind about *me*." She leant out of the window, turning her lovely map towards the fading light. This brought her closer to Commander Syce, who made a singular little ejaculation and was motionless. Nurse Kettle traced the lively figures through the map: the landlord, the parson, various rustic celebrities. When she came to Hammer Farm, there was the gardener's cottage and his asthmatic child, and there was Rose bending gracefully in the garden. Nearer the house, one could see even in that light, Commander Syce had used thicker paint.

As if, Nurse Kettle thought with a jolt, there had been an erasure.

And down in the willow grove, the Colonel's favourite fishing haunt, there had been made a similar erasure.

"I started it," he said, "some time ago—after your—after your first visit."

She looked up, and between this oddly assorted pair a silence fell.

"Give me six months," Commander Syce said, "to make sure. It'll be all right. Will you?"

Nurse Kettle assured him that she would.

# ★ ★ ★ ★ ★
# JOHN JAKES'
# KENT FAMILY CHRONICLES

*Stirring tales of epic adventure
and soaring romance which tell the story
of the proud, passionate men
and women who built our nation.*

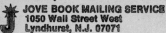